Enjoy the story!

Debbiann

Compromises

Debbiann Holmes

authorHOUSE®

AuthorHouse™
1663 Liberty Drive
Bloomington, IN 47403
www.authorhouse.com
Phone: 1-800-839-8640

© 2011 Debbiann Holmes. All rights reserved.

No part of this book may be reproduced, stored in a retrieval system, or transmitted by any means without the written permission of the author.

First published by AuthorHouse 3/3/2011

ISBN: 978-1-4567-3851-8 (e)
ISBN: 978-1-4567-3852-5 (dj)
ISBN: 978-1-4567-3853-2 (sc)

Library of Congress Control Number: 2011902511

Printed in the United States of America

Any people depicted in stock imagery provided by Thinkstock are models, and such images are being used for illustrative purposes only. Certain stock imagery © Thinkstock.

This book is printed on acid-free paper.

Because of the dynamic nature of the Internet, any web addresses or links contained in this book may have changed since publication and may no longer be valid. The views expressed in this work are solely those of the author and do not necessarily reflect the views of the publisher, and the publisher hereby disclaims any responsibility for them.

Photography by Eric J. Young

To my sister, Terri - you will always be a
part of my life and my best friend.

And for my infallible friend, Gina - thanks for
your honest feedback and support!

I

It was hard to take it all in, everything that Seth had told me a few short hours ago. I lay on my side, watching him breathe deeply while sleeping next to me. I moved a lock of curly long black hair from his handsome face, realizing just how much I hadn't been living these past few months. How I thought I could ever live without him, I didn't know. I knew the past few months without him had been pure hell. I was truly only half alive when I wasn't with him.

I had so many questions! I needed some space to figure it all out. I let him sleep as I crawled out silently from under the covers. I had arrived in a fancy dress, so I opted to throw on the shirt that he had worn earlier in the evening. It was as long as any nightgown I would wear anyway. I breathed in his cologne as I smelled the collar of his shirt and looked back at him sleeping so soundly in bed. I loved him, yes, but I still had to wonder about the recent turn of events. He had told me, "no more secrets," yet why did I feel like there was more to come?

I went up to the kitchen in search of some water and a bite to eat. I hadn't eaten supper earlier when Seth had told me the truth about not being a pirate, but playing the part of one. My stomach started to growl in protest. I opened the fridge and, as usual, it was well stocked with everything I needed to satisfy my hunger. I made my sandwich and grabbed a bottle of water. I sat at the counter in the kitchen thinking of the recent events. Luke walked in, surprised to see me.

"Hey there, did he let you up for some air?" Luke chuckled, as he tousled my shoulder-length, wavy brown hair.

I had always had a good rapport with Luke, since the beginning. He was charming, absolutely gorgeous, funny, and my best guy friend.

"He sleeps," I laughed, speaking of Seth.

"I can't say as I blame him. Not being around you for the past few months made life unbearable for all of us, let me tell you! He probably is making up for all the lost sleep."

So he wasn't as unaffected as I believed he was. I smiled in spite of myself. "And how miserable was he, Luke?" I questioned, wanting to know more.

"You have no idea! I swear; Robert, Jake, and I have been walking on eggshells! We were forbidden to contact any of you, even to let you know we were okay. He wanted a clean break so you wouldn't suffer."

"So I wouldn't suffer?" I asked incredulously. "You don't know the half of it!"

Again, Seth's stupid protection, or what he thought was protection of me, had made me suffer so much these past months. Did the man not know how much I loved him? Didn't he understand that my life wasn't worth living if he wasn't in it? Oh, it made me so frustrated and angry with him.

"Uh oh, I recognize that look," Luke said as he shook his head and chuckled. "Last time I saw that was when Lisa was hanging all over Seth at Christmas."

I remembered the night well. That was when I was still trying to

Compromises

keep Seth at a distance; I was afraid of the intense feelings I had for him. Lisa, Seth's old girlfriend, had set her sights on Seth, once again. I had been totally frustrated with Lisa and her actions around Seth. I was jolted back to the present. "You'd do well then to tell your friend to think of other ways to protect me," I said in a huff as I crossed my arms over my chest.

"He doesn't listen to anyone, you know. I tried to tell him," Luke said as he shook his head back and forth. Seth was truly stubborn when it came to me and my protection.

"Well, he's gonna start listening," I said angrily.

"Start listening to whom, about what?" Seth asked as he came into the kitchen, kissed the top of my head, and went to the fridge for a bottle of water. He looked absolutely gorgeous in just a pair of pajama bottoms, leaving his muscled and toned chest bare.

"Me, and about everything," I said, still angry.

Seth looked at Luke, confused by my reaction, and Luke said, "Somehow this kitchen has gotten really crowded all of a sudden." He got up out his chair, pecked me on the cheek with a quick kiss, and walked out of the kitchen, leaving me alone with Seth.

"Aw, love, what's the matter now?" He chuckled as he leaned against the counter next to me while opening a bottle of water, taking a large gulp.

"Don't you 'aw, love' me, Seth Hanson," I said, still angry as I got up to pace in front of him. "You . . . you . . . you," I sputtered until he grabbed me by the arms and made me stand still and face him. He frowned, trying to figure out why I was in this current dilemma. "You didn't come for me!" There, I finally had said it!

"Shhh," he said as he brought me to his chest and held me there, kissing my hair and rubbing my back. I should have known better. I should have kept my distance. I couldn't stay angry when he held me like this. The fire that consumed me whenever he held me made it difficult to think, let alone be angry. "I wanted to protect you. I still do," he said.

Uh oh, what was that supposed to mean, he still does? Alarm bells started to go off in my head. "What are you saying, Seth?" I asked as I pulled back just enough to look up into his beautiful blue eyes.

"What I am saying is I realize it does neither of us any good to be apart. I know that now. I went through hell staying away from you all these months, and I know you did too. I saw it in your face even though you tried to hide it. Last night when I walked in to that bar and saw you, I knew I would never have the strength to leave you again, ever."

"Why do I feel that there is a 'but' coming?" I said, still not trusting that his over -protectiveness wouldn't get in the way of us being together.

"But," he continued, "I still need to worry about your safety. I don't know yet what that means, or how to do it."

"Seth, I can't 'not' be with you. Ever! It was pure hell these past months. I won't let you do that to me!"

"I know, love, but I won't put you in danger like you were the last time!"

"Well, Luke will have to get better information," I pouted. I was referring to the information that Luke had gotten from his old pirate contacts, so they could pass it along to the Coast Guard.

"Cassandra," he said, bringing me back in his embrace, "I wish it were that easy, but these pirates are getting trickier. They are keeping information closer to home. It's like they won't trust anyone anymore. Thus, we had no idea that we would have had trouble on that last trip. You were there. You know how it all went down."

"So where does that leave us, Seth?" I asked, pulling back again to look into his eyes. I couldn't leave him, not when I had just found him again. Especially since I knew he was an honest man and not a thief.

"I don't know, love. I truly just don't know. Can we just enjoy each other, and we can talk about it tomorrow?"

"I'm not leaving," I said determinedly.

"I was counting on that," he smiled down at me. He lowered his head and kissed me deeply. I wrapped my arms around him and he scooped me up in his arms, heading down to his stateroom. "By the way," he grinned as he looked down at me, "you look better in my shirts than I do."

"I could make it a permanent part of my wardrobe," I smiled teasingly back up at him.

"Tempting," he smiled back while making his way to the master stateroom.

I didn't care what he thought about protecting me. I wasn't going to let him go. He would just have to find a way to make this work. There was no way I was going to live the past few months over again.

As he lay me down onto his bed and crawled in next to me, he whispered, "Let's just enjoy right now. We'll figure something out; promise." He nuzzled my neck.

Yes, we will figure this out, I thought. We have to! I kissed him and let the emotions that I had so often held in check before come out with no restraint. I rolled him on his back and straddled him as he grinned up at me.

"Promise me, Seth. Promise you won't leave me," I asked, still concerned how we would work out a compromise between my wanting to be near him and his overwhelming sense of protection of me.

"Love, I won't leave you, but I will protect you. I won't have you put in danger. I will think of something, but right now I have more important matters that need my attention," he said as he pulled me down to kiss me.

Later, after awakening from the deep sleep I fell into after our lovemaking, I reached over only to find that Seth was gone. I jumped up; alarmed that he had left, and threw on his shirt. I was on my way to go find him when he came in the door. He grinned at me as he set my luggage down beside him.

"I thought you may need more than my shirt to wear so I took the liberty of going to your rental house and getting your items. I settled up with the agency there so Mandi and Jackie won't have to pay for the week you won't be there."

"You are pretty sure of yourself," I said as I came and wrapped my arms around him.

"Well, if the past night didn't give you away, I don't know what else could have."

"You scared me when I woke and you weren't here," I said, still holding him close.

He held me as he ran his fingers through my hair, "Trust me, I won't leave you."

"Ever?" I said as I pulled back to look into his beautiful blue eyes.

"Ever!"

I broke away and went to sit on the bed and he followed me, sitting down beside me. "Any reason you need to get out of bed yet?" He asked as he grinned at me.

"Well," I giggled, "it is my vacation and I really do need a tan." I looked down at my pale skin.

"Lucky for you, I have a meeting with one of my distributors today in town and I am running a bit late. You can sunbathe while I am out." He kissed me, moaning in protest when he had to untangle himself from me as I refused to let him go. "Love, don't tempt me! I'm already late," he grinned as he got up. "See you for dinner . . . and dress fancy. We have some celebrating to do!"

I watched him leave and fell back on the bed with my arms outstretched. Life just doesn't get any better than this, I thought to myself. I was on vacation in Florida, I was in love with the most perfect man in the world, and I was going to spend the week with him on his gorgeous mega-yacht.

I jumped up and got ready for the day. Before heading out to the beach, I called the girls to let them know what had happened to me yesterday. I was sure that after talking to Robert and Jake they would be full of questions. I wasn't sure how much they knew; I had never mentioned the whole pirate thing before. I didn't think a phone call would be the right time to explain how Seth and his crew pretended to be pirates in order to catch them. I was right in thinking they would be full of questions; they wouldn't let me talk for fifteen minutes while they went on and on, handing off the phone to one another. They were excited that I had met up with their "boys" and that they had finally been able to get in touch with them.

"So," Mandi said when it was her turn on the line, "I heard from the rental agency that we were refunded and our bill was paid for by a certain Seth Hanson?"

"Yes, you know Seth, won't take no for answer," I giggled.

"Like you would have said no," Mandi laughed back. "So you are back to your old self and with the love of your life?"

"Yes, and yes," I answered in excitement.

"Well, I won't keep you on the line, but the boys said they plan to take a trip to see us soon."

I hadn't heard that, so I wondered when they were making the trip up and how long they would stay. I hadn't given much thought to what would happen next, as I was so caught up in the moment. Would he relocate and live in Portsmouth, or expect me to travel with him? I pushed these thoughts aside; I was still just too happy to drown that out with the thought of possibly not seeing Seth for any length of time. I said goodbye to the girls and went upstairs. Luke was in the kitchen, eating a sandwich. I hadn't realized that it was nearly lunchtime. I made myself a sandwich and sat down next to him.

"What's the plan for today, my darling?" he asked me.

"Well, I am pretty darn pale and the weather here is perfect for tanning," I answered back before taking a bite of my sandwich.

"Want company?" he asked as he grinned with that sexy smile of his.

"You know your charms don't work on me, Luke," I smiled back at him.

"Give a guy a break, will ya?"

"I am. I will let you join me," I answered back.

He jumped up and said, "Give me a sec to change and I'll be right back." He ran toward the crew's quarters and I finished my sandwich. I had already dressed for the beach, so I checked my bag for my towel, suntan lotion, and sunglasses. Luke came back up wearing swim trunks and a T-shirt, a towel thrown over his shoulder and sunglasses on his head. Luke was really a sight, and he would turn more than one woman's head on the way to the beach.

"Ready?" he asked.

"Ready."

We headed down to the beach just a few blocks from the marina. It was good hanging out with Luke again. We had an easy rapport and the fact that I now knew how much of a good guy he was, protecting Seth from the very beginning, made me love him even more. We were laughing and joking all the way to the beach, enjoying the sunshine.

We failed to notice that we were being followed. Two men, with their hair pulled back in ponytails, watched our progress to the beach. They knew they would have to wait, wait for a moment when they could catch me alone. They had plans for me; yes, they had plans. I would be their leverage, their hostage. I knew nothing about the sinister plot that was about to unfold as I continued on my way to the beach with Luke by my side.

Luke and I settled onto our towels and I dug my feet into the sand as I rubbed suntan oil over my legs. 'Ahhh, this is the best,' I thought as I put my head back and let the sun bathe me in its warmth. Back home in Portsmouth, it was still spring and still cold. I was relishing the warm day and the sunshine here. Not to mention that I was back with Seth.

"Need help with the lotion?" Luke asked, breaking through my thoughts.

"Not on your life, Luke," I laughed as I grabbed the suntan lotion and lathered up my arms and midriff.

"You'll burn," he shrugged.

"Okay, but I'm warning you," I trailed off, leaving the threat hanging in the air. Luke was careful to do only my back, fearing my wrath if he tried anything. Besides, on our previous vacation, when Seth had thought there was something between Luke and me, Luke had told me how uncomfortable it was when Seth had been upset with him. He really enjoyed Seth's friendship, and avoided anything that would drive a wedge between them.

As he finished and laid back to soak up the sun, I turned to look at Luke while shading my eyes from the sun's glare. "Luke?" I inquired.

"Yeah?" he answered as he turned his head to look at me.

"How does it all work? I mean, how do you stay in touch with, well, you know?" I said, whispering, being afraid of anyone who would overhear our conversation.

"Well," he said as he settled onto his side facing me, "I have some contacts that I call every now and again. I just ask a few questions, letting them know what area I am in to hopefully avoid running into them. They think Seth and I are working in a certain area so they don't duplicate efforts, so to speak. See, pirates are greedy and don't want to share. If they work the same area, they might not get good pickings on yachts or boats to steal from."

"So it's kind of like getting them to tell you where they are so you can then alert the Coast Guard."

"You got it," he said as he turned back to lie flat on his back. "Except," he continued, "it didn't quite work out well the last time," referring to the run in we had with the pirates.

"Seems like dangerous work," I commented as I settled onto my back.

"It is, but not nearly as dangerous as the position I was in prior to hooking up with Seth," he said, alluding to when he was a pirate himself.

"It must have been horrible for you," I said as I rolled again on my side, intrigued by the life he had led prior to Seth, and curious. "Why did you ever get into that line of work anyway?"

"Well, see, I was a young and impressionable kid. These pirates are tricky. They talk to you about how you can make so much money that you never have to worry about ever holding a nine to five. They talk it up and it makes it hard to say no. Well, once you are in it, yeah, the money is good, but they aren't nice people, Cass. When I saw how they treated the women and how dangerous it was, not only with the Coast Guard always on the lookout, but because the pirates have itchy trigger fingers and short tempers, I started to lay low, but they don't let you out so easy. I was getting sick of it, and short of being shot dead or going to jail I didn't see a way out. That was, of course, until I met your Seth. Well, you heard the rest. He promised to help me get out of pirating, in the true sense of the word, if I helped him get information about where they were." Luke rubbed a hand across his face, wiping away the memories, or so it seemed.

"I'm glad you got out of it," I said as I leaned over to kiss his cheek.

"Hmm . . . ," he smiled, "so am I. Besides, I got to meet you because of Seth."

"You did, and I am glad I got to know you." I was sincere. He was a great guy.

I lay back, deep in thought about what Seth might do now that I was back in his life, but he still had the urge to protect me. Would he give up the pirate act? Could he? It was honorable, trying to help the Coast Guard clean up the riffraff in the Caribbean, but it was dangerous. Would he feel it wasn't worth it now that I was back in his life? I dozed after a while, just enjoying the sun and figuring tonight would be a better time to dig into Seth's intentions.

Much later, I awoke. It was getting late. I could tell by the beautiful oranges, pinks, and purples that colored the sky. I nudged a snoring Luke beside me, trying to contain my laughter.

"Was I loud?" Luke grinned back at me.

"Excessively so," I laughed back. "It's getting late and I have a hot date tonight."

"Yeah, rub it in. I swear, everyone around me has someone special and I have just little ole me," he tried to pout, unsuccessfully.

"I love you, Luke." I stressed the *I* and smiled as I got up to gather my belongings.

"Yeah, but not like that," he got up, shaking his towel to throw it over his shoulder.

"Oh, poor Luke, no one to love him," I said as we walked together arm in arm making our way up the beach, back to the street.

"Yes, poor Luke," he grinned.

"I find it hard to believe that you can't find a girl," I said as we continued on our trek back to Seth's yacht, watching the glances girls threw his way.

"I don't want just any girl now that I met you, Cass," he grinned as I lay my head on his shoulder and he pulled me in close.

"You know how much I love Seth," I grinned back.

"Yeah, and I would never want to be the one to cause a rift between you two. But, if he ever hurts you, not only will I kill him, but I will be there for you."

I laughed, "And . . . if he ever hurts me, I will come to you for consolation."

Watchful eyes, and not just the girls at the beach, followed our progress, mixing easily in the crowd, careful not be noticed. They were good at what they did. They took note of every little detail so they could report back to their employer. One would be inclined to laugh at that term, employer, as one wouldn't think of pirates that way.

2

As we approached the yacht, I grabbed Luke's hand and ran up the stairs, laughing. We entered the salon, out of breath and giggling like children. Seth came out of the kitchen and joined in the contagious laughter as I ran to him and gave him a kiss. He didn't let go of me, quickly deepening the kiss.

"Come on, you two," Luke laughed, "can't you contain yourselves?"

"Never," Seth said as he kept me in his embrace.

"You had fun, I see," he said as he smiled down at me.

"Yes, I always do with my best buddy," I answered as I looked back at Luke.

"Well, if you want dinner, you are going to have to wear more than this," Seth said as he trailed a finger down the strap of my bikini top.

"And, if you keep doing that," I said as his touch left a trail of heat, "we will be starving for the rest of the evening."

"Okay," Luke said as he pushed past us to go to the stairwell that led down to the crew's quarters, "I think I have seen enough. I will see you two later."

I giggled as I grabbed Seth's trailing hand. "I need to shower."

"Want company?" Seth asked.

"Most definitely," I replied.

We entered the stateroom. I still couldn't believe I was with Seth. I felt like I was in a dream. I stopped short and pinched myself.

"What on earth did you do that for, love?"

"Just making sure I'm not dreaming," I giggled in response, as he joined me in laughter.

Seth shut and locked the door behind us. We stripped on our way to the shower and jumped in, letting the water run over us. He took my sponge from my hand saying, "Allow me." He took his time soaping me, as I did with him until the passion overtook us and we ran from the bathroom, grabbing towels as we fell onto the bed. Our lovemaking was spontaneous and beautiful. As we reached the peak of our pleasure, I cried out his name.

Afterwards, he lay on top of me as I gazed into his beautiful blue eyes. He smoothed a stray piece of hair back into place as he asked, "Are you hungry, love?"

"Well," I smiled, "I am really enjoying this interlude with you, but I think I may need sustenance if I need to keep my strength up." My stomach growled as if to solidify what I had just said, and we both laughed. He rolled over and got out of bed as I leaned up on my elbows to watch him make his way to the closet to pull out clothes.

When he noticed I hadn't moved, he turned around and grinned. "Love, your stomach is growling. I need to feed you."

"I was just enjoying the view," I said, still not wanting to move.

He walked back over to the bed as I got to up my knees and hugged him close. He kissed me deeply. "Want me to order in?"

Compromises

"Hmm," I said, contemplating that idea. "Well . . . I think I may be able to contain my passion for you for about an hour . . . two at the most."

"Then, darling, you must get dressed, or we will be dining in."

I kissed him quickly and jumped out of bed. We dressed, watching each other. I loved this man. Loved him more than anything or anyone I had ever felt for in my life before.

He took me to a beautiful restaurant that overlooked the water. We sat at a table outside and listened to the music from a lone guitar player off on the side of the deck. I was eating heartily, so hungry from the day that I hardly spoke.

Seth laughed. "I hope I haven't been starving you."

I laughed. "Sorry," I muttered as I wiped my mouth with a napkin. "I'm just really hungry." I leaned forward so only he could hear, as I took his hand in mine, "Besides, I am hoping to get back some of the energy I will need for this evening."

Seth squeezed my hand as he, too, leaned in. "Love, you keep that up and you will have to skip dessert."

"Dessert," I teased, "is waiting for me back in your stateroom."

Seth caught the waitress as she was walking by, saying, "Check, please," and I giggled in response.

A lone man at the bar watched us throughout dinner, and although he couldn't hear the conversation, the way we were with each other made it obvious that we were a couple. It confirmed what he wanted to know. He drained the rest of his glass and laid down his money, making his way out of the restaurant, dialing his partners to firm up plans.

The next morning, Seth said he was going to be out for a short portion of the day again as he had some meetings. We were in the kitchen, finishing a breakfast of coffee and muffins. "What do you plan to do today, Cassandra?" he asked as he wiped his mouth and stood up, adjusting his tie and grabbing a lightweight jacket that matched his slacks.

"Well," I said as I wrapped my arms around his neck as he got ready to leave, "I do enjoy the beach, and since it will be a short meeting for you, I will meet you back here early."

Luke walked in, poured himself a cup of coffee, and sat down, straddling a bar stool. "I'll keep tabs on her if you like, Seth."

"I feel better knowing you are with her," Seth said. It made me think of how many things had changed since I first met Seth. Previously, he warned me to keep my distance from Luke. Now, Luke was my guardian. The thought made me laugh.

I shook my head, "I'm a big girl and have survived living in the big, bad world so far."

"Yes, love; it's not that I think you can't take care of yourself. I just worry about your safety. It wasn't that long ago that we were involved in an incident, and I just don't trust these pirates. They are thick as thieves. Who knows what could happen? Some of them could still be stewing over the fact that part of their crew is in jail awaiting sentencing. I just want to be cautious."

We hadn't ironed out any of the details about what would happen next. We were so caught up enjoying the companionship we had right now that I think neither of us wanted to broach more serious topics.

"Well," I said, as I reached up for another quick kiss, "if it makes you rest easier and work faster to get home quicker, I will let Luke be my bodyguard."

Luke laughed, "Never been called that before."

"Well," I laughed as I finally released Seth, "looks like you better get used to the job. I have a very nervous boyfriend who thinks I need one."

Seth grabbed me back in his arms and kissed me deeply. As he released me he chuckled, "So, boyfriend is what you think I am?" Before I could reply he walked out, laughing as he did so.

"What's that supposed to mean?" I turned around and looked at Luke.

"Who knows? Brits have a weird way of talking. I'm surprised he hasn't come right out and asked you to 'shag' with him. "

I laughed and nodded my head in agreement, but I was still baffled by what Seth had said. Maybe I misread the signals? No, no. That couldn't be it. He said he wanted to be me with me forever. Then why did he make the comment about me thinking he was my boyfriend. Sometimes, the man was an enigma. Maybe I wouldn't ever figure him out. Maybe that was part of the allure?

As I waited for Luke to change to go to the beach with me, I walked over to the baby grand piano. I hadn't asked Seth if he had learned the music I gave him at Christmas. I tapped a key and listened to it resonate through the room. I would have to ask him to play it for me later. It was a beautiful piece, and I wondered if he had practiced all those long months that we were apart. If he had, that would mean that he had thought of me often, as I had of him. I, again, was still wondering about his comment this morning about his being my boyfriend. Did he think of us as more? I dared not go down that path.

Luke ran up from the crew's quarters and chuckled when he saw me. "Playing chopsticks?"

"That's about all I could play," I laughed back as I gathered up my bag for the beach.

We spent the day lazily taking in the sun and chatting like old friends. We were "people watching" all day. We would laugh over some of the tourists, easily identifiable as they dressed so outlandishly in their tropical shirts and skirts. I was looking for a love interest for Luke, although Luke said it was hard to see anyone else when I was sitting there next to him in nothing but a bikini. He had more than several women look his way. They ranged in ages from fifteen to sixty-five. I teased him about it and he just chuckled, saying he couldn't help that women were so love crazed that they couldn't resist him. He reminded me that only I was immune to his charms. He was the perfect companion, and our relationship was growing stronger every day, even though he knew he and I would never be more than friends.

At the end of the day, we were making our way back to the yacht and I was joking about a particular busty redhead who had eyed him as we had packed up to head home. "Come on, Luke, she was literally lusting for you."

"I haven't heard it put quite that way before," he chuckled.

"What, women can't be visual creatures like men are?"

"I . . . ," Luke started to answer me when he stopped short.

"Luke," I questioned, picking up on his tense mood, "what's wrong?"

"You stay here," he ordered me as he kept his eyes locked ahead and walked off.

I watched where he was headed and saw two big, burly men with long ponytails. I knew the look of these two. Saw it in the pirates who had taken us over on the yacht. Fear coursed through my veins, and my heart picked up in tempo. I was so intent on watching Luke that I failed to see that another man with short-cropped hair had stepped up behind me. He was dressed casually in white linen pants and matching shirt, with a stylish straw hat that shaded his face. I felt the barrel of a gun in my side as he whispered, "Stay calm and no one gets hurt. Walk with me," he added as he steered me in the opposite direction from Luke.

I wanted to scream out, but the man had the gun in my side and Luke was deep in conversation with the other two, his back to me. The man led me quickly down a back alley. I was already thinking of how I could gain the upper hand in this tricky situation when he said, "Sorry, but I need your cooperation," and he hit me on the back of my head. As I slumped into his arms, my last thought before losing conscience was of Seth.

When I came to, I was lying in a bed. I looked up at a white ceiling with a fan whirling a light breeze across my skin. I lifted my head just enough to reach back to touch the back of it, and felt a small lump as I did. "Oww," I mumbled, as I struggled to sit up straight.

"Sorry about that," a man said as he watched me from a chair in the corner of the room. He rose and I shrank back into the headboard.

"I'm not going to hurt you," he said as he stood a few feet away from me. He wasn't the same man who had put the gun in my side. This one had shoulder-length brown hair. He was pretty good looking, in a rough kind of way. His brown eyes seemed concerned, but wary and watchful at the same time. He was tall and well built. "Let me amend that and say, I won't hurt you as long you give me no reason to."

"What do you want?" I asked boldly.

"You have spunk," he laughed. "I will give you that."

My head was pounding, and I put a hand to my forehead to try to dull the pain.

"Here," the man said as he came to the bedside table. He picked up an aspirin bottle and a bottle of water and handed them to me. I refused to take them from him and just glared back at him. "I won't poison you. Trust me, we need you alive and well."

"For what?" I asked, still refusing what he offered.

He put the items back on the bedside table and went to sit back in the chair. "Ransom."

"Ransom?" I asked incredulously, sitting up quickly and then wishing I hadn't as nausea set in.

"Yes. You see, I think that Seth will be more willing to comply with any requests we make if you are kept in good condition and unharmed in any way," he answered.

Oh, so this had to do with Seth. This was not good. I hope this man knew what he was in for. Seth would be livid, and no doubt would bring the whole Coast Guard down on this man and whoever was in it with him.

"Why me?" I asked.

"We have been watching Seth for the past few days. I can see that you mean a lot to him. Not to mention that my cousin, Jason, mentioned you were on the yacht before he was taken into custody by the Coast Guard. It seems either you fell in love with a pirate, or Seth isn't a pirate after all. Which is it?"

I wasn't going to answer that one, knowing that saying anything would put Seth in danger. So, this was Jason's cousin. It was starting to make sense. Jason was obviously in jail somewhere and looking for revenge. He would have shot Seth if I hadn't intervened last time. It seemed he was holding a grudge.

"I see you won't answer," the man smiled as he rose. I, again, was on alert. "I will bring you something to eat in a while. In the meantime, let me explain your circumstances so you don't try anything stupid. You were flown in by a private plane to a very remote island. There is no one but you, me, and few other friends on this tiny place. There are no boats and the plane was sent back to the mainland, which, by the way, is too far to swim to. So while you are here, feel free to roam as you wish. My name is Alejandro and I am staying in the room inside the next door down to your right. Oh, yeah, I always keep a gun on me, even when sleeping, so don't get any smart ideas."

With that, he left, and closed the door behind him. I surveyed the room. It was actually quite pretty. There were windows along one wall and white gauzy curtains that were long enough to pool at the bottom, which were pulled aside to show a stunning view of lush tropical plants and trees with a blue-green ocean beyond. As I moved to get up again, my head started pounding. What the hell had the guy hit me with, a ton of bricks? I looked at the aspirin bottle and picked it up. The seal was still on it, as was the one on the bottle of water. I pulled off the seal, opened the silver top, and shook out two aspirin. I swallowed both, drank the water, and lay back on the bed to allow it time to kick in.

My thoughts took over. So I was being held hostage. What did they want from Seth? Alejandro had mentioned I was being held for ransom. So did they want money? Seth! Oh my, he must be panicking! He surely must know what had happened by now. He was probably doing everything in his power to find me, of that I was positive. I needed to figure out where the hell I was and how I could get in touch with him.

I tentatively swung my legs over the side of the bed. My headache was getting better. I slowly rose and made my way to a door adjacent to the one that Alejandro had gone out of, hoping that it was a bathroom. I turned the knob and opened the door. I was right, it was a bathroom. It was very luxurious one, with a corner Jacuzzi tub and a shower stall off in another corner. It was done in very beautiful off-white tile and decorated with different shades of pinks, oranges, and bright blues. I went to the sink and checked my image in the mirror. "I look horrible," I said to myself, and then I ran some cold water on my face, feeling better by the moment. I went back into the bedroom and went to the window. I couldn't see anything other than the ocean off in the distance. I jumped, startled, as the door opened behind me. A pretty girl dressed in white came in carrying a tray full of food. Her long brown-black hair was braided and thrown off to the side, over her shoulder.

She set the tray down on the bedside table and went to go back out. "Wait," I said as I moved toward her. Her brown eyes widened, and she looked afraid. Alejandro walked in behind her and spoke to her in a language I wasn't familiar with. He gently laid a hand on her shoulder while he talked to her. She nodded at whatever he told her, and left.

"She doesn't speak English, so you won't get anything from her. Since she's the hired help, I'd prefer you don't scare the hell out of her either. It's hard to get help to come this far out from the mainland."

He stayed planted in front of the door, and I realized how big and muscular he was. I would be no match for him if he forced himself on me. Yet he had said I was to remain unharmed in any way so they could make a trade with Seth. I had to hope that he was right about that. I walked over to the chair he had sat in before and took a seat, still not quite myself.

"The headache should go away shortly. I see you took the aspirin. Good! I wouldn't want you to suffer for nothing," he said, as he sat on the edge of the bed. "I hope that you will eat. Like I said, we need you to remain in good health while in my possession. You are the bargaining chip we need to get Seth to comply with our demands."

"And what, pray tell, are those demands?" I asked, no longer able to keep silent.

"Let's just say, we need to know if Seth is truly one of us or not. We have our suspicions, but can't be sure. I meant what I said before, though; you will be perfectly safe as long as you don't do something here to harm yourself." He looked at the food and motioned with his hand, "Please eat something. When you are ready and feel up to it, come out to the living area which is off to your left. I will be happy to give you the grand tour of your vacation spot for the next few days." He took a half of the sandwich off the plate and ate it, probably to show me that I was not going to be poisoned. He rose, and strode back out of the bedroom, taking his half of the sandwich with him.

So they weren't sure yet if Seth was a pirate or not, and this whole hostage situation was to prove what? It wasn't really making any sense. Surely, they wanted money or something else from Seth. I walked over to the table where the food was and saw that it was a turkey sandwich, some fresh fruit, and another bottle of water for me. I took a bite of the remaining sandwich and waited to see if I would start choking or something- if they had indeed poisoned me. Nothing happened, so I took another bite. It was actually quite good, and I was starving. I continued to eat as I took stock of the bedroom. I opened closets and drawers, finding only women's clothing, but nothing close to some sort of protection or any device that would harm someone. It would have been nice to have the gun that Seth kept on board his yacht right now, I thought to myself. I moved into the bathroom doing the same, going through all the drawers and closets. The only things I found, other than towels and a few toiletry items, were a comb and a hairbrush. Well, I could always beat him to death with the hairbrush, but then what? I went back out to the bedroom and finished the rest of my food.

I opened the door and went down the hall to the left as he had instructed me. Sure enough, he was sitting there with a computer in front him, avidly typing until he saw me enter. He closed down the computer and rose. "I am glad you decided to come out," he smiled. I didn't respond. "Come," he said as he turned to go to the front door, "I will give you the tour."

We walked out into the bright sunshine. It was warm, with a light breeze, and I could smell some of the lush flowers that were everywhere. It would have been a beautiful vacation spot if I hadn't been abducted. He continued down a stone path until we reached a beach. I looked up and down the beach and realized that it was a tiny island, as he had said. In the center of the island, behind us, was a forest of trees. We were clearly the only ones here on this side of the island. There were no other houses, and I literally could see where the island began and ended. There was probably another beach on the other side of the forest of trees.

"See," Alejandro said, "I told you the truth. No escape, no boats, too far to swim, and we are the only ones here." I, again, didn't reply, but continued to take stock of my surroundings. "We are quite alone, and this place is extremely difficult to find as it is nestled in among other tiny islands. You won't be found here unless we want you to be," he continued to explain, as we headed back to the house.

My mind was spinning. I had to find some way to contact Seth. There had to be a phone, or maybe I could find a way through the computer to contact him. Then I remembered. I had never gotten his email address, if he had one, and I had never taken the time to get his phone number. But, I told myself, I could call the girls and alert them, as they surely had Robert's or Jake's phone number! We walked back into the house. He settled onto the couch and motioned for me to do the same.

"As I said before, you are free to roam. I would suggest that you do your best to behave while you are here. We want to return you to Seth in one piece," he smiled at me. I decided to explore the house to look for some way to communicate with the outside world.

Alejandro didn't move to follow me as I made my way into the kitchen. The girl who had brought me the food earlier was busy cooking. She looked up only long enough to see who had entered the kitchen, and went back to her task while she hummed an unrecognizable tune. I walked over to her and tapped her on the shoulder. Again, she looked at me with wide eyes, like she was afraid of me.

"Do you know where I can find a phone?" I asked in a whisper as I tried to gesture as if I was calling on a phone. I looked around quickly to ensure that Alejandro hadn't decided to follow me. We were still alone. The girl shook her head and replied in her own native tongue, which, again, I didn't recognize. "Phone," I tried again to ask her with no success. I surveyed the kitchen, finding nothing. The kitchen was light and airy. Like the rest of the house I had seen so far, it had white walls, with colors brought out in the furniture and paintings. The kitchen had all modern equipment, with an island in the middle. It immediately made me think of Seth and how he would have fun in this kitchen, as it was similar to the one he had in his California home. My Seth, I missed him immensely. I needed to find a way to get out of this predicament.

I continued to look around the kitchen and I did see that there were some sharp knives in a butcher block over in the corner of a counter, but the girl was watching me intently, and I had a feeling that she wouldn't stop at screaming out if she saw me take any. I had to shake myself and wonder what I was thinking I could with a knife, anyway. My captor was too large for me to overcome.

I walked out of the kitchen and saw that Alejandro was back on his computer. I needed to make sure that I paid attention to where he kept that laptop, so I could try to contact someone. I continued walking around the house taking in its luxurious furnishings and island feel. Obviously, whoever owned it didn't lack for money and had wonderful taste. There was a large dining room off to the side, and other than the kitchen, living room, dining room, two bedrooms and most likely two baths, there wasn't much else to the house. It was just huge and very open. Everything was decorated tastefully in the same theme that I had noted in the kitchen. Luscious plants decorated pots strategically placed around the corridors and gave off a wonderful tropical smell. It was truly a paradise spot. I wondered if everything here was obtained through pirate money- blood money. A shiver ran down my spine.

I didn't see any phones and no way to contact the outside world. The reality of my situation started to sink in. I was totally at the mercy of this man. I wasn't giving up by any sense of the word, but right now it looked pretty much like I had no choice other than to wait. Wait for whatever would happen next. Wait for them to contact Seth.

I knew Seth. He wouldn't stop at anything to save me. So wait is what I had to do. Seth was probably aware of the situation by now. Damn! Just when I had convinced him that we needed to be together, this had to happen! Would he now leave me as he had before in order to protect me in the future? The thought made me panic. I couldn't, wouldn't let that happen. I would have another battle to face when I finally got out of this thing, as I was sure that Seth would try to do just that!

I made my way back to my bedroom and sat in the chair, thinking about how I was going to convince Seth that I needed to stay in his life. No matter the danger, my heart couldn't handle another separation from him! And then another thought hit me: Luke. Oh my! How could I have overlooked how he must be feeling? I was with him when this happened. He must be going through pure hell right about now. Oh Luke! Luke, I'm so sorry you were there when this went down. I would have been taken sooner or later. Alejandro was determined to force Seth's hand. I was sure though, that Luke was feeling that this was his fault. Poor Luke! It made me even more determined to find some way to alert them both or find a way to escape. I didn't know how or when, but I had a feeling I had some time to figure it out.

3

Jenna Sawyer breathed a sigh of relief while changing into her yoga workout clothes. It had been a tough day at work and she was really looking forward to some downtime at the gym. Yoga always made her relax and unwind. Tonight she really needed it. It had been hectic for her lately. She had tried to reach out to a cousin of hers, Jason, who was in jail awaiting a trial for piracy. She knew some of her family had started to have untold wealth over the past few years, but she had never suspected piracy!

The thought made her sick to her stomach. She thought that piracy was the swashbuckling vagrants of the past or the contraband of men who recently had taken over large cargo ships off the coast of Africa. What she discovered, though, was that there were smaller bands of these pirates. They waited in the Caribbean for the unsuspecting traveler and took over their yachts and yes, even their women.

When she had tried to reach out to Jason, he seemed to have no remorse. He had just laughed at her and said that he wouldn't be in jail long, and therefore wouldn't need any of her visits. She had given up and avoided any further contact with him after several failed attempts to try to get him to see the wrong in his life. He was no longer the fun and carefree cousin that she had run around with in her earlier years. They had grown apart as they reached their teens, yet she still felt that childhood bond; thus she had tried to reach out to him. It still disappointed her, though.

Jenna's friend Kirsten was next to her in the locker room. Kirsten pulled on her workout shirt and slammed the locker door shut. She sat down on a bench and pushed her feet into flip-flops. Jenna's friend was petite, and very pretty. She had reddish brown, short hair that fell in waves around her oval face. Jenna and Kirsten were alike in that they were both pretty slim, but well toned. That is where the resemblance ended. Jenna was taller than her friend, but not overly so. Jenna had a heart-shaped face that was framed by long black hair, falling in natural waves to just below her shoulders. Her curvaceous body turned many heads when she walked by. She was immune to the reaction she had on men, and would have laughed if you had told her. To look in Jenna's blue eyes you would never be aware of the distress she had felt over the past several weeks. Jenna was an expert at hiding her inner thoughts and feelings. Very few could read her. Kirsten had heard Jenna's sigh, and had looked at her questioningly.

"Kirsten," Jenna said, "do you think we could go to the coffeehouse across the street after class?"

"Sure," Kirsten replied. "I don't have anything pressing going on. Still trying to wrestle with the news about your family?"

Jenna knew that Kirsten was referring to the recent reluctance that Jenna had felt about dealing with anyone in her family, especially now that she had found out about Jason's involvement in the piracy acts in the Caribbean. How could she be related to someone that cruel? "Yeah, it's just frustrating that I am related to people like that. And I thought I knew my cousin pretty well."

"Yeah, but they aren't like you," Kirsten replied as Jenna threw on her flip-flops. Kirsten stood up. They grabbed their yoga mats and headed out the door. "You can't help what your family does." Jenna had disclosed the mess about her cousin several months ago. Kirsten hated what it was doing to Jenna.

Jenna was such a kind and giving person that the news had really shaken her. She thought it was her duty to try and save her family, and so she had set out to visit with Jason. Only Jason wasn't ready to give up. He said he would get out of this thing, with full expectations of resuming his "career" once he was out. Jenna stopped trying after hearing that, and Kirsten knew it wasn't sitting well with her. Jenna thought somehow, that if she was related to someone like that it would haunt her, and affect her in some way.

"I know, but he's family," Jenna replied, as she struggled with the mat strap that was falling off her shoulder. She was so intent on their discussion and on wrestling with the yoga mat that she wasn't watching where she was going as they made their way down the corridor to the class. "Damn thing," she muttered as it dropped off her shoulder once again, and she looked down to grab the strap to pull it back up. She ran into something hard and very muscular. Arms went around her instantly to keep her from falling and she felt . . . protected and . . . safe. She looked up and gazed into blue eyes. The eyes didn't match the grin on his face, and she wondered how she even registered that fact, given how gorgeous the man in front of her was. He set her back away from him and reluctantly dropped his arms. She felt . . . alone . . . all of a sudden. It was like she was made to be in those arms. "And they weren't such bad arms to be in," she thought to herself as she took in his good looks and excellent physical condition. "Sorry," she muttered, and heard Kirsten contain a giggle beside her.

"No, don't be," the man answered her. "My fault, I'm sure."

She didn't know why it would be his fault when she was the one not paying attention. She wondered why her friend hadn't warned her that she was about to collide with this perfectly handsome man. But then again, catching a side glance at Kirsten's face, she thought she knew why. Kirsten wanted to meet him. It was evident in the way Kirsten was looking at him - or was that considered gawking?

"Ladies," he said as he excused himself and walked around them, heading to the men's locker room.

"Wow," Kirsten said as she gazed at his retreating back. The man chuckled before entering into the locker room, and Jenna slapped Kirsten on the arm. Kirsten was unaffected by the playful blow. "Where did he come from, and can I keep him?"

Jenna just shook her head as she grabbed her friend's arm to lead her in the opposite direction, toward the yoga class. She was afraid Kirsten would follow him into the men's locker room. Kirsten was just the type of girl to do that, too! They walked into class, making their way up toward the front right. They both rolled out their mats and discarded their flip-flops to the side. After settling down on her mat, Jenna started to warm up by stretching, bending over her long, lean legs to touch her perfectly manicured toes. She couldn't for the life of her think why she had reacted the way she had when she had bumped into the stranger. It made her scared that she could be affected so quickly by someone she didn't even know. True, the man was absolutely gorgeous. She had taken in the wavy black hair: a little long for today's styles, but it suited him. He had classic facial features, everything proportioned just right. His toned and muscled body had not only made her feel safe when he had held her, but stirred other emotions as well. She had suppressed those feelings for so long that she barely recognized the desire that ran through her blood. She tried to put him out of her mind and concentrate on stretching.

Kirsten was babbling, moving onto other topics. That was what Jenna loved about her best friend. She talked enough for the both of them that Jenna had time to think. However, this time, Kirsten stopped midsentence while talking about a new coworker she was trying to get to notice her. Jenna looked at her friend to figure out what had distracted her from her never- ending stream of conversation. Kirsten was staring in the mirror in front of them. Jenna looked into it as well, and froze. The man they had run into in the corridor was walking into the class. He grabbed a mat from the corner and made his way into the room, heading their way after he spotted them. Oh no, Jenna thought. Bad enough she had run into him and was trying to figure out these feelings, but now he was taking the same yoga class? How did this happen to her? She leaned forward and let her long, wavy black hair fall forward to hide her face, hoping he was headed for the other side of the room. No such luck! He rolled out his mat next to Jenna and sat down to stretch his legs in preparation for the class. His piercing blue eyes locked with Jenna's for a moment when she looked back up, and she took in a gasp of air. As he released her gaze, Jenna quickly looked away, and tried to focus again on stretching. The man smiled to himself, as he hadn't missed the quick intake of air.

"Hi again, ladies," he said. Jenna couldn't help but to look up and lock eyes with the man. She instantly thought of the way she felt in his arms.

"Oh, hi again," Kirsten said, peering around Jenna to get a better view. Jenna thought to herself, "Don't do it Kirsten!" Kirsten was a social butterfly. She would talk to anyone, and the better looking they were, the more she engaged them in conversation. Jenna told many people that Kirsten never met a stranger. In other words, she was just plain friendly to everyone she met. She would strike up a conversation with anyone in her path. It was an endearing trait, but at times Jenna could just strangle her when it came to good-looking men.

"You're new to this class, aren't you?" Kirsten asked.

"Yes, I am. So I hope you ladies will help me out through today's session," he answered Kirsten, while still looking at Jenna.

"Sure, we will be glad to help," Kirsten answered for her friend.

Jenna was glad for the interruption that occurred when the instructor entered the room and took up her position in the front of the class. She was able to avoid answering the stranger beside her. The instructor turned on mellow music and started to call out the first position, explaining all the moves as she did them, as this was a beginner's class. The man followed the instructions as he did the first move. He took in her graceful moves as Jenna followed the instructions. As they did the warrior pose, she could feel his eyes on her back. She stared into the mirror in front of her and he reluctantly moved his head to look into the mirror. Jenna refused to meet his gaze in the mirror, trying to concentrate. She didn't think that she would accomplish relaxation today, as he had set every nerve ending alive within her. Jenna tried to stay focused to the task at hand. There had been other good-looking men in her class before- in fact, there were some here today. But none of them had affected her like this man next to her. She could feel her pulse react and was slightly irritated that he would be interrupting the full relaxation she was longing for today. Damn the man!

She tried to block him from her mind as she focused on the instructor for the next move. He continued watching her through class. She was trying to concentrate, but wasn't quite pulling it off. She huffed out a breath of air in frustration, and he tried to contain his laughter. His reaction made her even more frustrated. Seriously, did he not have any manners? Did he like putting people on edge? Throughout the class Jenna didn't relax once. It was the most stressful yoga class she had ever been in! She couldn't wait to get out of the room and out of close proximity with this man who affected her so much.

As the class ended and they wiped off their mats, Kirsten approached him. "So . . . ," she began, "what are you doing after class?"

Jenna looked mortified. The man smiled at Kirsten before replying, "What did you have in mind?"

Wow, she hadn't realized how sexy his voice was. She continued to focus on cleaning up her mat and rolling it up. She was thinking how she would get out of going to the coffee shop, as she was sure that was where Kirsten was heading with the question she had posed to the stranger. She was going to invite him!

"Well," Kirsten said as she gently laid a hand on his muscled chest and then quickly pulled it away while he smiled, "Jenna and I are going for coffee and we would love it if you would join us, wouldn't we, Jenna?"

Jenna was stuck. She threw a black look at Kirsten, straightened, and faced the gorgeous man as he waited for her reply. It appeared he wouldn't answer Kirsten unless Jenna said she wanted him to join them. Short of being rude, and that was something Jenna never was, she couldn't get out of this one. "Yeah, it would be great if you could." She plastered on her best fake smile to hide her feelings.

"Well, then, how could I say no to that," the man replied. "The name's Luke. Nice to meet both of you," he said before turning his attention to rolling up his mat.

"I'm Kirsten and this is my best friend, Jenna." Kirsten kept the conversation going. "We just need to shower and change and we will meet you out front, say in twenty?"

Luke smiled as he straightened, tucking the mat under his well-muscled arm, "Sounds perfect."

The instructor walked over to introduce herself to Luke, obviously because he was so handsome she wouldn't pass up the opportunity to meet him. Kirsten grabbed Jenna's arm, walking quickly out of the room. "Hurry, we need to get ready."

"Yeah, about that-" Jenna started to reply, but her friend cut her off.

"You're going, Jenna. No ifs, ands, or buts." Kirsten continued to steer her to the locker room. Jenna was pretty sure that Kirsten would push her into the shower fully clothed if she didn't follow her, so she saved her argument for a better time.

In the locker room, wrapped in a towel after coming out of the shower, Jenna stared at her friend of the past five years with her hands on her hips. "What are you thinking?"

"I am thinking," Kirsten replied while gathering up all her makeup for her move to the counter, "that this guy is absolutely gorgeous, and I mean, beyond anything I have ever seen! I don't think it is an opportunity that I am going to let walk out that door without knowing more. Although he seems to have his sights set on you," she pouted.

"What?" Jenna asked as she continued to stare at her friend.

"Yeah, go figure. The guy walks into us in the hallway, and only has eyes for you!"

"He does not!"

"Yeah, he does," Kirsten said as she worked on putting on her makeup. "We don't have time to argue, but you are going with me. In case you don't pursue this thing he has with you, I want a second chance at him."

"Oooofff!" Jenna exclaimed as she angrily grabbed her makeup bag and joined her friend at the counter. She didn't wear too much

Compromises

makeup, mostly because she didn't need it, but also in the interest of time. "You really think he has his sights set on me?" she asked a little incredulously.

"Yeah, anyone could tell."

"Hmmm," Jenna thought. She wasn't sure if she liked that idea or not. Curiously, she felt something between them, but she wasn't used to feeling whatever it was. Not being sure of what it was, she was going to be very cautious around him. Luckily, neither girl was big on blow-drying their hair, leaving it to dry naturally. Jenna's hair had a little waviness to it when dried this way, and only enhanced the features in her perfectly oval-shaped face. They dressed in clothes they had brought with them for after their class, as they had been doing the coffee ritual for a few months now. It was Kirsten's idea of how to find eligible men. She said that the more intellectual types hung out in coffee bars rather than real bars. So far, it wasn't proving to be a good experience. Most of the men were either on their way to another meeting, or they were salesmen. Jenna was just glad that she had chosen a nicer top to wear after class. She didn't question why that mattered, but it did, somehow. The blue, silky tank top hugged her breasts, accentuating them and the slimness of her stomach below. The color really brought out her eyes. Her cropped jeans hugged her hips and her long, lean legs. She pulled on blue flats and pushed all her workout clothes into her bag. Kirsten wore a red tank top with a see-through blouse over top of it, and blue jeans. She looked pretty, but Jenna was just plain stunning.

They walked out of the locker room to find Luke patiently waiting, talking to the girl at the front desk. His dark hair was even wavier when it was wet. He was well built and his T-shirt left nothing to the imagination as it clung to his toned and slender body. It was evident he kept in good shape, but he wasn't like a bodybuilder type. As they got closer, Jenna got a whiff of his cologne. It was an expensive one, she recognized. She had splurged once to buy it for her dad, many years ago.

It was clear the girl at the counter was enamored of him. She was leaning over the counter and getting as close as she could. Luke, on the other hand, stayed a respectful distance away. When he noticed them walking toward him, he continued to answer the girl, but kept his eyes locked on Jenna.

Luke smiled at Jenna as she approached, and tried to think of an adequate response to the girl behind the counter. He had inquired about the membership program and asked if he could pay by the day. The girl had stated that although it wasn't customary for the gym, she would pull a few strings for him. He had replied that he was grateful, and continued to watch Jenna walk toward him.

"Ready to go?" Kirsten asked as she all but hopped up to his side.

"Absolutely," he answered and found he had a hard time breaking his stare into Jenna's beautiful eyes before turning to the girl behind the counter, who now was wearing a frown. "I think I will take you up on the offer to pay by day. See, I work on a yacht so I am not sure how long I will be here, but I hope to work out in the meantime."

"Oh," thought Jenna, "he works on a yacht; interesting!" She had never met anyone who worked on a yacht before. She wondered how life would be, traveling to all those different places. Maybe, just maybe, this coffee shop trip wouldn't be a bad thing after all. A smile started to play across her face, and Luke stared. The effect of the smile caught him by surprise. She was absolutely gorgeous. He smiled back. Jenna looked down, breaking the spell.

The coffee shop was literally across the street so they walked over together. Luke, being the perfect gentleman, offered his arm to them before crossing the street. Jenna hesitated before slipping her arm through his. She could feel the tension in her arm, and tried to keep a respectful distance. He held her arm tightly next to him, chuckling when he saw the response this drew from her, as she clenched her hands involuntarily. She wasn't so unaffected by him as she would like to make him think she was. Kirsten easily put her arm through his on the other side, not attempting to keep any distance between them. It made Luke chuckle to himself. They arrived at the shop, and he reluctantly let go of Jenna's arm. When he did release her, she felt like something had been taken away. Hmmm, that was a strange feeling for her. She didn't have much time to ponder that thought, as the shop was almost empty and they walked right up to the register to order their drinks.

Luke told the lady behind the counter that he was buying while Kirsten and Jenna tried to object. He smiled his perfect smile and said, "Under no circumstances are you to accept money from these two fine ladies." The girl behind the counter could do nothing else but smile at him; Jenna thought she would've run out in the street if he asked her to.

"So," Jenna thought, "he has this effect on every red-blooded woman. Good, it's not just me then." She didn't know why, but that made her feel a little better. They moved to a table off to the side after retrieving their coffees.

"So, Luke," Kirsten began, "I couldn't help but overhear your conversation with the girl at the front desk of the gym. You work on a yacht?"

Luke smiled at her, "Yeah, the life of a sailor. I get to go to all the great locations, don't have to pay a dime for travel, and get paid to do it."

"Wow," Jenna said unexpectedly and then realized that she had spoken her thoughts aloud. Luke just chuckled at her.

"It's okay. I get that response a lot from people when I tell them what

I do for a living. My boss is really a cool guy: not too demanding. And I have a lot of freedom. I have to say, it's a pretty good gig."

"I would say so," Kirsten smiled. "So are you in port long?"

"Yes, I would say so. The owner has some business here, so I think until he settles what it is that he is doing we should be here for awhile." Luke smiled and showed perfectly white, straight teeth.

"We've never met anyone on a yacht before, have we, Jenna?"

"No, we haven't," Jenna replied, trying not to give away too much of the turmoil that was going on inside her.

Kirsten could see that he was only interested in Jenna, and she was tiring of being the third wheel in this party. "If you'll excuse me a moment," she said as she left the table and headed to the back, where the bathrooms were.

Jenna was nervous all of a sudden. She looked down at her hands as they surrounded her cup in front of her as if she needed to warm them, avoiding his gaze.

"Say," he said as he turned his full attention to Jenna, "why don't I have you come over for a tour of the yacht?"

Jenna looked up, surprised at the invite. She could feel the heat rise in her cheeks as he continued to stare at her. "Ssssure . . . ," she stammered out while looking down at the coffee cup between her hands again. Damn, he made her feel like she was in the spotlight- like there was no one else in the room but her and him. How did he do that?

"Great," he smiled. "Tomorrow, then?"

Wow, so soon, she thought. What could she say? She did think it was kind of fascinating, the job he had. And she had never been on a yacht before. She wondered if the invitation included Kirsten or not. "What about Kirsten?" she asked.

"Oh," Luke said, "I was kind of hoping it would be just you and we could do dinner aboard the boat. The captain is an awesome cook."

Compromises

He touched the top of her hand that held the coffee cup, and electricity flowed between them. Jenna pulled her hand away quickly, not sure what to make of the sensation.

"Oh," she said. "Ummm, okay." After all, what harm would it do? Kirsten would probably complicate things, and make her stay longer than she would want if she was on her own anyway. Besides, how bad could it be if there were other people on board?

"I could pick you up at your place or you could come to the marina and I could meet you at the entrance; your choice." She was glad he was giving her some options. It made her feel safer about the dinner date. She answered that she preferred to meet him there. He told her the name of the marina, and she said she was familiar with where it was. They set six the next evening to meet.

Kirsten came back from the rest room and noticed that Jenna was starting to loosen up a little around Luke. She had a feeling that his interest had always been on Jenna anyway, so she wasn't as disappointed as one would think.

"You know," Kirsten said, "I think I know that guy over there." She pointed to a handsome man sitting by himself, typing on his computer, yet looking up to catch Kirsten's attention now and again. "I best go over and say hi. It was really great meeting you, Luke," she said as she held out her hand. She didn't make a move to sit down. It was clear that Luke was totally focused on Jenna, and Kirsten wanted to meet the man who, again, was looking at her.

"Yes," Luke said as he drained his cup and rose. Jenna rose as well. He shook Jenna's hand. He hung on to her hand just a little longer than Kirsten's; long enough to see the heat rise to her face. Yup! She was definitely affected by him. "I'll see you later," he said as he locked eyes with Jenna.

"Later," she replied as he finally released his hand. Before leaving he offered to walk the two girls back, but they declined. Jenna didn't want to prolong the goodbye, as she wanted time to figure out what was happening inside her when he looked at her like that. Kirsten obviously was looking back at the man with the computer, and he smiled; encouragement enough for her to start a conversation with him. Luke turned and walked out as they both watched him leave. Jenna sank to her chair and said, "Wow."

"Ditto," Kirsten replied. "But he seems totally taken with you, so . . . ," she said, as she once again smiled at the man across the room.

"Kirsten," Jenna admonished, "it never stops for you does it?"

"Never," Kirsten assured her. "Luke seems really taken with you. He's really hot!"

"Yeah, I know," Jenna smiled. She really didn't know what to make of it, but she knew she was looking forward to dinner tomorrow. She wanted to have more time to figure out what it was that was between them. She opted not to tell her friend about the dinner date. She wasn't sure why. Maybe it was because she was afraid this "thing" she felt between her and Luke was temporary and physical, soon to pass. She was definitely drawn to him. She had a feeling he knew the effect he had on not just her, but other women as well. Not that he was conceited, but he just knew it. He seemed like a sincere guy and she was just plain curious about him. Tomorrow suddenly seemed way too far away as she tried to regain her focus on her friend, Kirsten. The men in the room paled in comparison with Luke, and she found that disturbing for some reason. She tried to join in with her friend's enthusiasm about a man in the corner surfing the Net, but found her thoughts wandering back to Luke and the way he looked at her- the way he made her feel, like she was the only other living, breathing person in the room. She shook her head as if to clear the cobwebs and focused back on Kirsten.

"I'm tired and ready to head home," Jenna said.

"Are you okay walking back to your car by yourself?" Kirsten asked, staring at the lone man on the computer.

"Yeah, I'll be fine. Catch up with you tomorrow," Jenna said as she rose and made her way out the door. Kirsten made her way over to the other man. Jenna shook her head as she walked out of the coffee shop. "Kirsten is really something," she thought to herself.

Jenna found it hard to sleep that night. Luke's face kept her awake more than she would like to admit. She rolled to her side and tried to think of anything else, anything other than his handsome face. It was to no avail, and she ended up dreaming of him. She woke feeling tired, but excited about the upcoming dinner date.

4

The next day passed so quickly at work, Jenna barely had time to think about the evening. As she let herself into her "flat" above a series of stores, she breathed a sigh of relief. Putting her keys on the counter, she moved into the kitchen. She sensed that something was off- like someone was in her home. It was an eerie feeling, and she wasn't sure why she felt that way, but she wasn't about to ignore her instincts.

She made her way to a kitchen drawer and grabbed a knife in one hand and the phone in the other. She dialed 911, but didn't press the send button just yet, keeping her thumb on it. With the knife held above her head, she walked carefully throughout the flat, flicking on lights as she went. Her place was open, with large rooms. The walls partitioned the rooms, but didn't reach all the way up to the ceiling, which made it appear huge. The living room had a center fireplace that was open to both sides for visual effect. She opened closets as she went past, each time finding them empty. She only had two bedrooms and a bath and a half, so there wasn't much space to cover. Things didn't seem to be out of place, nothing was missing, and there was no one inside waiting to pounce on her.

When she finally made her way back out to the kitchen she let her arm fall and placed the knife back in the drawer, laughing as she did so. What a fool she was! She must be going crazy. It did seem like there was something amiss, but she couldn't put her finger on it. She walked back to her bedroom and stripped down to climb into the shower.

When she was done, she walked out with a towel wrapped around her. She found herself thinking of him again. Damn, he had made his way into her thoughts a million and one times throughout the day. She sat down in the chair in front of the mirror and brushed her black hair into some semblance of order. She decided to blow-dry it and style it just a bit. She put on just enough makeup to get rid of the circles under her eyes from lack of sleep the night before. After applying lip gloss, she headed to her closet. She chose a deep burgundy short-sleeved blouse that accentuated her ample breasts, threw on a black skirt that fell to just above her knees, and drew on some strappy shoes. Spraying perfume in the air in front of her, she walked into the mist. It was a trick she had learned to smell just enough of the perfume and to not put so much on as to be overwhelming. She wasn't sure exactly what one would wear to a yacht, but didn't want to be underdressed. Taking one more look in the long mirror, she smiled, approving of the way she looked.

Jenna locked up her place and made her way down the stairs. She jumped into her car. It was just a short ride over to the marina from where she lived. As she parked, she looked out at the marina, wondering which of the mega-yachts he was on. She didn't have to look long as she shaded her eyes from the setting sun and spotted Luke standing on the top deck of an impressive one. He wove as he noticed her and started walking down to meet her. She walked toward him, nervous as anything as she continued toward the yacht. She couldn't see anything but Luke. He walked up to her and stopped just an arm's distance away.

"Wow," he said as he looked her up and down.

"Yeah, ditto," she thought to herself as she took in the white collared shirt open at his throat, showing off a bit of the beautiful chest she had seen yesterday. He wore black slacks and boat shoes, looking every bit at home in the marina life. "Hi," she said.

"Welcome aboard." Luke offered his arm. She took it reluctantly, waiting for the electricity to start, and wasn't disappointed as she felt the warmth move through her body, making every nerve ending aware of him. "I have to warn you," he began as he turned to look into her eyes. He paused for a moment almost as if he was as affected by her as she was by him.

Jenna thought to herself that he should warn her that she was under his spell with every minute that passed as he continued to hold her arm in his.

"Um . . . ," he continued, "the chef and captain of the yacht is a little beside himself these days. See, he just went through a nasty separation from his last girlfriend and he is still suffering." (Well, it wasn't that far from the truth, Luke thought to himself.) "Just ignore him if he gets all melancholy or something tonight."

Jenna didn't know what to make of that. She followed Luke as he led her up the stairs and they entered into a large living room tastefully decorated and filled with comfortable couches and chairs. A large black baby grand piano sat off to one side of the room. She wondered who played it. He let go of her arm as they entered the room, and she immediately felt the absence of his heat. He motioned for her to sit on a couch as he moved to another counter across the room. She continued to stare at her surroundings, finding it hard to believe she was on a boat. It was huge! And it was extravagant! The yacht had to be worth well

Compromises

over a million dollars, or more like twenty million if she remembered correctly from the travel channel she watched now and again to get a taste of how the rich and famous lived.

"What's your poison?" Luke grinned, as he pulled out two glasses and the ice bucket.

"Wine, please. White if you have it." Luke grabbed a wine glass, filling it quite generously. He poured himself one as well. He walked back over to her and handed her the glass. Their fingers touched briefly, and again she felt the current of excitement as it moved through her. She held on to her glass with both hands, afraid her reaction to his touch would give her away as he let go.

Luke smiled as he sat a respectful distance away from her in another chair. It was almost like he knew when to pull back so as not to scare her away.

"This is . . . wow," Jenna said as she again looked around her.

"Yeah, quite the life I lead," Luke chuckled.

"Isn't it," said another voice from off to her right. Jenna turned toward the speaker to find herself looking at another absolutely gorgeous man. He was tall, with dark wavy hair and blue eyes. He had an English accent, and definitely would make more than one head turn. "Does every man that works on a yacht look like a dream?" Jenna wondered to herself.

"Excuse me," the man said as he entered the room; Jenna stood as he approached her.

"Hi," she said, at a loss for words.

"Hi," he smiled and she was dazzled for a moment by his good looks. He held out his hand and she shook it, but none of the electricity she felt with Luke hit her. Good thing, she thought- she couldn't stand it if that happened with every good-looking guy she came across.

"I'm Seth," this gorgeous man introduced himself. "Chef and captain of the yacht," he continued.

"Nice to meet you," Jenna said, once again sitting down as he made his way to the counter where Luke had been to pour himself a drink. Luke was watching intently when Jenna stole a glance his way. He was frowning, and looked worried. Why, she couldn't fathom. She wanted to tell him, "Don't worry, he doesn't have any effect on me." Instead she returned her focus to Seth.

"So, you must be Jenna," Seth said as he finished making his drink and turned back to face her. "I've heard a little about you from our mutual friend here," he motioned toward Luke.

"Yes," she answered, as she stole another glance at Luke. He seemed to be sending a silent message to Seth - one she couldn't decipher for the life of her. What was up? She felt safe enough, so what put Luke on edge?

"Well, it is nice to finally meet you," Seth said, taking a sip from his glass. "How did you meet Luke, again?"

"He ran into me at my yoga class," Jenna supplied.

"Yoga," Seth asked as he looked at Luke. Then Seth burst out laughing, setting his drink on the counter as laughter overtook him. Luke looked mad at first, and then he broke into laughter, as well.

Jenna thought they had gone mad as she looked between these two gorgeous men, doubled over. She didn't get what was so funny, but it was so infectious that she started to laugh herself.

Seth seemed to finally get control again, and picked up his glass, saluting Jenna as he did so, saying, "Thank you for that; I haven't laughed in quite a few days."

Jenna took a sip of her wine, wondering what could have made him so sad that he hadn't laughed, and then remembered what Luke

Compromises

had said about losing a girlfriend recently. "I'm glad I could lighten the mood," she replied.

"The thought of Luke in a yoga class," Seth said as he chuckled again. He walked over to Luke and slapped him on the back. "You really are a good friend," Seth stated as he walked back out of the room.

"Don't mind him," Luke said as he glanced at Jenna. "The whole girlfriend thing has made him kind of nuts."

"Did he love her a lot?" Jenna asked, curious.

"More than anything," Luke said as he turned serious. "We all do," he added absentmindedly, then realized he had spoken aloud and shook his head. "Would you like a tour?" He asked as he rose from his seat.

"I would love one," Jenna replied, not wanting to dig deeper into what he had said about Seth's lost girlfriend. It appeared this girl, whoever she was, had affected them both.

They made their way through a large dining room with a table set for dinner, and walked past the kitchen, where Seth was busy preparing dinner. He chuckled again as they walked past. They went down a hallway, and Luke showed her a well-stocked library. He walked in and ran his fingers over the spines of the books as he showed her the room. "Miss you, Cass," he said under his breath. Jenna didn't hear him as she gazed around.

"Wow," Jenna said. "I had no idea these yachts were so huge inside."

"Yes, and you haven't seen the best of it yet," Luke said. He took her to the driving station, called the bridge, and showed her the view from there. The sun was just a blob on the horizon, and the sky was lit up with blues, pinks, purples, and oranges. It was breathtaking. Jenna stood behind the wheel and couldn't fathom what it took to drive one of these things.

They went below, and he walked her through each of the rooms and their respective bathrooms. He explained that the large one was Seth's. She noted that a girl's items were still strewn about on the dressing table, like it was waiting for her to return. "Seth's absent girlfriend," Luke explained, as if that said it all. The thought of asking why Seth, captain of the yacht, would occupy what looked like the master bedroom never struck her. Then again, she wasn't used to mega-yachts or who slept where.

Luke brought Jenna back to the crew's quarters, where there were three rooms, a bathroom, a small kitchen, and dinette area. He walked into one room that held only one bed. There weren't any personal items to distinguish this from the others. "This is my room," he said, and then quickly led her back out as if he didn't want to make her uncomfortable. They made their way back through the salon and went up to the top deck and walked out onto a large area strewn with strategically set chairs to invite one to sit and watch the sunset. Another small bar was located off to one side. She walked over to the railing and looked at the sun as the last of its rays hit the water. "It's beautiful!" Jenna exclaimed.

"Yes, beautiful," Luke responded behind her. She turned and found he was staring at her. She had the distinct feeling that he was talking about her, and not the sunset. Crossing her arms, she rubbed them as the feeling of excitement went through her.

"Sorry," he said, "you must be getting a chill. Let's go back inside."

She wasn't about to set him straight that it wasn't the air that made her shiver, but the way he looked at her. They made their way back to the dining room and he held out a chair for her to sit in. Luke pushed her chair in gently, his hand brushing her back before he went to a chair across from her to sit down. That brief touch set her nerves on edge. She looked down at her clasped hands in front of her, trying to gain control of her emotions. What was it about this man that affected her so? He seemed to know he affected her, yet he was so careful not to make any advances, and was the perfect gentleman. She looked up to see him watching her intently. He looked away quickly.

"What happened?" Jenna asked.

"Excuse me?" Luke looked back to meet her gaze questioningly.

"To Seth's girlfriend," Jenna said. "I mean, I can see she clearly has affected him and he seems as if he is still so in love with her."

A look passed over Luke's face, and she wasn't quite sure what it meant. "It's a long story." Luke brushed her question aside. "Besides, now isn't the time or the place," he said as he concentrated on unfolding his napkin to lay it across one of his legs.

Jenna decided not to push the issue. It was obviously a painful topic. "What's for dinner?" she asked, deciding to change the subject.

"Steak, potatoes, veggies, bread, and salad," Seth answered for Luke as he started carrying in plates full of food. "Dessert, if you are interested, is strawberry shortcake."

Jenna watched in amazement as Seth continued to go back and forth with food. "You cooked all this?" she asked.

"It's a passion of mine."

Before Jenna could reply, two other men came walking in. They, too, were gorgeous. They had blond, messy hair, a style popular for the day. Luke introduced them. "Robert and Jake, this is Jenna. I met her at yoga yesterday."

The statement about the yoga class caught the two new men off guard. They stared at Luke for a whole minute before breaking into laughter, which made Seth join them. Luke laughed with them, and then controlled himself. "Okay, laugh's on me, I know," he chuckled as he tried to get control of the situation. Robert and Jake sat down at the table and dug in. Luke cleared his throat, causing them to pause and look at him. "Ladies first!" Luke stressed. They dropped their utensils, muttering, "Sorry."

Jenna felt herself give in to the laughter at the look on their faces. They joined in. She felt at ease in a room of gorgeous, strange men. It was weird, but she felt safe with them. She quickly filled her plate so they could dig in. They did so, filling their plates and squabbling like family. Seth sat down to join them, but toyed with his food. Luke looked at him, saddened to see him in such a state. Jenna could see that the man was truly in pain and wondered why this woman would have left him if he clearly loved her so much. If she had a man like that, she would never leave him. Especially if she was loved as much as this unknown girl was. It made her want to go out, find her, and tell her what a fool she was for leaving him.

She looked over at Luke, to see that he was watching her intently. Looking down at her food, she started to eat. It really was quite good. Jenna listened as the conversation flowed around her. They talked about the weather. Robert and Jake talked about their girlfriends, who were about to arrive here in Florida; they seemed excited about that. They explained to Jenna that they had been out to sea for a long while and hadn't seen them in quite a few months. For a moment she thought how that would feel- to be dating someone and not see them for months. She looked up at Luke and thought she wouldn't like not seeing him for months on end like that. He smiled at her, and it made her forget that last thought all together. To wait for him would be worth it, she realized suddenly.

After dinner, she offered to help clear the table and help with the dishes, but Seth waved her off, saying he needed to be occupied. Again, she had to wonder at this girl who seemed to have broken his heart.

Luke walked her up to the top deck, carrying their glasses of wine. She took her glass from him and moved off to the side, looking out

Compromises

over the water. Taking in the beautiful sight of the moon hitting the water below, she was beginning to see why Luke would like this job. The beauty of living on the water made you respect the beauty around you. She looked sideways to glance at Luke as he too, took in the sight. Yes, beauty was definitely all around her tonight.

Luke kept a respectful distance, for which she was grateful, as she still had to figure out what this sensation was every time he touched her. They stood in silence, and she heard the low melody of a radio coming from speakers set about the upper deck. She hadn't noticed this before, and thought that either Seth or Luke had turned it on when she wasn't paying attention.

"I hope you enjoyed dinner," Luke said as he turned, facing her as he leaned against the railing.

"How could I not?" Jenna replied, and then realized what she had just said. She had to be more careful when answering him, she thought. "I mean, the food was great." Luke just chuckled as if he understood her dilemma. "Luke," she questioned as she turned to face him, "why did Seth's girl leave?"

Luke was stunned into silence, not quite sure how to answer her. He tried to regain his composure. "Why do you ask?" He figured he would try to get her to talk more, rather than tell a lie.

"Well, clearly Seth loves this girl and she just up and left? I mean, it doesn't make any sense. Why would she leave?"

"There were unforeseen circumstances that got in the way." Luke tried, again, not to lie to her. Somehow he felt it harder and harder to keep things from her. He wasn't sure why that was, but it just was.

"You can tell me," Jenna said as she reached out to touch his hand before realizing what she was doing. The moment her hand touched his, electricity jumped through her again and she quickly pulled back. Her reaction didn't affect Luke. He set his glass down, grabbed hers and did the same. He did what he had wanted to do ever since he had held her in his arms that first time, running into her in the gym hallway. He pulled her to his chest and buried his head in her hair, breathing in the fresh scent of her.

Jenna was shocked at first, and then relaxed in his embrace. It was like she was "home." She felt she belonged there. She liked the way his lips were moving in her hair. He pulled back slightly, but only to keep kissing her along her jaw until finally taking her lips with his. The kiss was deep and sweet. She lost track of where she was. Returning his kiss, she moved further into his embrace, bringing her arms around him to keep him close. Luke moaned and deepened the kiss by entering into her mouth with his tongue. She let herself get lost in it. She only knew that this was where she belonged. She wasn't in a state of mind to question it.

Luke pulled back, reluctantly, and put some space between them as he picked his glass up and looked back over the ocean. He was quiet, and she had the feeling that he had withdrawn from her. She wasn't really sure what to say or do, so she picked up her glass and took a large gulp of wine before leaning on the railing to gaze over the water herself. They stood in silence for awhile. It was a comfortable silence.

Luke turned, and was serious all of a sudden. "So, tell me about you . . . your family."

"There isn't much to tell," Jenna said, still gazing out at the water. "I lead a pretty boring life, Luke."

Luke started pacing, and she turned to watch him. He was clearly agitated, and she couldn't for the life of her figure out why. "What do you want to know?" she inquired, figuring that he was wrestling with some kind of demon within himself.

"I just want to know about you, is all," he said; but she got the distinct feeling that his question was more important than he was letting on.

"Well, there are parts of my family that I don't, or you could say won't, associate with," Jenna said, wanting to be truthful and not sure why she was bringing it up. Something in her statement made Luke stop pacing. He stood in front of her again, the interest clear in his eyes.

"Why is that?" he asked, as he held his breath.

"Well," Jenna said as she turned to look out at the ocean, "some people in my family are not the nicest people, and it disgusts me." There! She had said it. She wasn't sure why she felt comfortable sharing this with Luke, but she did. It felt good to get that out.

He moved closer and turned her to look into his eyes. She saw pain and concern there. It touched her heart. "You don't have to tell me if you don't want to," he said, clearly serious. "You don't . . . ," he stopped as he took her mouth with his. She couldn't get enough of him, which scared her. She had never felt this way about anyone before. It was thrilling and scary at the same time. She gave in to his kiss and moved in closer. He, once again, moaned, pulling her in for a deeper kiss, and then finally broke it off as he kept her close in his embrace. She heard him cuss into her hair and wondered why. Was it because he wanted more, like she did, but wanted to take it slow, to be cautious, like her? Or was it something else?

He pulled back and smiled. She noted that the smile didn't quite reach his eyes. It made her sad. Something was bothering him, and she wasn't sure what it was, but she was sure it wasn't her. He finally let her go, and moved away to look out at the water. "It's getting late. Let me walk you to your car," he said as he moved toward the stairway, not waiting for her reply. She picked up her glass and followed him down into the kitchen. Everyone was gone, probably off in their respective staterooms for the evening, and they set their glasses on the table. Luke continued to walk down out of the yacht and to the parking lot where her car was parked, waiting for her. She fumbled with getting her keys out of her purse. Her hands were shaking slightly, so she had a hard time getting the key into the lock. Luke took it from her and deftly opened the door. She walked closer to the door and turned. He took her one more time into his arms and gave her a kiss that lasted forever. He seemed reluctant to let her go, and she was even more reluctant to let him go.

"I enjoyed your company," Luke said as he gazed into her eyes.

"As I did yours," she answered, truthfully.

"Can I see you tomorrow?"

She hadn't thought she would see him again so soon, but was grateful that he seemed to want to see her as much as she did him. "I hope you will," she said as she smiled at him.

"How about breakfast?"

"Sounds good," she said. After all, it would be a Saturday and she wouldn't be pressed to get to work or anywhere else.

"I can meet you at your place and take you out if you tell me where you live," he said.

Jenna was cautious about giving out her address to anyone. Yet she felt she could trust Luke, for whatever reason she felt that way. She gave her address, and they agreed upon nine in the morning to meet. She was already missing him, and she hadn't left yet. Weird! This guy was really getting under her skin. "Tread carefully," she told herself. She dropped into her seat, and turned the key in the ignition. He closed the door carefully, and she felt as though a huge piece of her life had just been sealed away, taken from her. She shook her head to clear the thought and drove away from the man who made her feel more than she ever thought she could or would ever feel in her life.

Later, she entered her own home, throwing the keys on the counter as she made her way to her bedroom. She stripped and walked into the bathroom. After brushing her teeth, she made her way to the bed, flicking off lights as she did. She tripped on the white bear rug that had been a gift from her grandfather, laughing as she stumbled over it. Damn rug, it was always tripping her up, but she didn't have the heart to get rid of it. She had always been close to her granddad as a child, and many a time he had curled up on this rug in front of the fireplace in his home to read her a bedtime story.

As she curled up to her pillow, her thoughts returned to Luke. Something about him was sad. It was evident in the way that his smile didn't quite reach his eyes. In fact, she felt that same sadness with all of them. Could it be Seth's girlfriend? Was it something else?

Jenna wanted to make Luke's smile reach his eyes if it was the last thing she did. She closed her eyes, and it was the last thing she thought of as she fell into a deep sleep. She was going to make the smile reach his eyes.

5

Days had passed lazily and uneventfully on the little island where I was being held hostage. Alejandro was good to his word. He was going to keep me in good health as long as I behaved. The food was always delicious and I had free rein on the island. He also made sure there was no way I could escape.

As I stepped out of the shower and dried off, my thoughts turned to Seth. He must be so worried! I could only imagine what this would do to our relationship. Knowing how protective he was of me the last time there was an incident with pirates, I knew this wouldn't turn out well. He would either leave me for good this time or become so overprotective I wouldn't be able to move. Damn Alejandro! The thought made me angry and even more anxious to find a way to contact Seth.

I dressed in a bathing suit and cover-up, knowing that another day on the beach would be my only pastime. Well, I thought, at the least I am getting a lot of rest. I was fed well and I took long walks along the beach early in the morning and late at night. Alejandro didn't join me, which was something I preferred. As long as I didn't try anything "stupid," I was unharmed.

I made my way into the kitchen and filled a bowl with fresh fruit that the girl who worked in the kitchen had just finished cutting up. As I sat down and forked a piece of mango, I looked over at her. She smiled, which was getting to be more regular once she determined I wasn't going to scare her. She still couldn't communicate, as she didn't speak very much English. She knew some of what I said, I knew, but very little. "Good morning, Stella," I said.

She nodded her head and answered in broken English, "Morning." She turned to clean up the dishes she had used to make breakfast.

Alejandro walked in and sat down opposite from me. "Good morning, Cassie. I trust you slept well?"

"I'd sleep better if I was home," I replied sarcastically.

Alejandro laughed as he shook his head. "Seth really has his hands full with you. Does he know you are such a wildcat?"

I remembered the day Seth had called me a wildcat. He had surprised me on the boat when I was leaving, just about to lock my door. Seth had come from nowhere to push me back down inside. He had called me *wildcat* when I had struggled against his hold. Coming to warn me about Luke, he had ended up kissing me. That was our very first kiss. The memory made me miss him even more. I brought myself back to the present.

"How long is this going to go on?" I asked, wanting to know when I could get back to a normal life.

"Well, it depends on your boyfriend," Alejandro said as he took a sip of the coffee that Stella placed in front of him.

"What does he have to do to get you to release me?"

"Of course, there is money involved, but he has more than that I need him for."

"What on earth can he do for you that you can't do yourself?" I said, hoping that I could somehow bring this abduction to an end.

"I wonder," Alejandro said as he stared off into the distance. "How did the Coast Guard find you last holiday season?"

"I don't know," I answered, lying through my teeth. Of course I wasn't going to tell him about how Jay and Seth stayed in contact with each other. "I do know that Seth was taken by surprise just as everyone else was." It wasn't an all-out lie. He was surprised by the pirate attack at sea.

"How did you go from being an abducted member on the yacht to his girlfriend?"

Oh, that was going to be tricky. I wasn't sure what or how much he knew about my relationship with Seth. He obviously knew we were together. "I fell in love." It wasn't a lie, but I wasn't giving anything away either.

Alejandro laughed as he rose from the table. "See? You give me nothing. Thus, your stay here will be for awhile longer."

He left the room and I lay my head in my hands. Oh! This was so frustrating. I felt absolutely useless! I had to find a way to get to Seth.

Later, I walked along the beach, looking for shells that caught my eye and putting them in the pocket of my cover-up. As I bent down to pick up yet another blue-green shell poking out of the sand, I heard an engine. I looked up to see a small boat approaching the island. I walked quickly toward the dock that was down at the other end, near the house. As I got near, I stayed close to the side of the house and watched as a man got out of the boat and made his way up to the front entrance. I heard Alejandro greet him and they walked inside.

Ah! Finally, a way off the island! I ran down to the dock, taking furtive glances back toward the house to ensure that Alejandro didn't see me. I reached the boat and jumped inside. I looked down at the keyhole to see it empty. Damn! I looked around the small boat and opened a bag down beside it, looking for a phone or anything I could use to contact the outside world with. It only held some ropes and boat items. I looked around for a handheld radio, thinking I could get on it and give out a Mayday signal. I was so intent on scoping out the boat that I failed to recognize that Alejandro had made his way outside and run down to the boat dock. He and his visitor stood by, waiting for me to realize they were there. He had a smile on his face. I finally realized that I wasn't alone, and slowly turned to find them standing there, obviously amused by what I was doing.

"Do you think I am so stupid as to allow you a way off the island?"

I dropped the bag that I had been digging through and stood up. I ignored the hand he held out to help me back off the boat. He chuckled as I huffed my way back into the house. I heard him compliment the other man on remembering to take out the key and the handheld when he came to the house. I wished I knew how to hot-wire a boat to start it without a key. Maybe I needed a lesson in hot-wiring when I got out of this thing.

As I made my way back into the house, I noticed that the computer was out and sitting in the living room. I looked back outside and saw that Alejandro and the other man were still talking by the boat. I sat down and looked at the computer. It was open on email. I clicked the Sent folder and saw a message that had been sent to Seth. I knew I wouldn't have time to read it, so I took note of the email address. How did these pirates know these things? They certainly were a smart breed. I made sure I put the email back to the state it was in, and quickly went to my room. I found my purse and wrote down Seth's email address, then tucked it behind one of my credit cards to hide it. Even if Alejandro found it, he wouldn't think anything of it, knowing that I was Seth's girlfriend. Now I would just need to get the computer to type a message to Seth. That was not going to be easy.

Alejandro never said anything more about my failed attempt to escape. As we sat down to dinner later that night, we ate in silence.

"Do you have family?" I asked Alejandro after awhile, curious to see if he would open up.

"Do you mean to ask if I have someone in my life that would turn me away from pirating?" He was clever and not about to give away anything.

"I was just trying to make conversation," I said demurely while looking back down at my food.

"I don't have any girlfriends, at the moment," he answered, laughing as he did so. "Why, you interested?"

"That's not what I meant." I looked back up at him. He was handsome, so he obviously did have girlfriends in the past. I wondered if they knew what he did for a living. The thought of his profession made me sick to my stomach, as I was sure it would for many. Either his girlfriends were kept in the dark or they were of a type that it wouldn't matter what he did, as long he bought them things. I shivered, thinking about it. "I meant," I clarified, "family. Sisters, brothers, mother . . . ."

He interrupted my stream of conversation. "I have a cousin, besides Jason who you've already met. We aren't close, as she was only made privy to my occupation when Jason was arrested."

"Oh," I said, realizing that maybe I had an ally in his so-called cousin.

"Jason is the closest thing I have to family now, and he is in jail, thanks to your Seth."

It was making more sense now. If that was the only family that Alejandro had left, I could see why it was important that he had some kind of revenge thing for Seth.

Compromises

"Maybe, if you weren't in such an illegal profession, you would have your cousin safe and sound."

Alejandro laughed. "Trying to get to my conscience? Well, don't waste your time. That ship sailed a long time ago."

We finished eating in silence. I couldn't grasp the mind of a thief. Was nothing other than money important to him? I was glad I wasn't like that. Money couldn't buy love. Even though Seth was extremely wealthy, I would have loved him even if he wasn't. In fact, I fell in love thinking he was just the captain of a yacht.

"What about your Seth?" Alejandro asked, breaking the silence. "Isn't he a pirate as well?" Tricky! I had to be careful even in casual conversation.

"Yes, but I put that out of my mind when I am with him. I just love him," I shrugged my shoulders for effect.

"I can't tell if you're serious or not, Cassie. You are very adept at hiding things."

"So are you," I answered as I got up from the table and went to my room, not wanting to give anything away. I lay down on my bed and thought of Seth. Maybe I could get a message to him tonight. I would have to try.

Later that evening, something woke me. I wasn't sure what it was at first, and then it came to me. I was dreaming about Seth. We were making love and I was in pure heaven. In my dream, Alejandro walked in as we were making love and shot Seth in the back. I shivered as I tried to bring myself back to reality. I found the pillow I had been holding close crinkled beside me. I got out of bed and looked out through my window at a dark night. I tip-toed to the door and slowly opened it, soundlessly, to make my way out to the main part of the house. Everything was dark and quiet. I didn't see the computer anywhere. I made my way down the hallway, careful not to make any noise.

Alejandro slept with his door open, probably to make sure that he could hear me if I got up and around. He snored loudly in his bed and rolled to his side, facing away from me. I stepped in cautiously, looking around. I noticed a black bag in a chair off to the side. I grabbed the bag, feeling the weight and hoping it was a computer. I remembered that Alejandro warned me that he slept with a gun. The last thing I wanted to do was get shot.

I crept out soundlessly and went back to my room, closing the door behind me. I opened the bag. Bingo! It was the computer. I went to grab the slip of paper out of my purse. I brought the computer up. Lucky for me it came right up with no passwords needed, and he was signed into his email. You would think that thieves would be a little bit smarter about things like that. Then again, they usually got caught, so maybe not.

I typed in Seth's email address, excitement rushing through me. I couldn't give him much. I typed . . .

"*Seth. Love, it's me, Cassandra. I am being held by Jason's cousin, Alejandro. I am okay. Just do as he asks, as he knows you are a pirate, like him.* I added this piece of information just in case Alejandro ever came across this email. *I can't tell you where I am. I think . . .*" I continued as much as I could as I finished my email.

I cleared out the item after I sent the email. Putting everything back into the bag, I made my way back into Alejandro's room. I set the bag back and was heading back out the door when I heard the click of a gun. I put my hands up in the air and waited.

Alejandro breathed out, "Cass? Shit! You have to be careful. I could have shot you." He flicked on a light and I turned to face him. "What the hell were you doing in here?"

"Looking for something to escape with," I answered, somewhat truthfully.

"Damn, girl, don't you know I am smarter than that? There is nothing here or anywhere on the island that you could escape in or with. Did you want to get shot or something else . . ." He smiled as the sentence trailed off.

He still held the gun as he got out of bed. I was relieved to see he was wearing PJ bottoms. He walked toward me and let a finger trail down my throat. I stood perfectly still, my eyes trained on his gun until he took his hand to bring my chin up to stare into his brown eyes. Passion was evident. He took hold of my chin, forced a kiss on my lips and moved in closer, so I could feel how excited he was.

I struggled against his hold and pure reaction took over as I slapped his face. Instantly realizing the danger I just put myself in, I brought the hand that slapped him to cover my mouth. I waited.

"Good thing I need to return you unharmed. You best get back to your own bed before I change my mind," Alejandro said, leaving no doubt in my mind that he would follow through with that threat. I quickly ran back to my own room. I had gotten a message to Seth. There! I had accomplished one thing. I crawled back into bed and hugged my pillow tight and waited for my heart to slow down after the scare I had just had, glad that I was still safe and unharmed. I needed to be careful around him in the future. After all, he was a man . . . and a pirate.

6

Seth was getting anxious. He wanted to find Cassandra and put Alejandro in jail, where he belonged! He knew that Luke wanted the same thing, but it was taking some time. Luke had been seeing Jenna every night. They were spending every moment they could together. Sometimes he brought her there to the yacht, and every time he did, Seth had to control himself. Seth wanted to shake her and scream at her to get her to tell him where he could find Alejandro. Luke kept telling him that he couldn't rush this thing. He needed time to get Jenna to trust him enough to tell him what she knew. It was frustrating, but Seth knew that Luke was right.

They all missed Cassandra so much, and feared for what she was going through. It didn't help things much for Luke to know that this is exactly why Seth had stayed away after the pirates had taken over the yacht this past Christmas when Cassandra was aboard for a trip to the Caribbean.

Seth had called Cassandra's parents, and they were making arrangements to come back to the States. He told them that the Coast

Compromises

Guard was involved and they should just sit tight until he had more information about where she was. There was really nothing they could do here, and besides, he and Luke were working on a tricky situation. If her parents were here it could delay finding Cassandra. With nothing much else to hang on to, they had to trust Seth and his judgment. But they wanted to know the minute Seth had concrete information and a rescue was imminent, so they could fly in right away. He promised them that he would. It was the least he could do.

Seth heard the computer alert him of incoming email. "Damn, not that blasted Alejandro again," he stated to himself as he made his way over to it. The man was exasperating! He had only said that he needed Seth's assistance now that Jason was in jail. Seth didn't know how he was going to accomplish that and look for Cassandra at the same time. He told Alejandro as much. Alejandro said that pirates have a way of getting things they want. He would trade Cassandra for Seth's help, after Seth solved a particular tricky situation with him. He said he would alert Seth to the where and when. After all, Alejandro said, pirates have to stick together- unless, of course, he wasn't a pirate.

Seth opened his email and he read the first line. His heart stopped. He sat down and read the full email. Cassandra had gotten a hold of a computer somehow and had sent him a note. She ended with . . . *I may be somewhere tropical, a small island. There is only this one house and there is no way on or off except by boat or helicopter, maybe a small plane. I miss you terribly. Promise me not to do anything rash! Love you so much.*

Seth was finally able to breathe. He was relieved that she was fine. He had to believe it was her, as she had used his term of endearment, "love," at the beginning. He could read between the lines to see that she wasn't giving away anything to Alejandro about his true status of not being a pirate. She didn't give him much information. There were so many little islands that could be in a tropical place. He'd search every single one if that is what it took to find her! He couldn't reply to her, but he hoped that maybe he would continue to get little clues as to where she was. She was fine; that, at the least, was comforting!

Then he thought about the email. Obviously, Alejandro wasn't aware that she had typed the message. Alejandro wasn't stupid, and wouldn't have left the computer out for easy access. That means that Cassandra was taking risks. Damn that girl! She was really something else. She'd taken the risk to get a message to him. He couldn't have her in danger, doing stupid things like this. And, she was warning him not to do anything rash! He remembered when they were on the yacht and the pirates had taken over. He had caught her contemplating taking the small boat to escape out on the open seas. He hoped she wouldn't do something like that now! He got up to pace around as he thought about his risk-taking girlfriend.

As Seth was pacing in the salon, his mood becoming darker as he thought of these things, Luke and Jenna entered the room.

Jenna felt the tension she always did when around Seth. The man was clearly in pain over the loss of his girlfriend. It just wasn't healthy, loving someone who had left you just like that. They were all pretty closemouthed about what happened. Not to mention that it was freaky how her things were still set out in Seth's stateroom. It was like he was waiting for her to show up at any moment. Whoever this Cassandra was, they were pretty well involved with her. Even Robert and Jake loved this girl. She had touched their heart in a very special way. Jenna had a sneaking suspicion that the sadness she felt in Luke had to do with Cassandra's leaving. It appeared that they all had a very special bond. Jenna would have been jealous of this girl if it wasn't for the very clear and evident fact that Seth was the one that loved Cassandra the most and they were in a very special relationship.

Jenna smiled at Seth, letting him know that she felt for him too, as she entered the room. He nodded his head in a gesture of greeting and quickly strode out of the room. She saw that he was really upset and guessed correctly that he was probably thinking about Cassandra again.

Luke had been spending all his free time with Jenna over these past few days. Since he worked on the yacht, it wasn't as if he had a job to go to every day. She did, though, which made her days at work painfully long. He would surprise her by being at her house, waiting for her to come home. She hadn't invited him in as of yet, afraid of what would happen if they were truly alone together. He would wait patiently outside while she dropped her work items inside and then run out to go with him to dinner or wherever he wanted to go. Sometimes he would take her to the beach and they would walk along the shore, feet in the sand, watching the sun set. They talked about her job, his day, or other trips he had made in the past to Florida. He would regale her with stories of when he was in exotic places, traveling with Seth on the yacht. He made her laugh as he told her that he wasn't a fan of excursions at those tropical places. He'd had an incident one time where a dolphin wanted to be quite friendly with him. She doubled over in laughter, knowing how the poor thing must have felt, as she had a hard time trying to contain her feelings inside, as well.

Her feelings for him hadn't diminished in the least, and she knew that her heart was getting more attached every time she saw him. It was both scary and exciting at the same time. She didn't know where this was going, but never one to shrink at the chance of living life to its fullest, she continued to see him.

Luke watched Jenna now, and saw her look as she watched Seth leave, and he frowned. He hadn't disclosed anything else about Cass or how she had left or why, and he knew that Jenna was baffled at how hurt they all seemed over her leaving. "It's not you," he said.

"I know," Jenna said as she sat on one of the luxurious couches and settled into the back cushion while Luke went to get her a glass of wine. "I wish he would let go. He needs to start living again. It's just not healthy to want someone that has left you."

Luke had his back to Jenna, and he tried to hide the look of hurt at her statement. They all wished that this was over and they could start living again. He had purposely led her to believe that Cass had left of her own free will. He needed her to think that, and couldn't tell her the truth.

He hadn't gotten Jenna to open up about her family in the few days he had seen her. He knew Seth was getting antsy and wanted him to move quickly, but he also wanted Jenna to trust him. He needed her trust. He turned with a smile plastered on his face, which contradicted everything he was feeling inside. "You seem to be in a good mood tonight. Let's not spoil that with talk about Seth's love life, or lack of it, that is."

Jenna saw, once again, that Luke's smile didn't quite reach his eyes. She hadn't been able to get past the sadness in him these past few days. Whoever this Cassandra was, she wished she could find her and tell her to get back here, as the whole place was a mess without her. "Well, that mood is changing pretty quickly," Jenna said, and then realized she had spoken her thoughts aloud.

Luke sat down beside her and handed her the glass of wine. "Sorry about that. What can I do to change that?"

Jenna smiled and placed her glass on the table. "Just being with you makes my mood better."

Luke smiled back, "Good. I like to know I make a difference."

"What's for dinner?" Jenna asked, trying to change the subject and keep herself from wanting to take him in her arms and erase the pain and sadness that she felt he was hiding from her.

Compromises

"Pasta- Seth's specialty," Luke smiled. "He made some homemade garlic bread sticks and salad on the side. It's pretty awesome."

"He definitely has a talent in the kitchen," Jenna agreed. She had eaten at the yacht for several nights, and Seth's culinary skills never ceased to amaze her. The guy was an excellent cook. She might just have to give in to Kirsten's pleading, as she was always asking Jenna to invite her to come with her one of these nights. Maybe Seth needed the distraction of another woman to help him get over this girl.

"So," Luke said changing the subject to try to get her to open up, "we have been seeing a lot of each other lately, yet I feel there is so much I don't know about you."

"Not much to tell you, Luke," Jenna replied as she reached again for her glass of wine, to give her hands something else to do rather than reach out to him. "I've told you, my life is pretty boring."

"Hardly," Luke answered, "you are in excellent shape; you do charity work, you work hard at your job to excel, you've been spending a lot of time with me . . . "

"Where is this going, Luke?" Jenna asked, gazing into his beautiful blue eyes, straightforward as always.

"Well, what about your family? Don't they miss you? I mean, I really have been taking all your time."

"I don't have much family left in the area. And some, I prefer not to see," Jenna said as she looked down into her glass once again.

Luke thought he was on to something now, "Why is that, again?" He wanted to sound innocent, casual even, and tried to keep from leaning in, hanging on her every word.

"Let's just say there are some skeletons in my family closet that need to stay there."

"We all have skeletons," Luke said. He had a few of his own. He wondered how she would feel about that once she found out. He pushed the thought aside, intent on keeping her talking about her family.

"Do we have to talk about this?" Jenna looked up again, meeting his gaze.

"I just want to know all about you," Luke said as he moved closer to her.

All her nerve endings were alive. She waited as he moved in. He grabbed her glass and set it on the table next to him. He moved closer to her and gently kissed her. She let herself dissolve into the kiss. It was like this every time. It started out gentle and then a fire burned within her. One of them always backed away after a few moments, putting the distance between them, and this time was no different. He sighed as she moved and got up from the couch to run her hands across the top of the baby grand piano, thinking that she hadn't seen anyone play it. Pity, that something that could make beautiful music should sit empty, waiting. It was like everyone else on this yacht, waiting, waiting patiently.

She brought herself back to the conversation. "I have told you before, there are some people in my family that I am not proud of," Jenna said. She was trying to fight the fire within her as she looked back at Luke, and talking about her unsavory cousins was one way to do it. Luke scooted to the end of his seat, intent on every word as she continued. "See, there are some criminals in my family and I recently learned about that. I have a hard time coming to terms with it," Jenna said, missing the sudden interest that Luke displayed as she was caught up in her feelings of disgust of being related to such scoundrels.

"Do they live here?" Luke inquired.

"Some, yes, and others, no."

"Well, where are they? I mean, don't they have contact with you?"

"Well, a cousin of mine was recently placed in jail here locally and is awaiting trial." Jenna hoped that this information wouldn't turn Luke

Compromises

against her. It wasn't a pleasant thing to tell someone you were just getting to know that you had family with a sinister background. "Other cousins, doing similar illegal things, are in the Caribbean."

"The Caribbean; okay, it's a start. Keep her talking," Luke thought to himself.

"I don't think we should keep talking about this," Jenna said, as she moved over to pick up her glass and take another sip before sitting down.

"I just don't want you to feel that you can't talk to me," Luke said, reaching for her empty hand as she sat down close to him. She let him take it, enjoying how her hand felt in his. "What kind of illegal things are they into?" Luke asked as his thumb played with the pulse that was racing in her wrist.

"Piracy," she said as she looked down at his hand, afraid to meet his gaze.

"You mean like the ones off the coast of Africa that have held a few of the large cargo ships hostage lately?"

"Well, there are those as well, I guess. My cousins tend to stay closer to home and pirate the Caribbean islands south of here."

"I am aware of them," Luke said, and then when she looked up in surprise he responded, "We travel a lot in the Caribbean, so we have heard the stories. We have been lucky enough to avoid them in our travels, though," he added nonchalantly. He didn't want to add that her cousin, Jason, had been aboard this very yacht a few short months ago- thus the reason Jason had been caught, and the reason Luke had sought Jenna out.

"Oh, yes, I guess you would have," Jenna nodded, realizing that boaters surely must share stories about their travels.

"Dinner is ready," Seth stated as he walked in, breaking into the conversation. Jenna wasn't positive, but she thought she heard Luke sigh, as if he was irritated at the interruption. "I'm sorry that I won't be joining you," Seth continued, "but I have some things I need to attend to."

"Thanks, Seth," Luke said. "Oh, can I catch you for a moment?" he asked before Seth could leave, and then turned to Jenna to add, "I will only take a moment."

Luke and Seth walked off quickly together. Jenna looked down at the hand that Luke had just held, thinking how odd it was that she felt much more at home when Luke was holding it. Jenna hated talking about her family, yet it helped to get this frustration out about how she felt about them. Luke was being so sympathetic about this whole thing! He let her talk about herself a lot.

She wondered what skeletons he had in his closet. No doubt they involved women, as the guy was breathtaking and hard to resist. She smiled as she thought how it was getting harder and harder not to invite him in at night when he left her at her door.

In the other room, Luke caught up with Seth. He told him that Jenna just leaked information that she had a cousin in the Caribbean. Seth, in turn, told Luke about Cassandra's email.

"Damn, the girl is good." Luke saw the pained look on Seth's face and correctly guessed he feared that Cassandra was taking risks that could mean she would end up getting herself hurt or . . . dead. "She's not that stupid, Seth. She won't take risks that will endanger her life. She's careful. You don't give her enough credit. She's a strong girl. She will make it through this thing . . . and mostly unscathed."

Seth stared at his friend, desperately wanting to believe him, and failing miserably. "We need to get to her. See if you can't nail down the location of this cousin. I will start looking at maps of the Caribbean, but there are tons of little populated islands."

"I'm on it, Seth."

Compromises

Luke walked back into the salon and broke through Jenna's thoughts, noting her smile. He held out a hand to help her stand up. He pulled her close once she was standing, and took her mouth with his once again. After he stopped, he said, "I wish . . . ," and left the sentence there between them, unfinished. Jenna wasn't sure why, but she felt she didn't want to know what he was going to say. She let the sentence dangle there in the air between them and followed him to the table as he sat her in her chair, then made his way across from her, before sitting down himself. She thought how nice it was to be treated like a real lady. Most guys wouldn't open your door or hold out your chair for you anymore. They left you to your own devices. She wondered if it was because he lived with Englishmen and they seemed to have more manners than most. Or maybe he was just trying to impress her. Well, it was working, for whatever reason he was doing it.

Dinner was delicious, as usual. They chatted about other non-significant things, steering away from the topic of her family. After they finished their meal, Jenna offered to clear the table and do the dishes, but Seth walked in as she offered, and absolutely refused to let her assist.

Luke asked what she'd like to do. Jenna said that she would love to head on home since it was a work night for her. She said her goodnight to Seth, again complimenting him on the delicious meal.

Luke drove her home. They rode in silence as the warm night air blew Jenna's hair around her beautiful face. Luke would turn and watch her periodically. She would close her eyes, tilting her head up to enjoy the breeze, as it was still quite warm at night. When they arrived at her home, he walked her to the door. She turned, not letting go of his hand this time. She asked, "Would you like to come in?"

Luke smiled. It was a seductive and sexy smile. He realized he was making headway in their relationship. "I would love to," he answered as he quickly followed her in, just in case she changed her mind.

She dropped her keys on the counter and offered him a drink. He said he was fine for now and then he moved in close, trapping her against the kitchen counter. She could feel every inch of his hard and muscled body and it started that fire inside of her again. She wrapped her arms around his back and pulled him in close, reveling in the feel of him. Luke didn't waste any time, knowing that her resistance was down. He took her lips with his own and then twined his tongue with hers. She let out a soft moan, which only seemed to increase the fire raging between them. His hands moved up and down her back. She pulled back, saying, "Luke, I . . ." She didn't get much further as he leaned back in to take his time with another long kiss. Damn him! Why did he have to make her feel this way? It made her want more.

"Can we take this somewhere more comfortable?" Luke finally asked.

Jenna didn't trust herself to speak, and just nodded her head in agreement. No use in fighting the inevitable. She had invited him in knowing full well what that implied. And yes, she wanted to sleep with him, be intimate. She took his hand and led him through the living room and down the hallway to her bedroom. As they entered the room, Luke started to strip off his clothes, pausing only long enough to watch her strip hers off, as well. They left a path of clothes and shoes as they fumbled and stumbled moving closer to the bed. Luke fell on top of her as they finally reached it with very little left to discard. He again kissed her deeply, and she moaned in response. Luke leaned up and smiled down at her. She realized that the smile actually reached his eyes for once, and that made her extremely happy. She had, for the moment, pushed away his sadness. For that, she was glad.

Compromises

"Will you respect me in the morning?" Luke asked as he teased her.

"Come here, you . . . ," Jenna smiled back at him.

There was nothing more said as their lovemaking took over and the rest of their clothes were discarded. Luke was a masterful lover and took his time, seeming to know when to slow down and when to move ahead. He made her feel like there was no other living, breathing thing on this earth but the two of them. She clung to him, never wanting this feeling to end.

Later, as Luke was making his way to her adjoining bathroom in the dark, he tripped and stumbled, hitting his knee on a chair as he steadied himself. "What the hell . . . ," he cursed.

Jenna sat up in bed and flicked on a light to see him hopping, cursing, and nursing his knee. She realized then what had happened and she doubled over in laughter.

"What the hell is that?" Luke asked as he found the culprit that had tripped him and pointed to the white bear rug at the end of Jenna's bed on the floor.

"That," Jenna said, gasping for air, "is a gift from my grandfather. The bear's head does have a way of reaching out and grabbing you," she said while still trying to control her laughter.

"Damn thing nearly killed me," Luke said while starting to smile. "Are you sure the thing is dead? 'Cause I swear I felt teeth."

This only made Jenna laugh more. Luke made his way back to bed and laughed with her, still holding his knee. Jenna finally was able to control herself and said, "Are you hurt?"

"Yes, terribly so, I am afraid. I may not be able to drive home tonight with this injury," Luke said, playing the injured soul perfectly, shyly smiling back up at her like a little boy asking for permission.

"Well, then," Jenna stated with a chuckle, "I don't suppose I could have you drive, being injured and all. You will just have to stay the night."

Luke crawled back under the covers and pulled her against him. As the heat started to build between them again, Luke said, "I think I need to be nursed back to health . . . very slowly."

"I'm not much of a nurse," Jenna giggled as she playfully kissed his face.

"You'll do in a pinch," Luke said before taking her mouth with his own; the giggles subsided as the heat took over.

Much later, Jenna was soundly sleeping, curled up to Luke. He disentangled himself from her hold, carefully moving a leg here and an arm there, while slowly climbing out of bed. He was sure to watch for the bear head as he made his way around the room. He located her purse and grabbed it, bringing it to the bathroom before closing the door and locking it. He had snuck into her house several times in the past few days while she was at work. He was always careful to leave everything like it was prior to his snooping, trying to find anything to lead him to Alejandro's location. After all, he had been a professional pirate for a long time, and he had a knack of getting through locked doors. He had forgotten about that damn rug, though, tonight when he was moving about in the dark. He had wondered why she had the thing when he had snuck in. Now, at least, he understood her attachment to it.

He felt bad about having to deceive Jenna, and it didn't feel right going through her purse now. Yet he had to, for Cassie's sake. He tried to remind himself that if Jenna knew what trouble Cassie was in, she probably wouldn't have minded. He kept Jenna in the dark for good reason. He was a pirate; he knew their lifestyle. They protected their own. If they felt that Jenna had helped in any way to bring down Alejandro, she would never be safe. He reminded himself that it was better this way. She couldn't know what he was up to, why he had sought her out in the first place. He frowned at the thought of how she would feel if she knew that he had purposely sought her out after Cassie was taken. He pushed this out of his head as he thought back to that dreadful day walking back from the beach with Cassie.

7

They had been heading home from the beach, laughing and carefree, enjoying the sunset and a shared joke about a buxom redhead who had showed interest in Luke at the beach. Luke had stopped short when he noticed two men leaning against one of the posts out front of a popular store, staring at them. He had told Cass to wait while he moved forward. As Luke approached the two men, leaving her behind him, he was already dreading this interlude. It couldn't be good when two pirates showed up in broad daylight to contact him out in the open like this. "Easy," he told himself, "see what's up and get Cassandra out of here." Even in times like this, when it was broad daylight and she was sure to be safe, he worried about her.

"Hey, what's up?" Luke inquired as he reached the two men. He took a quick moment to look back at Cassandra, noting that she had stopped and dropped her bag, waiting. He turned his attention back to the two men in front of him. They were among the contacts he kept so he was in the loop on where pirates would be patrolling in the Caribbean. He didn't know why, but the smile on their faces made him wary.

Compromises

"Luke! Good to see you. We have some important information for you."

Luke was cautious, but now eager to learn what was important enough to meet in broad daylight. "Should we take this conversation somewhere else?" he asked.

"Nah, what we got to say won't take too long," one man replied as he held Luke's gaze.

"Spill," Luke said, waiting for them to get on with it.

"We have a message for you and the captain of that vessel you reside on these days," the other man said, pulling Luke's attention to him now. He didn't like the way this was going. Everyone thought that Seth was a pirate and that they had stolen the yacht they were on. So far, it had been a good ploy. Usually, when someone had information about pirating, they didn't mention much about Seth. It made him wonder, why the change now?

"I don't have all day, fellas," Luke said, trying to appear cool, calm, and collected.

"You may have more time after you hear what we say," the man said with a laugh.

The first man who had spoken said, "Tell Seth, we need him to prove himself."

Uh oh, Luke thought. I smell trouble. "Prove himself? I'm not following!"

"Well, see, it's like this. Jason found his way into prison for piracy somehow," the first man continued. "Seems like you and Seth didn't end up in prison, but you were on the same yacht when overtaken by the Coast Guard. Wonder why that is?"

Luke could feel the dread creep up his back like icy cold fingers trailing up his spine. He wanted to turn around and check on Cassandra, but he didn't dare. He didn't want to draw their attention to her. He tried for stupidity, "I didn't know that! How the hell did that happen?"

"We were hoping you could tell us, since all of you were arrested at the same time. Yet you and Seth are free as a bird!"

Luke thought quickly. "They didn't have anything on us. The Coast Guard couldn't prove that Seth wasn't the captain of the yacht and we were the crew. Unfortunately for Jason, they must have found something in the small boat they used to reach us." He hoped his lie sounded plausible enough to be true.

"Interesting," the first man said. "Well, you see, we just have to make sure we know who we are dealing with, and Jason's cousin, Alejandro, was none too happy to hear the fate of his cousin. So, as a deal, we are willing to do an exchange."

Baffled, Luke replied, "Exchange? What kind of exchange? What does Alejandro have that we could possibly want?"

The second man chuckled, "How about Seth's little play toy?"

Luke asked, "His play toy? Like you mean the yacht?"

The first man said, "No. I mean the girl."

The dread weighed heavily on Luke now. He turned slowly and scanned the crowd. Cassandra was gone. Maybe she had gone into a store? Maybe she realized the danger and was hiding? Somehow, he didn't think so. Luke grabbed the first man by the front of his shirt and practically spit in his face, "Don't you touch a hair on her head or you will have to worry about far greater things than the Coast Guard and jail." The second man grabbed Luke from behind, but Luke shook him off. "Where is she? What have you done with her?"

The first man stepped back and straightened his shirt as Luke backed off. Luke had a suspicion that killing this man would not help Cassie, and might put her in even greater danger. No, he had to wait his turn at getting to these men another time. "No harm will come to her as long as everyone does as they are supposed to. Tell Seth to expect a message from Alejandro shortly. All will be explained in that message," the man in front of Luke stated. They turned and left.

Luke ran back to the spot where he had left Cassandra. He looked around again in the crowd, to no avail. He knew their kind. They would have made sure she followed without a fight until they got somewhere to drag her away. His heart dropped in his chest, and he felt physical pain. He ran all the way back to the yacht, and when he got there, ran into the salon screaming for Seth. Seth came out of the kitchen. "Hey Luke, did you tie up my girl on the beach all day? I was just about to come looking for you two . . ." Seth stopped midsentence as he took in the look on Luke's face. "What's wrong? Where's Cassandra?"

Luke tried to catch his breath after running all the way, fearful for Cassandra. "They took her, Seth! Took her!"

Seth grabbed Luke by the arms. "Who took her?"

Luke said, breathlessly, "Pirates, a cousin of Jason's. He wants us to prove we are pirates and that we didn't have anything to do with the Coast Guard arresting Jason and the rest of this crew this winter. They want something in exchange for returning Cassandra."

Seth tightened his grip, but Luke couldn't feel past the pain in his heart. "Where - where did they take her?"

Luke shook his head, "I don't know. They said you should receive a message soon."

Seth let go of Luke and started to pace. He knew it! He knew that having Cassandra back in his life was dangerous, and yet he had put her in danger, once again, because he had fallen in love. Stupid! How could he be so selfish as to put her through this! He continued pacing, thinking of how to get to her before any real danger came to her. If they wanted a trade, they were smart enough to keep her safe . . . for now. Of that, he could be sure. But how long would they wait?

What kind of act would they ask Seth to perform? How dangerous would it be? Would it cost lives? He picked up his phone and dialed Jay, his friend in the Coast Guard, who was aware of the double life he led. "Jay! It's Seth. I have a problem. I need you to come over right away. Dress in plain clothes, though, would you?" He hung up and faced Luke. The color had drained from his face, and Luke could tell that Seth was suffering as much as he was. "Tell me what happened," Seth said. "I want to know everything."

Awhile later, Jay showed up at the yacht. He found Luke, Jake, Robert, and Seth all sitting in the salon, drinks in their hands and looking like death warmed over. Seth rose and shook his hand. "Glad you came so quickly!" He motioned for Jay to take a seat, and offered him a drink. Jay took a beer and sat down, thinking he hadn't seen his friend look this awful since before Cassandra came back into his life. He immediately knew it couldn't be good news. Did she leave him? He thought they were both very much in love, so he doubted it. Curious, he waited until Seth refilled his glass and sat down.

"They've taken her, Jay, and I need your help," Seth said, looking very tired.

"Who has taken her?" Jay knew without a doubt that he was talking about Cassandra.

"A cousin of Jason's, Alejandro, has her. He wants a trade. He wants me to do something for him. Prove that I am a pirate or something. I think he may be shorthanded, or he wants revenge on me. Either way, this doesn't look good," Seth said as he paced around the salon. "This could be really bad. I don't like the way it sounds."

"We will have to play along, Seth," Jay replied, seeing the magnitude of the assistance Seth was asking of him. "We can't let on that you are an informant. We will just have to be very careful about what it is he wants you to do. We don't have any guarantee that they will return Cassie either."

"I have to find a way, Jay. I need your help. We need to find a way."

"Can we find out where this cousin is?" Jay asked, seeing no way around this situation.

"We are working on that, but I need alternatives. I need some options. I can't let anything happen to Cassandra," Seth said.

"I will see what I can do, but Seth — we have to be realistic about this. This might just be the most dangerous thing you will have to do. This Alejandro obviously is going to ask you to fill in for the lost men. You and I will have to stay in touch more frequently, but we will have to be underhanded about it. We may be able to get more information about the ring of pirates than we were ever able to get before."

"I don't like the sound of this! If he feels for even a second that I am not a pirate . . . ." Seth realized that screaming at his friend wasn't going to solve anything. Jay had just reconfirmed what he feared. Alejandro was asking for proof that Seth was who he portrayed himself to be. "Sorry," he said to Jay. Jay got up and put a hand on his friend's shoulder.

"I'll do what I can to make sure you stay protected. In the meantime, we need to look for her. There has to be a way we can get to her."

Luke got up and faced them. "I can't sit here any longer. I am going out to do some digging of my own. I'll keep in touch," he added as he slammed his glass down on a table, grabbed the keys to the rental car, and took off at a near run. Jay and Seth just looked at each other, wondering what Luke could possibly do that they weren't doing already.

As Luke left the yacht, his mind went into full gear. He couldn't approach the two men he had seen today, but he sure as hell had other contacts in the area. He headed toward a seedy side of town. He was apprehensive and worried that he might not find out anything, but he couldn't sit by and idly wait for things to unfold.

He pulled into the parking lot of a rundown motel off the beaten path for the usual vacationers. The low, one-story brick building was in bad need of a paint job, and the whole area around it just screamed for an overhaul. Of course, the clientele it drew in didn't care much about what it looked like; it was a bed and a place to hide, for the most part. Luke got out of the car and walked down an alley. He knocked at a red door, on which the paint was peeling to expose the white underneath. The number on the door was 619, although the 6 had lost its top screw and was dangling precariously as if it would fall off the next time the door opened. The place practically screamed, "Stay away, danger lurks inside!" It reminded Luke of a motel you would see in a scary movie. No one with half a brain would want to stay there, unless you were hiding from someone or something. As he knocked a second time, someone from inside hollered, "Enter at your own risk!"

Luke knew it wasn't an idle threat. He announced, "Its Luke!" and then opened the door and walked in. He let his eyes adjust to the change in lighting. It was still pretty sunny outside, but the room was darkened as there were no lights on in the room and the shades were drawn. A light flicked on and he saw a large, burly man sitting in chair next to a table with the lamp that was barely illuminated. Luke shut the door behind him and walked farther into the room. The carpet was an ugly dark green, and a TV in the corner flickered from commercial to commercial, with the volume turned down low. Off to one side was a queen-sized bed that looked like it had been tussled in, and there was a small kitchen off to the back of the room.

Luke brought his attention onto the man in the chair. He was in his late thirties, unshaven, with long dark hair braided down his back. The cut off T-shirt showed massive arms, with tattoos running down the length of them as well as on the side of his neck. One of the tattoos was a pirate symbol with the skull and crossbones. Luke remained standing as he looked at the man who was seated in front of him. The man held a gun, which was pointed at Luke's chest.

"Well, well," the man said, while putting down the gun before picking up his beer can from the table and taking another swig. "What brings you around here?"

"I need some information," Luke said.

"What do I get in return," the man said as he smiled, showing off a gold front tooth.

Luke wanted to reply, "You keep living," but knew that this man was invaluable to him right now. The man knew all the pirates. He kept in touch with all of his buddies. He'd been in pirating long enough to know not only the pirates, but their families as well. Luke was hoping beyond hope that he had some information about Jason's cousin, Alejandro.

"Name your price," Luke said, knowing he would give his own life if that was what it took to get Cassandra back.

"Depends on what you want to know," the man stated.

"I need to find out about a family of a certain pirate," Luke stated.

"Hmmm," the man thought. "That will be expensive. You know how private we are."

"I don't care about the cost," Luke reiterated. "I will pay you half now and half later, when your information proves to be correct." He knew from past experience that you never paid in full until you checked things out. Also, Luke knew that if you paid well enough, the information was kept secret, so Luke could continue to work as an informant for Seth.

"You got cash on you now," the man inquired.

"Mike," Luke smiled, "you know I never come empty-handed."

"Who's the family?"

Luke thought about his reply. If he asked straight out about Alejandro he couldn't be sure that there weren't already some rumors flying around about a potential pirating act going down. Alejandro, if a smart man would have seen to it that no one, and that meant no one, would leak out his location. So Luke tried another avenue. "Jason Cartier," Luke said as he watched the man's face closely.

"Jason's in jail," Mike replied.

"I know this," Luke said, trying to keep his cool and his patience. "I want to know if he has any women in his life." Luke knew that if he could find someone who knew Jason, he could find out about other family members through them, and possibly where this Alejandro lived.

"Well," the man grinned, "why didn't you say you were looking for some company?"

"It has to be someone Jason is related to." Luke wanted to be sure that there was a family connection; otherwise, the information could be pointless.

Mike stated his price, "Five hundred grand."

Luke took out his cell phone and called his investment broker. A short dialogue ensued in which Luke stated he needed to wire two hundred fifty thousand." Luke looked at Mike and Mike, always prepared to make money, grabbed a slip of paper with banking information to an offshore account, handed it to Luke. After supplying the information to his broker, Luke hung up the phone, waiting for Mike to make the next move. He knew that Mike had information; otherwise he wouldn't have named a figure so quickly. Luke was just happy that working for Seth these past years had been lucrative enough and that living on a boat didn't allow him to spend a lot of money, so that pulling out this kind of

Compromises

cash wasn't difficult. He also knew that if he needed more, Seth would pay whatever was needed to find Cassie; he loved her that much.

Mike offered Luke a beer, but Luke declined. "Once I get confirmation that your money has hit my account, I will text you the information." Luke shook his head, and without a word, he left.

Later, Luke received a text from Mike. It stated, *"Her name is Jenna. She's a cousin of his and lives right here in Florida. I don't think she keeps in touch with the family much, as she abhors the fact that some of them are criminals. However, she has a really good heart and has taken to visiting Jason since he was put in prison. Guess she is trying to change his ways or something."*

"Huh," Luke laughed to himself, "like that would help."

The text continued, *"Here's her address. You should be able to catch her down at the gym close by. She takes a yoga class there."*

The man was unbelievable. It made Luke wonder how much they kept tabs on both him and Seth. Good thing they were always so careful to keep their secret, never letting on their ties with the Coast Guard. Still, it reminded him that what Seth and he did was in fact very dangerous. It just reinforced why, when Seth had given the order to never contact Cassie after the pirate episode while vacationing in the Caribbean, Luke hadn't tried to contact her. Even when he knew the pain she must have been going through, as well as Seth, for keeping apart.

Luke texted back, *"I'll give you the rest when I have the chance to check her out."*

"I know you're good for it," Mike answered, *"or I'll come find you."* It wasn't an idle threat.

Back in the bathroom at Jenna's house, Luke was startled back to the present moment as Jenna called out his name from the bed. Quickly flushing the toilet, he turned on the water in the sink as he answered,

"Be right out, babe." He would have to wait to look through her purse later. Turning off the light, he opened the door, and since it was still so dark in the room, set her purse off to the side and climbed back in bed with Jenna.

"I missed you," she mumbled, half asleep.

"I was aiming for that response from you. Want to show me how much?" Luke questioned as he pulled her close again, letting himself relax.

8

The next morning, Jenna didn't want to wake Luke, he looked so peaceful as she slipped out of bed and made her way to the shower. She tried to be as quiet as she could as she got ready for work. She dressed quickly and was grabbing her purse when he rolled over.

"Sneaking out on me?"

"You looked so peaceful, I didn't want to wake you," Jenna said as she walked over to lean over and kiss him.

"Want me to drive you to work today?"

"No. I am finding it hard to leave you as it is," she giggled. "Take your time and lock up when you leave. Help yourself to anything you want to eat in the kitchen."

"You trust me alone here with that bear?" he laughed.

"Try not to kick him in the head again. He hates that," she laughed back.

"I'll try," he said as he grabbed her hand to pull her back down and kiss her one more time.

"Luke," Jenna admonished as she pulled away, "you're gonna make me late."

"Hmmm, tempting," he said.

"Yeah, well, we can't all have the job you do, mister carefree and wild."

"Well, better go make a living, darling, so you can get your cute little backside back in this bed where you belong."

Jenna shook her head as she smiled. He smiled back, and again she was glad to see the smile reach his eyes. The sadness was still there sometimes, but at least she was breaking through some of it. She rushed out the door, not wanting to be late and not trusting herself to call in a sick day if she stayed any longer.

Luke took his time going through every place he hadn't been able to search before, as he had always feared she would come home and catch him when he snuck in before. Now that she knew he was there, he could take his time. He still felt that she probably kept any address information in an electronic device, like most people did these days. That was what he was after in her purse. He continued to look, going through drawers and closets. He played old messages on her phone, but most of them were from him calling to verify dinner arrangements or from Kirsten asking if she was still so busy with her new "hot" guy that she couldn't break away for a moment of girl time. He smiled to himself as he heard that one. Kirsten even complained that she hadn't made it to the gym. Well, Luke thought, he was taking up all her time. He had planned it that way!

He finally let himself out of her home late that afternoon. One of the neighbors saw him get into his car, and he just waved at her. Good, let the neighbors get used to seeing him come and go. It would make his so-called breaking and entering that much easier.

Compromises

When he got back to the yacht, Seth was sitting with his head in his hands.

"Seth?" Luke inquired, getting alarmed.

"Alejandro is getting impatient. He says he wants me to come down soon. He hasn't gotten anything in particular just yet, but he says no need to wait. Luke, I can't go down there now. I need to continue to look for Cassandra."

"Seth," Luke said, louder, "I am making progress. I think I have her trust. I plan to get everything out of her tonight. I promise you, I will have it tonight."

Seth looked up finally. "Let's just hope it's not too late!"

"It's not, Seth! I know it. I know our girl, Cass. She's tough. She is going to be fine." Luke willed for it to be so. He couldn't even think otherwise. The alternatives were too depressing to think about.

"Yeah, well for Alejandro's sake, I hope you're right," Seth said back, angrily. "I'll kill the guy if he lays a hand on her."

"You won't be alone my friend, not alone at all!" Luke meant every bit of it, too. He knew how much Cass meant to both of them and it wouldn't take much for either of them to end Alejandro's life if she was injured in any way.

Later that night, Luke let himself back into Jenna's apartment. He had a plan, and was hoping that it would work, so he rushed there just in time. She came home shortly after. "Hi, sweetheart," Luke said as he took her into his arms.

"Hmmm," Jenna muttered as she hugged him back. "I could get used to this."

"I hope so," Luke said. He let her go as she put her work items down. Turning to get her a drink from the fridge so she couldn't see his face, he said, "Hey, someone called today while you were gone. I tried to get to the phone, but I hit the wrong button and erased the message." He hated lying to her, but they were feeling the pressure from Alejandro, and felt they were on borrowed time.

"Oh," Jenna asked, "who was it?" She turned to face his solid back as he took a glass from the cupboard and poured her some wine. "Luke?" She wasn't sure he heard her.

"Someone named Andrew, Angelo; something like that."

"Alejandro?" Jenna seemed truly surprised. Luke felt even worse deceiving her now. He turned to her and put on a neutral face, giving away none of the intense feelings he was experiencing now.

"Yeah, that may be it." He handed her the glass of wine.

"Wow, I don't ever talk to him." Jenna sat down at the table, truly stunned. Luke sat down across from her, waiting. "It's just that he's part of the family that I told you about before. I believe he is involved with piracy. I don't try to keep up with any of them, due to that fact. Did he say what he wanted?"

"I'm afraid I cut him off before I could get that far," Luke said, and she mistook his sadness about lying to her for feeling bad about cutting off a family member's call.

"Luke, seriously, it's okay. I never keep in touch with him. I can't imagine what he wants."

"Where does he live? Maybe we could drive over so I could apologize face to face."

Jenna laughed. "Seriously, Luke, we don't keep in touch. Besides, he owns his own small island off the coast of Antigua, in the Caribbean, so driving there is out of the question."

Luke jumped up from the table and walked around to her and lifted her into his arms. He kissed her deeply, and she melted into him. When he finally released her, she had to catch her breath and steady herself. "Wow, keep that up and we will have to skip dinner."

Luke smiled at her, and he seemed really excited about the idea of skipping dinner. In reality, she had just given him a huge clue on where to find Cassie. "Why don't we do that; but you go shower first. I need to call Seth," he said, and then added, when he saw her curious look, "you know, to make sure he isn't expecting us for dinner."

"Okay. Want to order in?"

Luke smiled as she walked out of the kitchen and answered her, "Sure, whatever you want."

Luke called Seth quickly, relaying the information that Jenna had just unwittingly given him. Seth was quick to get off the phone, no doubt to call Jay and arrange a way to get the Coast Guard involved in getting to this place where Alejandro lived. There were only a few inhabited islands off Antigua, so finding where he lived would not take that long. Luke was ecstatic. He had done it! He had found a way to get to Cassie. It would only be a matter of time now, and then she would be safe. He owed it to the wonderful woman in the other room, and she didn't even know it. Luke made his way into the bedroom, and then leaned in the doorjamb of the bathroom, listening as Jenna showered.

"What do you want for dinner?" he called out to her.

"You!" she giggled from behind the curtain. Luke stripped off his clothes and surprised her by jumping into the shower with her.

"You asked," he said, as he pulled her in close for a kiss.

"I know," she giggled as she matched his enthusiasm, "but I wasn't expecting this. How about you wash my back and I'll wash yours?"

"Deal," Luke said as he smiled, and this time the smile stayed in his eyes.

Hours later they sat on the bed, dressed in PJ's, he with just sweatpants on and Jenna with a long T-shirt, with empty Chinese takeout boxes on the bedside table. Luke had conveniently packed an overnight bag to bring with him tonight. She hadn't asked him why, as she was just glad to know that he thought enough of her to want to spend so much time with her. He avoided bringing Jenna to the yacht, as he knew it was probably a madhouse there right now, with the guys working out the plans for their rescue trip. Luke figured he would be leaving to go and find Cass with the rest of them, and wasn't sure how long he would be gone. He was thinking of how to break this news to Jenna.

"I have some bad news," Luke said as they sat facing each other as she broke the Chinese cookie to read her fortune.

"Oh?" Jenna looked concerned as she set her cookie down on the bedside table without looking at the little white paper, waiting patiently for what Luke had to say.

"I have to go out of town for a bit. I'm not sure how long it will be. Seth has some business and he is taking the yacht to travel there. Of course, since I am part of the crew, I am obligated to go," Luke said as he watched her intently.

"I see," Jenna said as she looked down at her hands. After all, what did she expect? She knew he worked on a yacht and that they traveled a lot. It was only a matter of time before this was bound to happen. Yet now that it was, she was disappointed and feeling at a loss for words.

Luke grabbed her hands and she looked up into his gorgeous blue eyes. "I promise to come back as soon as possible," he said.

"It's okay. I understand," Jenna said with a nervous laugh. "It's just that I have gotten so used to seeing you every day."

"I'll miss you too," Luke added, truly meaning it. He hadn't meant to get involved with her, but she was finding a way into his heart. Yet he worried. What would she think of him when she knew his past? Would she be forgiving of how his meeting her was a scheme to find information? He didn't want to find out at the moment, although he knew it was probably inevitable some day.

Compromises

"Luke, I'll be fine," she said, clearly mistaking the long look on his face as he pondered these thoughts.

He tried to smile. "Think of Cassie," he thought to himself. "I did it all for her safety, and that is what is most important." Finding Jenna was a bonus he hadn't counted on. He leaned over and kissed her. She smiled at him.

"Maybe you should go away more often, if this is how you treat me before you go," Jenna smiled.

"I'm not relishing the thought of not seeing you for days," Luke said, surprised that he actually meant it. "I hope to make it quick and come back soon."

"Well, I hope you do," she responded as she smiled into his eyes, glad to not be the only one who was going to hate this small separation.

He stayed the night, and they made love several times. Luke knew that what he was about to do was going to be dangerous. It always was when pirates were involved. The gun-toting lawbreakers didn't care much about the carnage they left behind, as long as it was a means to an end.

Much later, they were both so exhausted that they fell asleep in each other's arms. Luke awoke a few hours later and pushed a lock of hair off Jenna's face as he watched her sleep. He wasn't sure what was happening between them, but he knew that he felt for her. He did want to continue seeing her when he returned; he knew that. He also knew that he would probably have to come clean about the whole ordeal with Cassie, too.

He kissed her gently on the lips and disentangled himself from her arms and legs. She shifted slightly, smiled, and fell back into sleep. Luke wasn't good at goodbyes, especially with how he was feeling about Jenna. He threw on his clothes and made his way into the kitchen. He wanted to leave her with something to remind her of him, make a statement. She had left a sandwich in her refrigerator for tomorrow's lunch, in a plastic bag. He grabbed a black marker to write on the bag she would use. He wrote, "Miss you already."

He knew she would find it in the morning. He let himself out, locking the door behind him, and drove back to the marina.

Seth was up and talking with Jay, looking over a map, when Luke arrived. There were red lines all over the map. Seth looked up as Luke walked in, then came up and clapped his hand in Luke's, trying to keep the emotion out of his voice and failing miserably.

"Luke, I can't thank you enough," Seth said.

"No need, Seth. I love her too, you know," Luke answered.

"Yeah, I know," Seth said, joining Jay back at the maps as Luke followed him. "We have planned out which islands couldn't be inhabited. That's the ones with the red X's on the map. We figure that Alejandro is pretty smart so, he wouldn't keep a plane or boat on the island, not wanting to chance Cassandra escaping. Jay pulled some strings and sent out a Coast Guard rescue helicopter to search the area under the pretense of looking for a pirate group. So far, we narrowed it down to these three islands here," Seth said as he circled three small dots on the map. "We need to be in stealth mode while we look for Cassandra. We can't let on or clue Alejandro in on the fact that we are anywhere in the area. In my last conversation with him I told him that I was working on a plan to get to some very expensive cargo that was going to be transported in the Caribbean very shortly. You haven't let on to Jenna, right?"

"No," Luke answered abruptly with emotion, but Seth was too preoccupied to notice. Jay wasn't though, and looked at Luke. Luke just shook his head as if to indicate that now was not a good time to get into it. Jay nodded and looked back down at the map, redirecting his focus.

"I think we could use one of our fast boats and cut the engines off a ways out and then paddle in under the cover of darkness. It will take longer, but we don't want to alert anyone," Jay said. "Again, the Coast Guard is thinking we are about to round up a band of pirates, so they will work with us."

"So we go together then?" Luke asked, getting more involved as he pushed aside his thoughts of Jenna and her reaction to all this.

"Yes," Jay answered, "we go together. I figure one of us will need to get to Cassandra and get her away safely to take away any danger of getting her caught in between as things go down. Then the others will have to handle anyone else that may be in on this. The tricky thing will be to get them out on the water where we have the authority to arrest them. I haven't figured that part out yet, but I will."

"Who else will be with us?" Luke asked as he heard Jay mention "others".

"Robert and Jake are going," Seth said. "Jackie and Mandi flew in tonight so they are currently otherwise engaged," Seth said, smiling, "but we can catch them up when they get up in the morning. By then we should be ready to get going."

Luke hadn't realized that Cassandra's best friends were planning to come, but it made sense that they would be here as soon as they knew that it was looking like they were getting her back. He thought it was a good idea to have them here when she came back, as God only knew what might have happened to her in Alejandro's company. The thought made him angry, and he was hoping that he would be the one to find Alejandro when they finally did.

"I want to go after Alejandro," Luke said as he clenched his fists.

"Oh, no, you don't," Jay answered as he caught Luke's reaction. "Neither you nor Seth are getting close to this guy. We need to do this the right way, the legal way," he said as he correctly assessed the situation they would be in if he let any of them near Alejandro. "For that reason I am bringing two of my own men with us. They won't be as . . . um . . . emotionally involved as you two are."

"Jay," Seth said, as it was clearly a surprise to him, "I want to make sure this guy doesn't walk away."

Jay knew that Seth meant it, literally. "Look, guys, I know you all love Cass, as I am fond of her, too. But it won't do you any good to end up in jail on any complications, okay?"

Seth looked down, knowing that his friend was right. He wouldn't be able to trust his emotions; but he still wanted to be close to let this guy feel his anger and know that he wouldn't ever be able to mess with him or anyone close to him again!

Jay sensed he had won the battle, for now. But he also knew Seth well. He knew that Seth wasn't going to let Alejandro leave that island without something to remember him by. He couldn't blame his friend, but it was his job to ensure that Seth, Luke, or any of them didn't end up getting caught in the legalities of the system. This was already so risky that he hadn't disclosed the whole reason for the operation to the Coast Guard. He had pulled a few strings on the flyover by the Coast Guard helicopter. He wondered if Seth had any idea how much he was risking pulling in the authorities like this. Somehow, he knew it would hit Seth sooner or later. He hoped later, because Seth would worry about his longtime friend. He had purposely kept Seth focused on the task at hand: finding Cassandra. Besides, if Seth was to get closer to Alejandro and what he wanted him to do, they might be able to arrest a large part of the pirates who operated in the Caribbean.

"Well," Jay said, noting the hour as he looked at his watch, "We better get some sleep, as we will be getting very little of it soon."

Luke looked at Jay like he was crazy, wondering how anyone could get sleep tonight, but he knew he was right. He clapped his hand on

Seth's back, saying, "He's right. We won't do Cass any good if we aren't at one hundred percent."

They departed and headed to their respective cabins. Luke crawled into bed, anxious to get this under way. Soon, Cass would be back. He felt so guilty for putting her at risk. He had been the one with her that day she was taken. He should never have left her side! He would never forgive himself if anything bad happened to her during this whole ordeal. "Almost have you now, Cass," Luke whispered to no one in particular. He never thought sleep would find him, but it soon took him over and he dreamed of getting revenge on Alejandro.

9

When Jenna woke, she rolled over to grab for Luke and felt an empty side of the bed. She bolted up and looked around. His clothes were gone. She grabbed a sheet to wrap around her naked body as she ran to the window and looked out to where he had parked the rental last night. It was gone as well. Her shoulders slumped as she realized he had left. Well, she couldn't blame him. The last thing she wanted to do was to cling to him, crying or begging him to stay, which might have happened. Jenna sat down on the edge of the bed. "'Now what," she thought, at a total loss as to what to do with herself. Glancing over, she happened to see her Chinese fortune cookie from the night before, on the table where she had left it when she learned he was going to leave. She grabbed the little slip of paper, and read her fortune.

"Nothing is as it seems."

Well, wasn't that just peachy? Something made her shiver as she read the words. It was almost like a foreboding of something she should know. Jenna shook her head to dispel the omen. She needed to get preoccupied with something else. She had been so tied up with Luke that everything had gone to the wayside.

She looked around her room and realized she hadn't spent any time cleaning since they had met. That was the first thing she set out to rectify. She threw on some old clothes, turned up the radio, and cleaned the whole place until it was spotless. Surveying her work, she smiled, feeling better having had something to do and to keep her mind off Luke. She showered and changed, trying not to remember how empty her place felt with just her in it. It was a Saturday, so she thought she would see what Kirsten was up to. No doubt her friend was feeling the loss of her company, as she had been so wrapped up with Luke these last few weeks that she hadn't given any thought to spending time with anyone else. She picked up the phone to call, hoping that it wasn't going to be too bad between them.

"What's the matter? Mister handsome dump you?" Kirsten asked when Jenna called her to see if they could meet for lunch.

"No, he didn't dump me," Jenna chuckled. "He's out of town for a bit, on business."

"I see," Kirsten said, clearly still hurt that Jenna had only contacted her because Luke was out of town. "So you called me because now you need some other company."

Jenna stopped giggling, and said seriously, "Look, I know that I have avoided doing anything other than be with Luke, and I am truly sorry for that. He kind of came like a whirlwind into my life and knocked the breath out of me. Can you forgive me?" She really hoped that Kirsten was just pouting and not seriously upset with her.

"Damn, Jenna, I thought you would never call," Kirsten said as her voice lightened, and Jenna knew that things were going to be fine between them. "Let's meet for lunch, and you can tell me all about him," Kirsten added, seeming more like her old self as the moments ticked by.

They made plans to meet at a nice little restaurant and bar called the "Blue Sky Bar" which was known for its famous martinis. Jenna arrived first and ordered a round of drinks for her friend and herself. Kirsten came bouncing in, her usually bubbly self. She came over and gave Jenna a hug before setting down her purse and then sitting in the chair across from Jenna.

"So," Kirsten said, "you are glowing! Tell me all about him."

"We got intimate," Jenna said, smiling.

"No way!" Kirsten looked absolutely shocked as she looked at her friend across the table. "Jenna, I'm so surprised. You never move that fast with anyone. What happened?"

"I don't know," Jenna looked, clearly puzzled about this turn of events. "I just felt, well, I really don't know what I feel. I just really like being with him, and only seem half alive when I'm not."

"Wow, girlfriend," Kirsten said, "you got it bad!"

"Yeah, and it's scaring me half to death," Jenna confessed, glad to finally admit to someone that she had fallen for Luke.

"Well, how does he feel? Did you tell him?"

"I haven't said anything, but he may have a clue, I think . . . I don't know," Jenna said, confused now whether Luke might not know how she felt.

"You will have to clear that up when he returns," Kirsten said, as the waiter arrived with their drinks. "You ordered already?"

"I owe you one," Jenna smiled apologetically at her longtime friend. "I'm sorry I haven't been keeping in touch."

"Forgiven; seeing you went and fell in love with one of the most beautiful men on earth," Kirsten said dramatically, as they touched their glasses together in a toast, before taking a taste of her martini. "How long is he gone for so I know when the void is going to hit me again?"

"He wasn't sure. I guess it is part of the world that he lives in. It will be hard getting used to that, I can tell you. I never gave it much thought when we were together, but this sucks," Jenna said as she also took a taste of her martini.

"Yeah, well, if that is the guy's only downfall, I'd say you have it pretty good," Kirsten giggled, and Jenna joined her.

"I guess so."

Back on the yacht, Luke woke up early. He went to the kitchen to find Seth making a cup of coffee and on the phone. The guy was at full speed already. He turned, "Morning. Want some?" as he motioned to the pot and hung up the phone.

"Yeah, thanks."

"Jake and Robert are up. We are just about ready to roll," he said, and seemed anxious to get going.

Luke knew exactly what he was feeling. "Let's roll then," he said, as he took his cup with him to the bridge.

Seth followed him, and things were a flurry of activity as everyone ran around tossing off lines and moving the yacht. Jay had left after they retired to their staterooms last night. He had the Coast Guard moving out to the Caribbean with the directions to head into the center between the three islands they had narrowed down to as where they believed Alejandro had to be. Mandi and Jackie joined Luke and Seth in the bridge or driving station. Luke exchanged hugs and kisses and then returned his attention to the task at hand. Everyone was quiet and yet excited to finally be doing something. Luke pushed Jenna out of his mind as he kept his attention on the waterway and on getting closer to Cassandra's rescue.

It took several days to get where they wanted to be. Seth and Robert had taken turns at the wheel, never letting one or the other tire too much before switching off. At times, Luke had to forcefully move Seth away from the wheel. It was as if Seth felt that being there would make the yacht go faster. He knew that Seth probably slept little, but that he had to force him to get some rest or they would never be ready to act when they got to their destination. As they finally reached the islands, they saw the Coast Guard cutter off in the distance. They stayed a good distance away. A fast boat came out from the cutter. As it got closer, they recognized Jay and two other men. Seth went out to meet them and help them aboard. Jay made introductions as they shook hands. They moved into the dining room and laid out the map.

Jay said, "So, this is the closest island," as he pointed to one of the red circled dots on the map. "We'll have to get about a mile off before we cut the engines. It will be tough work rowing in by hand, but we need the cover of night to sneak up and try to scope out the island."

And so it began. They waited until dusk, and then loaded into the small fast boat and made their way out to the island. They cut the engines just as darkness fell, and used a compass and the GPS map to continue on their way by manual power. They took turns at the oars, as it was no easy feat to push a boat full of men closer to the island. They were lucky that there was no moonlight for the next few nights so they could make a stealthy landing without fear of being seen. When they made landfall, they jumped out and pulled the boat onto the sand. After much argument over who was going to stay with the boat to alert the others, one of the Coast Guard men who came with Jay was ordered to stay with the boat. They each had a walkie-talkie to keep in contact with each other and relay information. Jay was hoping that he would get Luke or Seth to stay behind, worried about keeping them out of conflict with Alejandro, but they wouldn't have anything to do with that. They

Compromises

set out in groups of two to walk the island. Robert and Jake had stayed behind on the yacht to keep it on course and keep the girls safe. Several hours later, the landing party met back at the small boat. No one had seen or heard anything that would lead them to Alejandro. The island had a few small homes, but as they scoped out each and peeked through lit windows, they saw no sign of Cassandra.

Seth threw his flashlight into the boat, and it bounced around on the bottom due to force of his throw. "Damn it!" he exclaimed.

"Seth," Luke said as he laid his hand on his friend's shoulder. "We know it will take some time. We are really close, though. Don't lose faith."

"I just want her back." The last few days and weeks were taking their toll on Seth. Luke knew exactly how he was feeling.

Jay propelled the group back into the boat. He picked up Seth's flashlight, and while handing it back to him said, "tomorrow's another day."

When they arrived back at the yacht, Mandi and Jackie rushed down to meet them. Their faces fell, though, when they realized that Cassie wasn't with them. They told the Coast Guard men to stay aboard, as it was easier this way than having them run between the two larger boats.

Later, as dinner was done and everyone was relaxing, Luke found Seth up on the top deck, looking out at the distant islands lit up by a sprinkling of house lights. "We will have her soon," Luke said, as he laid a hand on his friend's back.

"Not soon enough," Seth said as he turned to look at Luke. "What if she hates me, Luke?"

"Cass? Why would she hate you?" Luke was genuinely surprised by the question.

"It was because of me that she was taken. It was because of me she was put into danger last Christmas. I am just really bad news for her. How could she not hate me?"

"Man, you have got to know her better than that!" Luke said as he leaned against the railing looking out at the water toward the islands. "Right now, she is probably giving Alejandro a run for his money." They both laughed, knowing that Cassandra was probably doing just that. The girl did have a strong will and a mind of her own.

"Have you thought about how you are going to break the news to Jenna?" Seth asked curiously, changing the direction of their conversation.

"I'm trying not to think about that," Luke said honestly. "Right now, Cass is number one on my mind and I don't have much room to think of anything else."

Seth shook his head in agreement. He slapped Luke on the back as he said, "Well, it's late and we got another day of this ahead of us. I am going to head down in."

The next night came soon, but not fast enough for Seth. He had maneuvered the yacht farther down to the next set of islands. One of these was close enough to Antigua that Seth could anchor the yacht at a marina there. They set about going into the village. Luke tried to do some digging around, without being too suspicious, about any of the surrounding islands and their inhabitants. He thought that one of the islands a little farther off was most likely the best place for Alejandro to be.

As he was walking back to the yacht he saw a quaint little store, and something in the window caught the sun's glare, and his attention. He stopped and made his way inside. The item that had glinted in the window lay on a display cloth. It was a necklace of white gold with a small white gold bear dangling from the chain. It made Luke think of that ridiculous rug at Jenna's. Damn, he couldn't keep her out of his thoughts for long. He found himself buying it and stuffing the box in his pocket as he continued on his way back to the yacht. He'd never been one to buy such an expensive gift on a whim like that. He tried not to think too deeply about why he had.

He met up with Seth and Jay poring over the map again, rethinking some of the islands they had crossed off before. Seth looked up as Luke walked in. "Any luck?"

"Well, without coming right out and asking about Alejandro, it's pretty hard. I do think that they won't be on the closer islands, though. One man at the local grocery store said that they get visits from the farther islands off to the right of here who come in for supplies and food."

"Where's the cutter positioned now?" Seth asked Jay.

"We are positioned here," he pointed to the map, "just waiting to get the order where to take custody of Alejandro once we find him and lure him out to open water."

"So we do the same drill tonight?" Seth looked at his friend patiently.

"Yup. I think you are good to stay docked here, as the fast boat can make the distance and we don't have to worry about leaving the yacht out there in open water."

And so they waited for nightfall once again. They had catnapped through the day, trying to save up their energy, knowing it was going to be another long night. Seth and Luke both hoped it wouldn't be another futile search like the night before. They climbed in the boat once again and set out to get to the farther islands while Mandi, Jackie, and Robert stayed behind on the yacht. Robert wanted to be on the smaller boat with the guys, but he was the only other captain really capable of moving the yacht should there be a need. Mandi was glad he wasn't going out there. It was bad enough worrying about her friend

Cassie that she didn't need the added pressure and worry about Robert. She hugged him close while they watched the boat disappear.

Once again, the small rescue party cut the engines and had to paddle into shore under the cover of darkness. Once they hit land, they again split up to search the island. This one was at least a lot smaller, and held only one large, sprawling house. Luke was with one of the other Coast Guard men that Jay had brought along. They landed on the other side of the island, and the beach was secluded from the house that lay on the other side by a forest of trees in the center. Jay and Seth had taken a path to loop around the other side and make their way in from that end. When Luke got close to the house, he flattened himself against it as the man with him did the same.

"Look," Luke whispered to the other man, "I'm going to scope out this side of the house and see what I can see or hear. It would be easier if you just stayed put," Luke said, hoping he could do this part on his own. The other guy was slowing him up a bit, and he was in no mood to have to babysit someone tonight.

"Don't do anything stupid," the man said. Luke just smiled and shook his head as he thought to himself, "Depends on what you consider stupid."

As he got closer to a window he leaned his head around and peeked into the lit room. It was luxurious and beautifully decorated. The view of the ocean from here was probably fantastic, as he could hear the waves gently pounding the shore. He could see that the room was empty, and was about to move on until he heard voices arguing. As one voice got closer, his heart stopped. He would recognize it anywhere. He waited, just to be sure. He heard someone enter the room and slam a door shut. "Oooooh," he heard the girl say in utter frustration. He peeked in the window quickly and saw Cassandra pacing back and forth.

She hadn't seen him, and Luke had to stop himself from hollering

Compromises

out to her. He pulled back quickly, leaning back into the wall, breathing heavily. He wanted to go to Cassandra so badly, but he knew the plan. He stayed against the wall for a moment and saw from the lighted window as she moved to the open window. He held his breath as Cassie called out the window, to no one in particular, "Damn it Seth! Where the hell are you?"

Luke waited until she retreated from the window and then moved away from the house as quietly as he had come. He had to alert the others that this was the right place, and come up with a plan to get her out safely. "Soon, Cass," he whispered to the night air around him, "Soon."

Luke and other man made their way back to the boat, waiting for Jay and Seth. They didn't have to wait long, as they saw them running down the beach toward them.

"She's here," Seth said as he stopped in front of Luke, leaning over with his hands on his knees, taking large gulps of air.

"I know," Luke said as Seth straightened up.

"Did you see her?"

"Yeah, it's Cass alright," Luke said, remembering her heated argument prior to slamming the door shut just moments ago, as he listened under her window.

"Is she okay?" Seth tensed for Luke's answer.

"Yeah, she's great."

"Let's get her out of there," Seth said, and Jay had to grab his arm from keeping him from going any further.

"Seth," Jay said as he detained his friend, "we have to do this right. We can't put her in any danger and we need to make sure we can put Alejandro in custody."

"You want to explain just how exactly you plan to arrest Alejandro? On what charges?"

"Pirating, of course," Jay said.

"What evidence do we have? He's on his own private island right now," Seth said, still looking like he was going to sprint off any minute.

"We have to lure him out on the water to commit an act of piracy. Hoping that he will do so," Jay said, avoiding looking into Seth's eyes as he added, "and we are going to need your help to do that."

"Jay," Seth said surprised, "how am I going to lure him away from Cassandra right now? I doubt he would go anywhere. And I have to pretend to be a pirate, remember?"

"Well," Jay said as he took in their surroundings, "we can talk about it when we get back. We have to leave her here for now, though. We need Alejandro to believe everything is still going as planned."

"Damn it, Jay!" Seth said, still not wanting to leave, now that they had found Cassandra.

"I know, buddy," he said as he clapped him on the back, "but believe me, in the long run this plan will be better, as it will keep Cassie safe for a long time."

Seth looked defeated, as did Luke. They both knew Jay was right. The Coast Guard had authority on the water. They couldn't just steal her away, as they would have no charges to bring against Alejandro. They needed to catch him in the act. Only, there was no guarantee that he would leave her to do any pirating. It had to be a really attractive job for him not to pass it up.

"I trust you, Jay, but I'm not happy about this," Seth said as he climbed back into the small boat.

They paddled back out and away from the island as Seth kept looking back. Jay had a plan, and they did need to ensure that Cassandra would be safe after this thing was over. That was the only reason Seth was leaving now. He wanted to just go in there, shoot the guy, and get his girl back, but he knew the consequences of a rash act would separate them forever.

They rowed out, powered up when far enough away not to be heard, and made their way back to the yacht. The girls were anxiously waiting as they had in the past, only to see that Cassandra was still not with them. The guys explained that they had found her. The girls were surprised she wasn't with them, until they explained they were thinking long-term about Cassandra's safety and had to ensure that Alejandro was put away.

They all went into the salon as Jay started telling them the idea he had that would help lure Alejandro out to take part in a large act of piracy. It had to be really attractive to Alejandro, one that he wouldn't just send his guys to do without him: it had to involve a yacht with very expensive cargo on it. Since Seth had told Alejandro he was working on a large takeover, Seth started to get excited, thinking that the plan might just work. The plan meant it would be a few more days without Cassandra, leaving her in Alejandro's custody a little longer. Seth had to trust Jay on this one. He was right. Her safety depended on capturing Alejandro and putting him away forever where he wouldn't be a threat any longer. But he wasn't so sure that he would be able to stay away from Cassandra now that he had found her . . . .

10

I had just argued, once again, with Alejandro. He was pressuring me about the other night, being in his room, when I was caught returning his computer. He was sure that I was hiding something. I finally used anger to cover up my actions, stormed into my room, slamming the door shut for emphasis. I leaned against my closed door, taking in a large breath of air. If only Seth was here! This man was dangerous, and I didn't know how long he was going to keep his hormones in check. Pirates wouldn't think twice about raping their victim. The only reason I had escaped it so far, was that he wanted to be sure Seth would do as he wished, whatever that may be. I went to the window and looked out into the dark night, cursing Seth and asking where he was. Of course, I didn't expect him to answer. Silence greeted me and I turned away, looking forward to another day closer to being taken out of this situation. I wondered how it would turn out. Would one of us get hurt in the process? What would Alejandro do to Seth? What was his ultimate goal?

Alejandro wasn't letting on about any time frames. He said he was

Compromises

in contact with Seth. I hadn't been able to steal the computer again, as he slept even lighter now, or so it seemed, waking up every time I even wandered out of my room at night. I only knew he was keeping in touch because of his little comments that Seth was working on a plan for a really large takeover of a yacht. I wondered how Seth planned to do that. Would he really do an act of pirating? That would be so dangerous! What if he got shot? I knew Seth wouldn't stop at anything to get me back; of that I was sure. I just hoped he wasn't taking any risks.

The next afternoon, late in the day, I made my way out to run around the island, as I had been doing lately. I came to an area on the other side of the island and saw something that made me pause. On the beach, something looked out of place. The tide had clearly wiped away whatever was toward the lower part of the beach. Farther up, near some brush, I found what looked like prints, and where something larger had been slid onto the sand: a boat, maybe?

Who would bring a boat on this side of the island and not come to the house? Seth? Could it be? I tried not to get my hopes up. I took a palm frond and wiped away the evidence, making note of where I was. If I had to do it again, I would get out here before Alejandro would see it. I wasn't sure why, but I felt that whoever or whatever was here wasn't a friend of Alejandro's. And anyone who wasn't a friend of Alejandro's would most certainly be a friend of mine.

As I ran back to the house, my steps were a little lighter, and hope set into my heart for the first time in a long while. The skies were coloring with the sunset, and I thought how beautiful the island was; if only I wasn't being held captive, this island would be a perfect spot to relax and unwind.

Alejandro was waiting as I ran back to the house. He smiled as he walked down to meet me. "Good afternoon, did you have a good run?"

"Yes," I answered cautiously as I wiped the sweat from my brow, wondering what he was up to.

"Isn't today a special day?" He let me pass as I made my way into the house, with him following behind me.

"Why?" I asked, not sure what day it was, as I continued on my trek to my bedroom. "What's the date?"

"It's the 14th." I paused just a moment, staring straight ahead, and then continued on my way to my bedroom without turning around.

"Nope, nothing special," I answered, as I closed the door to my room and leaned against it. "At least, not special this year," I said to no one in particular.

Alejandro knocked on my door, making me jump. I was just about to get into the shower and change for dinner. I answered, "What?" I never was overly polite to him. Tonight wasn't any different.

"Dress nice for dinner," he said through the closed door, and walked away.

"Just who the hell does he think he is?" I asked myself as I moved away from the door and stripped down on my way into the bathroom to get into the shower. Did he think I was in a celebratory mood just because of the date? Knowing that I had no choice but to follow his orders, I made my way to the bathroom. It was late; it was already getting dark as I adjusted the water in the shower. Surely he didn't think that I was going to celebrate, even if it was a special occasion- which, to me, didn't feel very special.

The shower was a huge open space with no curtain or door, as it was deep and wide enough that none was needed. It reminded me how luxurious this place was. The shower had what they refer to as a rain bird, located above your head. It was like standing in the pouring rain, which matched my mood now that Alejandro had reminded me of the date. I adjusted the temperature even colder, as it was warm that day, stripped off the rest of my clothing, and stepped in to allow the water to cascade over my naked body.

The place was so secluded, and no one ever visited, so I never bothered to lock my windows. The only thing I did lock was my bedroom door. Not that Alejandro had made any advances, except for the other night; but I still didn't trust him. Never knew when a guy would get lonely enough to try something stupid.

I immersed myself under the semi-cold water and closed my eyes. I relaxed and dreamed of how special this day should have been, if I had been with Seth. I could imagine him playing for me at the piano as I watched the muscles in his back move under his shirt. And we would have wine with a dinner that he had prepared especially for me. Tears mixed with the water as it cascaded down my face. And later, we would make love until the sun came up . . . .

As I let the water wash away my tears and the cares of the day, a hand covered my mouth as a hard, clothed body pushed up against me. I instantly started to struggle as I was pulled into a hard chest. The shower continued running over my eyes, so I couldn't see. I continued to squirm against the hold I was in. Whoever held me was strong, as they pinned me against their body and I panicked, knowing that I was helpless. I thought to myself, "No! This can't happen to me, not on this date!" Damn, Alejandro had changed his mind. He wanted me and now, for some reason, he was going to take me against my will. What did I think? That a pirate would have morals? I would have laughed at myself for even thinking that, if I wasn't so afraid. It became very evident that the man who held me was extremely aroused. Pinned so tightly, I panicked and tried to think how I was going to injure him long enough to get away.

"Shhh, love," a familiar voice whispered in my ear.

I moved my head out of the stream of water to see more clearly. I must be dreaming. I shook my head again, but his hand stayed over my mouth. I went limp and moved closer.

"I am going to take my hand away, but you need to be quiet - hear me?" Seth said as he continued to hold me close.

I shook my head in agreement to let him know that I was going to do as he said. His hand came down slowly and I instantly threw my arms around him and kissed him. He returned the kiss with the same urgency he felt in me. The kiss started to turn more sensual, sexual. I moaned and pulled myself closer to his soaking wet, clothed body. He started to strip off his shirt and only broke off the kiss long enough to drop it to the floor. I assisted him, wanting to feel him against me, to take me away from all these horrible long days without him. He pulled me up as I wrapped my legs around him in the shower and we lost all conscious thought of where we were. We were together, and that was all that mattered at the moment. Our lovemaking was urgent, with a fervor built up from our long separation and the long absence from each other. I moaned as we reached the height of passion together.

Later, as he wrapped me in a towel, drying me off slowly, I finally had the chance to ask him how he had found me and what was happening.

He took the towel to my hair, gently drying my curls before running his hands through it. "We actually found you last night, but Jay wouldn't let me come for you. Believe me, it was one of the hardest things I have had to do in my life. I couldn't stay away."

"So it was you," I said, absentmindedly.

"What?"

"Did you drag a boat up on the other side of the shore?"

"Yes, how did you know?"

"I saw the prints there during my afternoon run. Don't worry, I wiped away all the evidence, hoping that maybe it was you. How the

Compromises

hell did you find me?" I couldn't believe my eyes. He was here! Seth was here!

He sat down on a stool at the counter while I moved over beside him to apply a little makeup.

"Luke actually got the information on where to start looking for you. It's a long story, but for now, I need to tell you the plan."

"I'm not leaving with you, am I?" I asked, already sensing the answer as I dropped my makeup back on the counter and stood to look at him, gazing into those beautiful blue eyes.

"Jay made some good points about keeping you safer, longer, if we are able to arrest Alejandro."

"And . . . ," I prompted him to continue, crossing my arms in front of me.

"And, we need to catch Alejandro out on the water, in an act of piracy."

"So I am still a prisoner." My head dropped down as I stared at my bare feet.

Seth moved to stand in front of me. He leaned against the counter as he pulled me between his legs and held me in his embrace. He kissed me as he chuckled, "a prisoner with benefits."

I smiled, "What exactly do you mean, Seth Hanson?"

"Well, I can't take you with me, but I sure as hell won't be without you, or not let you know I was here to protect you."

"You're going to stay?" I asked incredulously, knowing how dangerous that could be.

"Well, only until dawn. I can't risk being found and you can't let on that I am . . . um . . . visiting you, so to speak."

"I'm a pretty good actress when I need to be, you know," I said as I hugged him, laying my head on his bare chest. "He will never have a clue, although I may smile a bit more than I have these past few weeks."

He moved a finger under my chin to bring my gaze up to his. He got serious all of a sudden. "This is dangerous, Cassandra, but I couldn't stay away."

"I realize that, Seth. I am glad you didn't stay away. Trust me, I can pull this off. Just one question . . ."

"And that would be?"

"How long do I have to do this?" He knew that I meant staying in Alejandro's custody.

"We are working on that. We are going into town tomorrow to start some rumors about an expensive cargo on a yacht that is transporting items close to the island."

Uh oh, I knew what that meant. "Your yacht's the one with the cargo, isn't it?"

"We hope to lure Alejandro out, to catch him in the act of piracy."

"Well, I will do what I can to see he does just that," I said as I kissed him.

Alejandro knocked on the bedroom door in the adjacent room and I jumped, holding a hand to my heart to steady myself as I pulled away from Seth. He stayed very still, listening.

"Yes?" I asked as I steadied Seth from moving as he reached over to the counter where he had set his gun.

"Are you almost ready?"

"Yes," I answered. "I'll be just a moment." I didn't want to chance Seth acting irrationally and shooting Alejandro. I knew that wouldn't be good situation, as he was the intruder in Alejandro's house and we were in a foreign land with foreign laws.

Alejandro said, "I have dinner waiting on the outside deck off the side of the house. I will wait for you there."

Compromises

I again leaned into Seth, hating that I had to leave him. He must have sensed it. "I'll be right here, watching from a distance. Have your dinner and hurry back to me, love. We have to let Alejandro believe nothing has changed."

"I am counting on the fact that you will be here, waiting. That is the only reason that I will be able to make it through the next few hours. Does Jay know you are here?"

"No way! Are you kidding? I had to sneak off by myself. I tell you, I am not relishing the thought of having to row that damn boat back by myself. But you are worth it, love. Just having this little bit of heaven with you makes it all worth it."

I smiled as I moved away from him, reluctantly, to get dressed.

"What's the special occasion?" he inquired about the dinner date with Alejandro, as he followed me into the bedroom.

"It's my birthday," I answered nonchalantly as I stepped into my dress. "He must have done his homework."

"Your birthday?" Seth was amazed that he didn't know that. He grabbed me to turn me back to face him. "I lost all track of the days since you have been gone." He took me back into his arms. "I'm sorry, love. This wasn't exactly how I had in mind you spending your first birthday with me."

"You just gave me the best present ever," I smiled, indicating the little interlude in the shower.

Seth smiled his sexy grin, "You are something. Most women want diamonds or some kind of trinket. You just want me."

"You are all I ever wanted, Seth, from the first day I laid eyes on you. I just didn't know it," I answered as I pulled the strings to my dress up to tie it behind my neck. The dress was made with a tube top that hugged my curves on top and flowed from there in a sheet of black to just below my ankles. Beads adorned the collar, with strings to hold it in place around my neck. Seth moved behind me as he grabbed the ties from me and tied them, leaning down to kiss the nape of my neck, and I leaned into him. "Seth . . ."

"Later, love. I would hate for us to get caught by your captor and ruin my chances for putting him away for a long time."

I turned and kissed him one last time. "Please be careful."

"Aren't I always?" he smiled. "You be careful as well." He looked concerned.

"I'll be fine, Seth. Nothing has happened thus far, and nothing will. Promise to meet me back here after dinner? I won't be late," I said, already regretting that I had to leave him. I knew he wouldn't stay and wait, and would in fact be out there ensuring my safety. It made me far more nervous knowing he was out there. It increased the chances that he would be caught.

"I'll be waiting, love."

I made my way out the door, closing it behind me as I did so. A frown formed across my brow as I thought about Seth. Having him here in the house wasn't a good idea. I was more worried that he would risk his own safety to protect me. The man took too many chances when it came to me. At least he was listening to Jay about permanently putting Alejandro away - the legal way that is. I would just have to be careful, knowing that he was watching, so that he wouldn't come charging out from the bushes to protect me. It could be tricky, as Alejandro was being more aggressive around me. This could be very, very bad.

I made my way out to the side deck. A white tablecloth was draped over a candlelit table. China and crystal of the highest quality adorned the top. The latticed covered area was strewn with little party lights that glittered in the dark night. A chorus of crickets and frogs kept time with the music playing softly from the speakers set into the patio. Alejandro was dressed in a white-collared, button-up shirt and tan linen pants,

Compromises

rolled up from the bottom, and was barefoot, looking every inch the pirate and very dangerous. He held a chair for me to sit in. I sat down and he moved to the other side. Almost on cue, Stella, the girl from the kitchen, came out with food. She curtsied as she delivered the first dish. Alejandro explained that was her way of paying honor to my birthday.

"I don't know why you are going to all this trouble," I said as I started to eat, eager to end this dinner and get back to Seth.

"One's birthday should never go uncelebrated. It signifies another year of your life, and life, my dear, is worth celebrating."

"Well," I said sarcastically, "why don't you let me go and I will really be celebrating."

"Cassandra, you know that I won't do that. Why not just enjoy what we have tonight, hmmm?" He raised his wineglass, but I ignored him. He shrugged his shoulders and took a large gulp of his wine. "Suit yourself," he said as he set it back down on the table to eat.

I stayed quiet and tried to look around without being conspicuous, looking for Seth. I didn't see him, but knew he must be close by, watching.

"Do you like the dish?" Alejandro asked as he took another bite.

"Yes, actually, it is quite good."

"It's a local recipe." The meal was made up of steak, pasta, sauce, and vegetables.

"It's quite good," I replied as I took another bite. I was anxious, and my hunger dissipated because of my fear of Seth getting caught.

Seth was indeed close by. He was well hidden from the house and from where Cassandra was on the deck. He was just ensuring things were going according to plan, and that she was safe. Concealed by the multitude of large bushes that kept the deck secluded, he was too far to hear their conversation, but he could tell by Cassandra's facial expressions that she wasn't having a good time. He heard something crackle in the bushes behind him. His heart stopped; he reached for the gun he had hidden on his side, but felt another gun in his side before he could pull his weapon from its holster. He quickly turned, arms raised, fully expecting a friend of Alejandro's to lead him out in the open. He was already formulating a plan, what he would do next, when Luke grinned.

"Thought you could slip away that easily, my friend?" Luke whispered as he holstered his gun.

Seth whispered back, relaxed now that he knew who it was. "Damn you! You scared the hell out of me. I could have shot you."

"Serves you right, sneaking off like that. Didn't you think that Jay and I would follow you?"

"Where did you get another boat?"

"Off your yacht, of course. We noticed you were gone, and when no one knew where you had gone, it only made sense you would come back here. Not smart, Seth; you could put her in danger, not to mention yourself."

"Yeah, well, I wasn't going to sit by and wait and not let her know that a rescue was planned in the near future."

"Are you coming back with me or do I need to drag you?"

"I am spending the night here, with Cassandra. I will head back close to dawn so we can move forward with the plan to start the rumors around town."

"That's really stupid, you staying here. What if you get caught?"

"I won't, so don't worry. I can handle this guy if need be." Something caught Seth's eye as he turned his attention back to the table and Cassandra.

Back at the patio, Alejandro and I had been discussing my birthday, and I was adamant that I just wanted to go home.

"Look, I don't know what you are asking of Seth, but I will tell you

Compromises

anything you need to know if it means that much to you, but just let me go. You have no right to keep demanding things from Seth," I said.

Alejandro had moved to my side of the table and grabbed my arm, forcing me to stand close to him. He looked down at me as he angrily retorted, "If your Seth would just do what I ask and get me a large vessel that will help settle me for awhile, I would release you. What kind of pirate, or man even, would take so long to get his girl back; unless, maybe you don't mean that much to him, hmmm?"

"My Seth," I spat the words back at him, "is more of a man than you will ever be."

I wasn't expecting the kiss that followed. Alejandro pulled me against his hard chest and kissed me as I struggled. He released me and I pulled away, surprised and angry. I spoke aloud as I knew that Seth was probably going to charge out of the bushes at any moment and put himself at risk. "Don't!"

At that same time, back in the bushes, Luke grabbed Seth, trying to contain both Seth's and his own anger. "Seth, wait. She's fine. Look, she's talking to you, listen."

From the patio, I hollered out, "It's not worth it," truly talking to Seth, willing him to remain hidden. Then, looking directly at Alejandro, I said, "You can't bully me and you don't want to damage me!"

"You may be right about that. But don't press your luck, little lady."

I walked up and got close to Alejandro. He smiled down at me. I smiled back and then promptly stomped on his foot with my high heel, wheeled around and walked away, leaving him to nurse his injured foot.

Watching from their hiding place, Luke chuckled, "That's my Cass!" He continued to hold Seth while watching Alejandro limp back to his seat, cursing as he did so.

Seth finally shook him off. "Okay, you had your fun. I should just shoot this ass and be on with it."

"You can't, Seth. Even if he is a pirate, killer, and whatever else, you would still be breaking the law."

Seth knew his friend was right, but didn't like it. He couldn't wait to get revenge on this guy, someday . . . .

"I want to get back to Cassandra and you need to get the hell out of here. Two boats on the other side of the beach will draw attention. I will catch up with you in the morning."

"Nothing I can say to change your mind?" Luke looked hopeful.

"Do you have to ask?" Seth said as he slowly made his way around back, crouching so as not to be seen.

"Guess not," Luke said to himself as he snuck back the way he had come, to get back to the boat. "Can't say as I blame you, either," he chuckled as he shook his head.

Back in my bedroom, I was pacing, and contemplating jumping out the window to go find Seth. Where the hell was he? Was he going to try and take over Alejandro? As I approached the window, I saw Seth coming around the corner. I stood back as he climbed through. He immediately took me into his arms and kissed me.

"I'm going to kill that bas . . . ," he trailed off, not saying the word. "I'll do it right now!"

"Seth," I admonished. "It doesn't do you any good to kill him. Where would that get us? I handled him, see, I am fine." He kissed me gently. "Seth," I pleaded, "please, let it go. I know it must have taken everything within you not to react . . ."

"Luke held me back. Otherwise, Alejandro would be lying in his own blood right now."

"Luke's here, too?" I asked, concerned that this was getting out of hand.

Compromises

"Was," Seth corrected as he took me back into his embrace. "I sent him home. I hate this, Cassandra." When I looked down, he mentally shook himself, remembering the importance of this day. He said, "Hey gorgeous, did I hear it was your birthday?"

"Yes," I smiled up at him. "Did you bring me something?"

"Did I," Seth answered as he moved me back to the bed and landed on top of me as we fell into it. "Did I ever."

I started to undress him as he continued to kiss me. He undid the strap around my neck, his fingers leaving a trail of heat where they landed. A knock on the door stopped us from going any further. Thankfully, Alejandro never came in without my permission. Seth sat very still. I motioned for him to stand behind the door. He did as I asked, and I held the top of my dress up and opened the door with the other hand. The door swung so that Seth was behind it, flattened against the wall. Alejandro stood at the other side, clearly oblivious to the fact that I had just been intimate with Seth only moments before and that he was standing on the other side.

"That was rude of me, at dinner."

"Forgiven," I said, wanting to get him out of here. "It was nothing."

"No," Alejandro said as he touched his hand to my face gently. I stood stoic, not moving. "It was wrong of me. I truly apologize and will try to behave around you from now on."

"Really, no need to apologize. Besides, I did stomp on your foot."

Alejandro laughed. "You have spunk. I can see why Seth fell for you." Uh oh, where was this going? I moved closer to the door with the intent to shut it if I needed to and keep Seth from forcefully pushing it into Alejandro to take him off guard.

"I'm really quite tired," I said as I faked a yawn. "Is there something else?"

"No. I will let you retire for the evening. I just wanted to say I'm sorry."

"Thank you," I said as I closed the door and then fell into Seth's waiting arms. He held a finger to my lips, waiting to hear Alejandro's footsteps retreat down the hall before speaking.

"I am going to make him pay," Seth said behind gritted teeth.

"Are we going to waste time talking about him," I said as I emphasized the word *him* and wrapped my arms around Seth's neck, "or are we going to celebrate my birthday? I think you were just going to show me something?"

Seth grinned, "Yes, I was. But now that I know he is so close, I have a better idea."

I was curious what he was up to. He grabbed the blanket off the bed and then my hand, helping me crawl out the window as he jumped out behind me. He grabbed my hand and we ran to the middle of the island into the secluded area with trees. He stopped, eventually, and laid out the blanket on the sand, dropping down on it and holding a hand out to pull me down next to him.

We lay back and looked through the trees and saw the beautiful stars as they lit up the sky. If I hadn't been in a hostage situation, this would have been a perfect night.

"This is beautiful," I said as I gazed up at the stars.

"Yes, you are," Seth answered and I turned to see him staring at me.

We made love slowly, cherishing the moment. Afterwards, I cuddled into his side. "I want to go with you, Seth."

"I want to take you," Seth answered. We both knew it was wishful thinking, and neither of us expected it to happen. It was just nice to voice it aloud.

Compromises

"How long?" I asked as I turned to face him and propped my head up on my bent arm.

"Too long for my liking. Jay's right, unfortunately. We have to do this legally so I know he is put away for good and can never harm you again. I can't get you back and then worry about where he might show up next."

"I knew you would hear the voice of reason," I sighed, as I lay back to look up into the starlit sky, wishing it weren't so.

Seth rolled onto his side and moved a lock of curly hair from my face. "I want to take you home with me. If you want me to, I will. We will find another way to capture him."

I knew he meant it. Yet I knew that Jay was doing the right thing. Besides, I had gone this long and with this little reprieve with Seth; I could last a few more days, if need be.

"Will you be coming back tomorrow?"

"I wish I could promise you that," Seth said. "Look, I can stay. I will hide the boat farther inland and stay until it's safe to let you leave."

"No, Seth, you can't. It's too risky. Besides, Luke and Jay need you. They would worry and maybe act rashly if you don't return. I have no reason to believe that Alejandro will treat me any differently. We need to stick with Jay's plan. By the way, shouldn't you be heading back?"

He reluctantly looked at his watch. He didn't have to answer; I saw the regret in his eyes. I knew it was going to be really hard to get him to leave me now. I got up and shook the sand from my clothes as I dressed. He grabbed my hand, forcing me to look at him.

"I can't leave you here, Cassandra. I thought I was strong enough, but I can't. I don't trust this guy."

I hugged him close, determined to do the right thing. "You can and you will. Now help me shake off this blanket and you head back to the boat. I know my way back to the house."

"No," he said as he pulled me close, "I can't do it, Cassandra. We will get him another way."

"Seth," I said as I held his beautiful face in my hands, "soon we will be together and nothing will tear us apart. Jay knows what he is doing. It's for our future. Seth . . . ," I pleaded. "Please . . . ."

He finally let go of my hand. "I don't like it."

"I know," I said and kissed him quickly before taking the blanket from him and running back to the house, not daring to look back to see if he followed.

Seth watched as I ran away, warring within and losing miserably. Finally, he made his way back to the boat to slowly row back away from the island, even more determined to take out Alejandro. He was going to make this guy pay, if it was the last thing he did.

11

The plan seemed like a good one. The girls, Robert, and Jake left early the next day and split up, heading into the small town. They went to restaurants, shops, and everywhere they could think of in which someone would overhear them. They spoke freely of a huge yacht that was traveling in the area for the next few days with expensive and unique artifacts being transported from Europe to the U.S. They made sure they were loud enough to be overheard, and hoped that the rumor would get out. They met back on the yacht to give Luke, Seth, and Jay an update on how their day had gone.

Jay, Seth, and Luke had purposely stayed aboard the yacht all day. They didn't want to be connected with the story that was getting circulated about the yacht. They only hoped their plan would work, and so they waited it out. They put together large boxes that would make the yacht look like it was carrying cargo. When Seth inquired where all the materials had come from, Luke laughed and said it was amazing what you could find when you needed it. They laid heavy rocks in the bottom, and filled the boxes with popcorn-looking packaging material, just in case the pirates sliced a side open. They left the boxes down in a holding area in the engine room. Luke looked over at Seth and said, "Just one last thing to do."

Seth knew what it was. He went to his computer in the lounge and brought up his email. He began typing to Alejandro that he had heard of a large cargo in Antigua and was going to scope it out.

Jay contacted the cutter that was still in the area to keep their eyes out for pirates, as he had heard there could be a possible act in the next few days. He wanted his men on guard and ready to act if and when Alejandro made his move.

Seth was going crazy. He wanted to go back to the island to check on Cassandra and see if Alejandro had heard the rumors they had spread. Jay was adamant in not letting him go, as he knew his friend well. He was already upset that Seth had snuck out there and spent the night, coming home only very early this morning. Unfortunately, Seth's hands were tied. He knew his friend was right. They had to do this the legal way.

They gathered in the salon as Jay laid out the next plan of action.

"Okay. We have laid the groundwork to get the rumors started. We need to let a day or so pass to let the word get to Alejandro. When we know Alejandro and his crew are ready to attack the yacht, you and Luke are going to take the small boat to the island and rescue Cassandra."

"But what about my yacht and everyone here?"

"We will relocate Mandi and Jackie to a hotel here in Antigua to keep them out of danger. Robert, Jake, and I will take the yacht out in the open water, where we will be waiting for Alejandro and his crew," Jay said. "The Coast Guard cutter is within easy distance to come in at my cue. We will be fine with protection close by." Seth knew that his friend was downplaying the risks they were taking. Anything could happen, and one of them could get hurt.

"Why are both Luke and I going to get Cassandra?" Seth asked, not sure why it would take both of them, and that he would feel better if one of them stayed aboard.

"Well," Jay explained, "I know you both are impatient to get Cassandra back to safety, and I don't want you anywhere near Alejandro when he gets here."

"I gotta miss out on the fun?" Luke asked. "Come on, Jay, you can always use another hand. Besides, I used to be a pirate. I would be invaluable to you. Not to mention, Alejandro would expect both Seth and I to be here since we said we were scoping out a large cargo."

"I don't want to send Seth by himself in case he runs into some problems once he gets to the island. Besides, I can't trust that you will let us get Alejandro the legal way. I also need Alejandro to be unsuspecting. So, if he comes to scope out the yacht, he can't see you or Seth anywhere on it just yet. You will have to come aboard much later, after he has taken possession."

"Damn!" Luke said dejectedly, "I'm not going to get a chance to introduce Alejandro to my fist." Luke slammed his fist into his other hand for effect.

Jay laughed, as did Seth. Seth said, "I know how you feel. I am still chafing at the bit from the kiss he gave Cassandra last night."

Luke laughed, and told Jay, "I am glad that I am as strong as I am. I wasn't sure I could hold Seth from reacting."

Seth realized what Jay had just said, and turned to him in question. "If you feel Alejandro is going to scope out the yacht and we can't be here, where will we be?"

"I want you to take Mandi and Jackie to the hotel here on the mainland until I give you the heads-up so that you can head over to the island."

"How are we going to know when we should leave to go to the hotel?" Luke asked.

"Well, I think everyone should leave tonight. We don't know when they will come to check out the yacht from a distance, and I can't chance them seeing either one of you. You will have to go now, and Robert will take the yacht out in the open waters as soon as you leave."

"Sounds like a good plan, if he falls for it. I just don't like having to sit and wait another day or two," Seth said. "I want to head back to see Cassandra tonight, and tell her what to expect."

"It won't be much longer," Jay tried to soothe his friend, moving close to lay a hand on his back. "We can't risk you running into them going back and forth to the island. You just have to be patient, Seth."

"Try not to mess up my yacht, though, will you?" Seth said as he rose from his seat, and Jay laughed as Seth headed downstairs to pack for the next few nights. Jay knew his friend well enough to know it wasn't the yacht he was worried about.

Seth, Luke, and the girls packed for several days not knowing when they would get the signal to get Cassandra. They reconvened in the salon later with bags packed. Jay thought it best they leave under the cover of darkness just to make sure that they were not noticed by anyone who might be watching already. They left to find a nice hotel farther inland, away from where the girls had been during the day, spreading the rumor. As they checked in and went to their own rooms, Mandi made sure that Seth would let them know the minute they left for the island to get Cassie. Seth assured them that if they didn't get word tonight, they would meet in the hotel restaurant for breakfast in the morning. He didn't want the girls to leave the hotel, in case anyone

Compromises

recognized them from earlier in the day. They were going to be prisoners of sorts in this hotel until things went down.

Seth made a phone call to Cassandra's parents. He had been in touch with them ever since she was taken, keeping them in the loop. They were on their way into Florida, and were on standby. They had arranged to fly in as soon as they knew where Seth was staying and when Cassandra was found, arriving soon, as Seth had sent his jet to fly them down from Florida once they landed there.

The next two days went idly by. Seth was on edge, even though Luke tried to pull him out of it by making jokes all day. He certainly kept the girls in stitches. Seth would smile, but that was about all Luke could get out of his friend.

The wait began . . . . Seth kept his cell close, waiting for Jay's call. He couldn't even chance trying to sneak out to the island to visit Cassandra again. He hoped she understood that it wasn't safe to return.

He did send another email to Alejandro, and said he was getting close to Antigua, not letting on that he was already there. He stated that he was going to be involved in getting to a large yacht with cargo that had untold wealth aboard. Alejandro replied that once Seth had the yacht under his control, he would contact him to make arrangements to trade the yacht for Cassandra. Seth knew better. He knew that Alejandro would probably try to take over the yacht before he could and then hold Cassandra for even longer, for more demands. He knew their type . . . . They were greedy.

Luke thought he had never watched so much TV in all his life. They couldn't venture out on the town, which left very little to do. At one point he decided to call Jenna, and found himself surprised that he missed her company. He was looking forward to getting back to Florida to see her. He took out the little bear necklace he had bought her, and watched the light bounce off of it as he dialed her number.

At Jenna's home back in Florida, Jenna picked up the phone, not recognizing the number. Tentatively she asked, "Hello?"

"Hi, baby," Luke said, really missing her now that he heard her voice. He lay back on the bed, his back propped up against the pillows, with his legs straight out in front of him.

"Luke?"

"Yeah, it's me. I had a free moment and was near a phone so I thought I would call." He squeezed the bear into his palm and then released it, watching the dents it left in his palm fade away.

"It's good to hear from you," she said as she sat down on her bed pulling a pillow close to her to hug it, wishing it was Luke.

"So, do you miss me yet?"

Jenna laughed. "What makes you think I miss you?"

She was teasing, of course, and Luke picked up on her playful mood. "Well, I thought that you may miss my warmth in your bed and someone to do your back in the shower. Was I wrong?"

"Well, there is that," she laughed. "But the bear misses you more. He hasn't been able to bite anyone since you have been gone."

Luke laughed. He really liked this girl, and was glad he had called. He watched the little bear twist in his hand as he let it dangle from the chain. "Well, we need to name him, 'cause I hear that tame bears won't bite, and I really have grown attached to my leg." He gently laid the necklace back in its box and put it on the side table, so as to lie back against the pillows and concentrate on Jenna's voice.

"I will leave that task to you, since you two are so close and all." Jenna was laughing now. She loved that about Luke. He was always so playful with her and kept her laughing. "How's work going?"

"Very productive. I hope we can wind things up here in about a week at the most, and I should be back shortly after that."

Compromises

"Well, good! I am cold at night and I am afraid that my back has been neglected in the shower since you have been gone."

Luke laughed. "So now I am the one who is going to have to take a shower, a cold one at that." They both laughed at his innuendo. Seth entered the room, and the determined look on his face gave Luke pause. He said to Jenna, "I got to run for now, baby, but I will give you a call as soon as I am back in town."

"Can't wait," Jenna said, smiling into the phone. "Bye for now."

Seth looked at Luke as he grabbed some keys off the counter. "Don't try to stop me," he said. Luke jumped up off the bed and stood in front of him, blocking his path to the door.

"Stop you from what?"

"I can't wait any longer. Cassandra's parents are flying in tonight. See that they get a room, and let them know that I am ensuring that no danger is coming to their daughter."

"Seth," Luke said, still blocking his path, "what are you going to do?"

"I told you! I am ensuring that Cassandra is safe."

"Look," Luke said, "I want to go in there and blast her out of that place too, but Jay is right. We need to make sure that we put Alejandro away. It was risky what you did the other night. We need to do this the right way. Alejandro's crew will be watching very carefully. You know the drill. Pirates watch their prey before they pounce."

Before Luke could say more, Seth's phone went off. They looked at each other, and Seth checked the display before he answered. "Jay, what's going on?"

"We've spotted them. There have been a couple of smaller boats passing by today. We noticed it was the same ones just a few hours apart, and then they headed back to the direction of the island that Cassandra is on. I think they are going to make their move tonight. I alerted the

Coast Guard cutter to keep a respectful distance as I don't want to clue them in that anything is up. I want you and Luke to take off tonight as soon as it gets dark. Make sure you keep watch to not cross paths with them on your way out there. Make sure you take care, as I don't know if they will leave anyone there on the island with her."

"Cassandra's parents are coming in from the airport. I had Mandi and Jackie pick them up and bring them here. I will want to meet with them before we take off."

"I wasn't aware they were flying in."

"I called them a few days ago and told them we were close to getting her back. I sent the jet, as I knew we were close to a rescue. I am sure they will want to be here when she is."

"Okay. But make sure it is just you and Luke that go tonight. I can't risk putting her father in danger when this all goes down."

"Wouldn't dream of it," Seth said as he hung up.

In anticipation of the evening and of rescuing Cassandra, Seth got a few things together in a bag and checked his weapon. He wasn't sure what Cassandra would need, so he grabbed a few of the items he had packed for her, clothes and such.

The girls picked up Cassandra's parents at the airport and then came back to the hotel. Seth arranged for them to stay in the penthouse suite. Jackie called Seth to let him know that they were back at the hotel.

Seth went up to meet them to express his sincere apology that he had gotten Cassandra into this situation. He knocked tentatively at the door, not knowing what to expect from them. They had been cordial enough on the phone, and happy that he had called them to let them know that they had found Cassandra and were close to rescuing her, but he still didn't know what they thought about him. What if they felt everything that happened was his fault? He did, so wouldn't they? He knocked again and waited his fate as the door opened.

Compromises

Mandi was the one who answered the door and motioned him to come in. She introduced Cassandra's parents, and he crossed the room to shake hands with them. Cassandra's mother smiled pleasantly, as did her father. Seth thought he might as well break the ice.

"I am so very sorry I got your daughter mixed up in this whole thing."

Cassie's mom said, "It's not your fault, Seth. We know that. We just want to be sure we are here when she gets back, in case she needs us."

Seth was extremely grateful that her parents didn't hold this against him. He hadn't wanted to meet them under these circumstances, and they were being totally gracious to him.

Her mom continued, "We were aware that things were strained when you and Cassandra split after the holidays. I knew she was in love with you, but she wouldn't open up to us. We figured she would tell us when she was ready."

Seth filled them completely in now. He told them about the Caribbean fiasco and how he had wanted to keep his distance from her because of his fear of this very thing happening, that she would be in danger. He told them how they had gotten back together, and how he realized that it had hurt her just as much to be apart from him. And, it was dangerous for her to be with him. He had still been trying to figure out that dilemma when she was taken so suddenly. The last thing he thought he would ever do was endanger Cassandra's life.

Cassandra's dad placed his hand on Seth's back. "My daughter is very strong willed. She wouldn't let on what was happening, but I do know that I hadn't seen her that miserable before when I saw her this past winter. I don't think you could have kept her away after she learned the truth about you."

"You're both very kind," Seth said. "I really don't deserve it. I promise, I will be bringing her back to you shortly," he walked out of the room, leaving them both to sit and wait things out with Jackie and Mandi.

Jackie and Mandi were not only anxious about the guys going to rescue Cassandra, but worried about their men back at the yacht about to deal with unpredictable pirates. Someone could get seriously injured tonight. They were beside themselves with worry, and waited with Cassandra's parents, hoping for the best. They sat together, hands clasped, and prayed . . . .

Luke and Seth jumped into the small boat just after the sun set. They had dressed for the part. They had on torn jeans, T-shirts, and baseball caps put on backwards. They looked dangerous and . . . handsome.

They once again cut the engine as they got closer to the island. Noticing a few fast boats were tied up at the pier at the front the house, they brought their boat out to the other side so as not to be seen and beached it, pulling it up on the beach, out of sight. Luke motioned for Seth to follow where they had been a few short nights before. They moved up to the window where Cassandra stayed. The room was empty. Seth motioned to Luke that he was going into the room. Luke shook his head, not sure that it was a good idea, but before he could say anything, Seth hoisted himself through the window and quickly made his way to the entrance of the bedroom. Seth flattened himself against the wall, listening, before making his way farther into the house.

Luke continued to stay close to the back of the house and work his way around front. He had his gun ready, waiting for anything that might happen. He stopped suddenly as he heard voices. There were several men leaving the house and heading down to the pier where the boats were tied up. He couldn't tell if any of them was Alejandro or not. What he did see made his heart skip a beat, and he held his breath.

12

The time since I had seen Seth had dragged by. I was spending my days lazily walking the small island, looking for any signs of Seth's return. I figured that something must be happening to keep him away. Maybe they were closer to rescuing me for good and getting Alejandro. I remembered that I needed to ensure that he went on this next pirating expedition. Alejandro didn't leave his computer anywhere that I would have access to it. Damn the man! He had thought of everything to keep me isolated on this island until he was good and ready to let me go. I could only wonder what it was doing to Luke and Seth at this point.

I knew that Alejandro had been in touch with Seth several times over the course of the past few days, and it seemed that he had escalated the threats against him recently. It made me angry that he would antagonize Seth that way; so angry that I was fighting nightly with Alejandro. These fights usually ended with me exasperated, knowing I wasn't getting anywhere with this stubborn-headed pirate, and I would make my way back to my room, slamming the door in my frustration.

Alejandro was true to his word, and he never touched me after the night of my birthday.

I was walking along the sand, thinking of these things, when I heard a small boat approaching. I looked up to see several small boats coming toward the island. What now? I stood watching them come closer as Alejandro came running out. We hadn't had any visitors in quite some time. It was odd that anyone was approaching. I could only guess that these were some of Alejandro's band of pirates. Whatever they were doing, it had to be pretty important to make their way to the island. Maybe this was the event that Seth was talking about.

"Time for you to go to your room," Alejandro said as he grabbed my arm.

I shook myself free and said, "Why? What do I need to be put away from?"

"Let's just say I don't want to tempt the company coming."

I couldn't argue with that, and went willingly back into the house and my room. Alejandro locked me in, which was unusual as I had always been free to roam before. But we had never had company before. So I pressed my ear to the door, trying to make out the faint voices out in the living room. I could barely discern their conversation. They were saying something about a large yacht in the area. Some girls were spreading the word all through town the past couple of days about valuables on this yacht. They were planning an attack- pirate attack on this poor unsuspecting yacht. Only I knew that the yacht wasn't as unsuspecting as Alejandro and his cohorts thought. I moved away from the door and sat on the bed.

Again I thought of Seth. Did he even know how dangerous it was for him to continue his charade of captain on his mega-yacht? To enjoy the Caribbean travels, was it worth it? Somehow I didn't think so. I would have to talk to my man once I was out of this, and get him to

Compromises

leave behind this whole pirate thing. It just was too dangerous for him. For me as well, it would seem! If it wasn't for the danger involved, I could understand why Seth carried on his charade and helped the Coast Guard. It made me love him even more. I just wasn't so sure that he should continue to do it once this was all over.

A while later, Alejandro came to my door and said, "Follow me."

When I made no move to follow, he grabbed me by the arm and dragged me unwillingly out the door, down to where several small boats were tied up to the dock. He held my arm tightly as he walked near the pier. I was angry and tried to get out of his grasp, but he only held me closer. Ever since these men had come earlier in the day, I had been locked in, and I was tired of the secrecy. I couldn't help feel that this turn of events had something to do with me. I could only hope that they didn't plan on bringing me with them. No one noticed the man up against the side of the house, watching patiently.

Flattened up against the side of the house, Luke stayed where he was, too far away to hear anything. He watched the events playing out in front him, keeping his hand on his gun in case something went wrong and Cassandra needed his help. Something moved behind Luke and he turned, aiming, ready to shoot. Seth held up both his hands. Luke lowered his gun and whispered, "Could have shot you, Seth. Don't ever sneak up on me like that again."

"They have Cassandra. I made my way throughout the house and there is no one else inside. Thought I would come back out here to see what you were up to. Are they going to take her with them?"

"Doesn't make sense. Why would they bring her with them?"

"I'm not so sure she is. Look, Alejandro is talking to the other man there. Looks like Alejandro is giving orders for that guy to stay with Cassandra." Luke shook his head in agreement as they continued to watch.

Down at the boat dock, Alejandro finally released his grip on my arm. He told me that I was going to stay with this new guy for a short time. The guy smiled at me until Alejandro made it very clear that I was not to be touched or harmed in any way or Alejandro, himself, would kill him. I shuddered; as there was finality in the way he said it. There was no question that he wouldn't follow through with his threats. I was glad to hear that Alejandro was going. This was exactly what Seth was hoping for!

Alejandro confirmed what I thought. "There is a lot at stake, and I am not going to let you guys mess this one up like that last one." He obviously didn't trust that these men would do it right. He wasn't stupid, though, and knew he couldn't leave me in the care of another without making it perfectly clear the consequences if I was hurt or endangered.

"Got it, boss," the new guy left in charge of me answered. Just as Alejandro had done, he grabbed me by the arm to lead me back into the house. Once again, I struggled against being manhandled like that.

At the corner of the house, still hidden from view, Luke and Seth watched the interchange. Luke put a hand to Seth's chest when he saw the man grab Cassandra by the arm. "Wait," he whispered, "she's alright. Remember, she can hold her own."Luke and Seth made their way to the back of the house, so as not to be seen as the new man made his way to the house with Cassandra in tow.

As the new man and I made our way into the house, I realized how much larger and stronger he was then I. He was practically dragging me back inside.

Outside the house, Luke motioned for Seth to follow as they moved away from the house, back to the small boat, to radio Jay when they were out of earshot. "We have to fill Jay in," Luke said. Seth shook his head in agreement.

Compromises

"Things are in place," Seth said to Jay on the phone. "They are coming your way. There are three boats and about six to seven pirates here who will be heading your way shortly. Alejandro is with them. You will know him when you see him."

"Great work," Jay said. "Cassandra?"

"She's here. They left her with a bodyguard of sorts. We are going to head back in to scope out the situation and get her out of there."

"Just be careful," Jay said.

"Always. You do the same, okay?" He was worried about all of them. They were about to be faced with a very precarious position, and a dangerous one at that.

"We'll be fine," Jay answered. "See you soon."

Luke and Seth made their way back to the house. Seth didn't want to get distracted, and couldn't chance putting Cassandra into more danger. He told Luke to head back to the bedroom window to grab her. He was going to take out the "babysitter." Seth was too angry, and was looking for revenge at this point. He wanted to get his hands on someone. This guy would do for now. Since Alejandro was out of his reach, he was going to make sure that one of his goons was going to pay, big-time. Luke didn't want to miss out on the action either, but he knew that he wouldn't be able to argue with Seth. Cass was his main priority now.

Seth snuck to the front of the house. He saw the last of the small boats off in the distance, moving farther and farther away. He snuck up to one of the windows and looked in, seeing nothing. Luke, in the meantime, headed around to the back where Cassandra's room was.

A prisoner back in my room, I contemplated the past couple of weeks. I was going insane, feeling helpless to reach Seth and now even more worried about the yacht out on the open water. I wished I could be doing something! I needed to distract this man they left behind and get out of the room, to see if they had left a boat behind. If I could get to the boat, I might be able to get off the island. I would figure things out after that. We had to be near some type of mainland, as food and such had been delivered on a pretty regular basis while I was here. Besides, Seth had come by boat, so that meant he was close enough to reach.

The pirate they had left to guard me had just put me back into the room, saying he was tired of hearing my mouth. I screamed and pounded on the door, oblivious to the fact that Luke was just outside and that Seth was making his way into the front. Luke slowly peeked his head up over the edge of the window to look in, and saw me pounding the door while screaming, "You pig! You can't keep me here. You just wait! You will rue the day you met me!"

Outside the window, Luke had to keep from laughing as he thought, 'Yeah, that's my Cassie alright."

Back in the room, I finally stopped ranting long enough that Luke could take a rock and hit the window. He waited. Nothing happened. He threw another rock. He didn't want to just crawl through the window; for fear that I would scream and alert the pirate in the other room that I had company.

I was catching my breath, wondering why the hell I thought that screaming at this pirate was going to do me any good. I thought that if I annoyed him long enough he might just open the door, and I could find a way out. Then I could escape and make my way out to the yacht, which surely had to be Seth's. Now I thought of the window that was never locked; why hadn't I thought about that before?

I heard a noise, and ignored it. Then I heard it again. It sounded like something hitting the side of my window. I walked slowly to it and looked tentatively out the open window.

Luke whispered from his hiding spot, "Hey gorgeous, waiting on your knight in shining armor to rescue you?"

Compromises

"Luke," I hollered, disbelieving what I saw, and then instantly went quiet, not wanting to alert the guy on the other side of the door. I whispered back, "Luke, oh my . . ." A knock made me turn around. "You pig!" I said as I went to the door to bang it again to distract him as Luke moved to the open window and pushed himself in. "Open this damn door, you pig," I screamed at the door, and then ran into Luke's arms.

The pirate on the other side replied, "Shut up or I will, and then you will be . . ." there was a thump on the other side of the door.

I wasn't really paying attention to him anymore. All I was focused on was that Luke had saved me! I ran into his arms and threw myself at him, catching him a bit off guard. He tried to steady himself then Luke caught me and our lips met as the door behind me opened.

I dropped my hold to turn, expecting to see the man left to watch me, fully expecting a fight to break out between him and Luke. Instead, my breath caught in my throat as I realized it was Seth who stood there. He was taking in my embrace with Luke, an unreadable expression on his face. The man left to watch me lay crumpled on the floor, next to Seth's feet.

I ran to Seth. He kissed me hard before setting me back on my feet.

"You're safe now," he said, holding me at arm's length.

"Seth!" I said, holding him close. It was really Seth. My Seth! I looked up at him and then started kissing his face. "Oh, Seth, tell me it's over."

"Not quite over yet, but let's get you out of here." He was waging a war within himself. I could see it. Perhaps it was the embrace with Luke, or perhaps it was something else. I could feel the distance between us.

"Seth?" I inquired, waiting.

Then he kissed me. It was like the floodgates opened as we clung together. Luke cleared his throat, but we ignored him. Seth held me close to his chest as he continued to take my mouth fiercely, showing me that he had been in as much pain as I had been. I twined my arms around his neck, matching his emotion with my kiss. Luke finally walked over and pulled me back.

"Luke," I admonished.

"I hate to break this up, but that guy is only knocked out, I am assuming?"

I looked past Seth to see the man in question. Seth looked down and answered, "Yeah, he's lucky he's only that and not dead."

"Seth," I said, afraid he would do something more. He looked back at me and smiled.

"Let's get out of here," Seth said as he grabbed my hand and took me through the house I had been held prisoner in for so long, and out to the beach. He held my hand tightly, not letting go. I had to run to keep up with his long strides. I was taking in his outfit, and thought how dangerously handsome he looked. If he was a pirate, in the true sense of the word, I would beg to be taken. I shook my head, trying to concentrate on the here and now and not on how appealing he looked.

Luke followed behind me watching over his shoulder, keeping guard. We made our way down to the back of the house and farther down the beach, where a small boat was waiting. Seth grabbed me back close and kissed me again, taking my breath away. "I am never, ever letting you out of my sight again!"

I laughed at that, but held on to him, trying to get close. We jumped into the boat and quickly made our way out. Luke turned toward the open water, running the engine at full speed, not worrying about drawing any attention at this point. The wind whipped at my hair, and I took in a deep breath of salty air. It was getting much darker, and I wondered how they knew where to go, not realizing that they had made this trek before.

"Where are we going?" I asked as I made out several lights in the distance.

"The island, just over there." Seth answered as he pulled my back to his chest and wrapped his arms around me.

"Island? Not your yacht? Isn't that your yacht out there that they are headed toward?" I asked, not really wanting to hear his answer, as I had a sinking feeling in the pit of my stomach that it was.

"Cassandra," Seth said, as he turned me toward him. He kissed me hard and I kissed back, still not sure I wasn't dreaming all of this. He finally pulled me back a little. "Cassandra, I need for you to do as I say. We are going to take you to the island, where we have a hotel room. Your friends and parents are waiting for you there."

His words were sinking in slowly. "My friends, Mandi and Jackie, and my parents are here?"

"Yes, they knew we were close to a rescue and wanted to be here for you."

"But you're not staying," I said, instinctively knowing that there was more to this rescue than met the eye, and he wasn't telling me everything.

"No, but I will be back soon. You will get filled in when you get back in the hotel room by your family and friends, but right now I need to ensure that you are safe. And, I have a score to settle."

"No, Seth," I said, instantly recognizing that determined look on his face, and I hugged him close, burying my head into his chest. "You aren't going to be put in danger. Luke either," I added.

Luke chuckled. "Same ole Cass."

"Cassandra," Seth with a warning tone, "you don't have a say in this case."

"Seth, please, let the Coast Guard take care of this one. Stay here, with me. I need to make sure you aren't put in danger." Thoughts of the last time he encountered pirates filled my mind. I remembered the gun going off, the blood, and Seth sinking to the deck.

"Love, believe me, no one will keep me from coming back to you. Now be a good girl and put my mind at ease so I can help Robert, Jake, and Jay."

A light-bulb went on in my head. Robert and Jake were still on the yacht, about to be taken over by pirates; and Jay, too. This was not good. My heart started to beat in triple time. Seth could tell I was worried.

"It will be okay, love. We have the upper hand this time. We were expecting them. Besides, the Coast Guard may already be there. They are alerted to the situation, and there probably won't be anything for Luke and me to do. I just want to ensure the guys are okay out there. Surely, you can understand that?"

"Seth," I said, while my breath came out in short blasts due to the worry and fear building inside me, "it's dangerous. You and Luke absolutely are not going to walk into this booby trap."

"Love," Seth said, using my endearing nickname, "you don't get a say in this one; besides, the girls and your parents need you with them right now."

"Damn it, Seth!" I didn't have much time to convince him that there was no need to put him and Luke in danger. Jay could handle it; I knew he could, especially since the Coast Guard was nearby. "Why do you always have to put yourself in the thick of things? Can't you think of me?"

Seth was dialing on his phone, and mumbled quickly that we were there and I was safe. He wanted them to meet us at the dock. He hung up and chuckled, "You haven't changed much, love. You still think that by coercion you can make me give up what I know I have to do?"

Compromises

"Luke," I said, trying another tactic, "please, Luke, I can't bear it." Luke almost looked like he wanted to say something to Seth, but thought better of it and then looked forward toward the dock.

"Damn fools!" I felt Seth chuckle as he held me against him. "If you won't listen to me, then let me go with you. I will stay on the boat, but I want to be near. I could help," I added as Seth stopped me by kissing me.

"Absolutely not," he said when he finally pulled back. "You are amazing, though. You would put yourself in danger to just be near me." Seth shook his head.

We got to the island quickly. My parents and the girls were waiting by the dock as we pulled in. My dad grabbed the line that Luke threw, and I was soon engulfed in hugs and kisses by the girls and my mom, as they all pulled me out of the small boat. I turned as Seth jumped back in, but wasn't given the opportunity to hug him before he left. My dad's strong hands wouldn't let me get back near the boat. He knew me well. Seth wove as he and Luke made their way out in the dark, and I watched as they disappeared from view, a sinking feeling in my stomach.

"Okay, okay," I said as my welcoming crew would not let me go. I shook them off, angry that Seth was once again being put in danger.

"Come on, sweetie," my mom said as she steered me back to the hotel, "let's get you inside."

I looked back over my shoulder and prayed that Luke and Seth would be safe as I was led back to the hotel. I didn't like this one bit. Seth knew I wouldn't let him leave, and thus he had arranged for me to be distracted once we pulled in. I really was upset with him! I had just got him back and now he was going to walk right into danger again! Damn the man!

After getting back into the hotel room, I told my friends and parents the story of how I was abducted and the boring, uneventful time I had

had waiting these past few weeks for rescue. They finally allowed me to shower and change into some comfortable clothes, after they were sure that I was fine. I walked back out into the main area, relieved to be finally out of being held hostage. Except now I had to worry about Luke, Jake, Robert, Jay, and . . . Seth.

What was happening out there? Would Seth get hurt like the last time pirates were on board his yacht? I was anxious. I knew that my dad had a cell phone and that Seth had promised he would call once everything was done back at the yacht, but still I paced nervously back in the room as I waited for the call. We were all in Seth's room, as that was where all my belongings were. It was clear where I would be spending the night. I smiled as I thought how I had waited for this moment over the past few weeks, and then frowned again as I thought of Seth and the danger they were all still in. We waited in silence for Seth's call.

13

Seth and Luke quietly made their way closer to the yacht. The Coast Guard cutter was out there in the distance somewhere. There were smaller boats also off in the distance, circling the area. "There was about six of them, right?" Luke asked.

"I think so. They should all be on the yacht now."

"We need to be careful. They will probably spot us coming up. They may know already if they are monitoring the electronics, as they will see our approach. We can only pray they don't suspect us ready to do anything other than an act of piracy." Seth knew instantly what that meant. Luke thought they would have to take out anyone who might be expecting them as they moved closer to the yacht. Since it was dark and they were dressed in dark clothes, they needed to ensure that the Coast Guard was aware of their presence. Seth opened his cell and called the man whose number that Jay had given him previously in case anything happened to Jay.

A man answered, and Seth explained who he was. "We are going in to ensure that things are going to plan."

"Not a good idea. We have it under control, Seth. You should just let us take it over from here."

"Sorry man, just want you to know that Luke and I will be in the mix when things go down." He flipped his phone shut, not allowing the man on the other end to reply.

As they approached the yacht, there was a guy standing at the back, holding a gun aimed at them. Seth put his hands in air and hollered out, "Hold on there, friend! Alejandro called in for reinforcement. We are just here to give a hand."

Luckily the pirate fell for the story and waited until they pulled closer, helping to tie them off. As they climbed onto Seth's yacht, Luke came up behind him and knocked him out. They quickly tied him up, gagged him, and then stored him in the back engine room area. Closing the door, they ensured he wouldn't be able to come out and alert anyone else.

Luke and Seth remained silent as they made their way up to the next deck. They kept as close to the walls as possible, their guns drawn. Luke peeked into the salon window, keeping close to the side so as not to be seen. He saw Jake, Robert, and Jay sitting on a couch together, facing them. There were a couple of guys standing in front of them with guns in hand. Luke squatted down, as Seth did the same.

"So what's the plan?" Seth asked in a whisper so as not be overheard, just in case.

"We need to scope out the rest of the yacht. I can make out a few smaller boats over there in the distance; do you see them?" Luke said, as he pointed to small lights in the distance. "It could be the Coast Guard and assistance headed in already. We will have backup pretty quickly. Alejandro only brought a small crew onto the yacht. They must have scoped it out and realized there was only a small crew on board, so he

Compromises

wouldn't need many men. We need to take a count to see how many are on board. But we can't be seen."

"Got it," Seth said, as he made his way up a stairwell to the next deck while Luke continued toward the front. As Seth made it to the top deck, there was another pirate standing guard- or he was supposed to be, but he was on his phone, looking at the Internet. Seth walked up silently behind him and hit him precisely in the back of the neck. The pirate slumped to the deck, and Seth made quick work of tying him up and gagging his mouth. He left him in a lounge chair, for the Coast Guard to get later.

Luke and Seth reconvened a short time later back in the same spot.

"How's it look?" Seth asked.

"I saw Alejandro in the bridge. There are the guys here in the salon, but I didn't see anyone else. You?"

"I took care of the guy upstairs who was supposed to be keeping watch; got to love the Internet. That's all I saw, though."

"Can you make your way around to the other side entrance so you would come in behind Jay and the guys?"

"Yeah, I can do that," Seth said. He pulled the gun out of his waistband and checked to ensure it was loaded and ready if needed, as Luke did the same. Luke then replaced it behind his back and signaled for Seth to keep low and move to the other side entrance.

Luke went around to the entrance and walked in casually, like he was late to supper. The men standing guard turned and took in the newcomer.

"Hey guys," Luke said. "I saw the yacht, but didn't know you all had already got to her. I heard there is a huge profit here just for the taking." He winked over at Jay.

One of the guys walked over and slapped Luke on the back. "Long time no see. I didn't hear you were down here."

"Yeah, well, I travel in all kinds of secrecy these days. Coast Guard almost got me a few months ago."

"Really?" The guys were getting so engrossed in Luke's story that they let their guard slip for just a moment and faced him, turning slightly away from Jay and the others.

"Yeah," Luke said trying to keep their attention on him as he saw Seth make a stealthy entrance behind Jay. "They have been getting better at predicting where I am at, or so it seems."

Seth walked up behind Jay. He made sure Jay, Robert, and Jake were aware it was him, and then untied their hands. He motioned to Luke that all was clear. In the next instant everything moved so fast that the two guys that were watching over them were taken completely by surprise. Luke pulled his gun and said, "No funny business guys. Nothing personal, but you see I just can't have you take this particular yacht."

Seth came up from behind and held a gun in another's back just so he knew that Luke was not alone. Jay, Robert, and Jake were quick to tie them up with the bands that had held them prior to Seth releasing them. Before they got much further, they heard another man approaching from the kitchen.

"What the hell is . . . ?" Alejandro entered from the bridge. Luke pointed the gun at his chest and made it clear that he would not hesitate to use it. Alejandro put his hands in the air. Robert and Jay retrieved the guns the other two had trained on them earlier, as well as the one Alejandro was carrying on his hip.

"Who the hell are you?" Alejandro said, looking at Seth, still cautious with his hands in the air.

"I," Seth smiled wickedly, "am your worst nightmare." He walked

Compromises

right up to Alejandro and cold-cocked him with his fist. Alejandro slumped over, holding his gut, moaning.

But they hadn't counted. There were six pirates altogether. The last one now came in from the rear deck after he had found the guy tied up upstairs in the lounge chair and released him; both of them were intent on finding the intruders. They walked up behind the large gathering in the salon, taking in the situation.

"Not smart!" one of them called out. Jake turned, and aimed his gun. The pirate shot him, but not before Luke got in a shot of his own at the pirate. The other pirate was out-numbered as everyone trained a gun on him. He dropped his weapon and put his hands in the air. Seth was careful to keep his gun trained on Alejandro, who was still trying to recover from the punch to his gut.

Robert came over and took Alejandro to tie him up with the others.

"Are there others?" Luke asked, as he moved toward Jake to find him holding his side, but otherwise still okay.

"They didn't come aboard, so they must be out there, waiting for the cue to come on in," said Jake in between deep breaths.

Luke dropped his weapon and pulled Jake's hand away to take a look. "You're lucky, looks like just a graze."

"Well," Seth said, "what are we waiting for, call the Cavalry," he said, looking at Jay.

Jay made the call to have the Coast Guard round up the others who were still out there. Robert went to see the condition of the man Luke had shot. He looked like he was hit a bit harder than Jake, but would live.

They didn't have to wait long, as it appeared that the Coast Guard had already rounded up the others that were standing guard around the yacht as things were unfolding inside. Soon there were men all over

Seth's yacht. They took the pirates into custody and made a call to local authorities to arrange a change of hands. As they were leading Alejandro out, he said, "You're Seth!" in a moment of recognition.

"Yeah, and don't ever, I mean ever, mess with my girl or my friends again. Got it?"

Jay didn't allow him time to answer as another man led Alejandro and the others off the yacht. Jay called down to a medic who had come aboard as a precautionary measure. "You need to take a look at our friend here," he pointed to Jake. "Get that one there to the medic out on the cutter," he said about the injured pirate, whom two men carried out as he moaned in protest.

Seth had run to Jake's side as soon as Alejandro was taken. "Jake," Seth said with concern, "are you okay?"

"Never been better," Jake said, and then coughed.

The medic pushed Seth and the others out of the way, to take a look at Jake. "You're lucky. Looks like just a minor wound. You shouldn't be laid up too long," he said after looking over Jake very carefully.

Luke sat down and Robert followed suit while the medic worked on Jake. "Never a dull moment around you, Seth," he chuckled, relieved it was finally over. He thought momentarily of Jenna, missing her and wanting to get back to her. The adrenaline from the past few moments was still running in his veins; as he got back up to pace for a bit, and then sat back down.

The medic confirmed Luke's initial sense of Jake's injury, and was quick to give him something for the pain and to wrap him up to stop the bleeding. "Bullet went right through and missed anything really important," he told Seth as packed up his supplies.

Jake laughed, and then grabbed his side in pain. "Good thing, huh? I am quite fond of my body parts."

The medic asked if there was a place they could move Jake to. Jake

Compromises

answered before Seth could say anything, saying he wanted to be taken to the bridge and sit on the bench for now.

"Wouldn't you rather go to your bunk?" Seth asked Jake, perplexed as to why he wouldn't want to get somewhere more comfortable.

"Look," Jake answered, "I'm not hurt that bad and I have a sneaking suspicion you will want the yacht to yourself tonight. I think the hotel will be just as comfortable."

Seth was flattered that Jake was thinking of him and Cassandra, but he wanted to make sure his friend was fine.

"Really," Jake insisted, "I want to go back to the hotel tonight. I really am not hurt that bad, Seth, and I think it's important that Cassandra be back on familiar ground tonight."

Seth knew he was probably right. She had been through a lot, and this was as close to home as he could give her tonight. Seth made his way back to the salon after he was sure that Jake was settled in the bridge and would be fine.

"I think I need a vacation," Seth said as he sat down in the salon.

"You deserve it. We all do," Robert said in agreement.

"I'd better call in and let everyone know we are okay," Seth said. He made the call to Cassandra's dad to let him know that it was over and that they had the pirates in custody and everyone was fine. He didn't want to relay the news about Jake, as he didn't want to cause unnecessary concern before they could see that he was fine with their own eyes.

Back in the hotel room, as soon as my dad said Seth's name, I grabbed the phone from his hand. "Seth! Seth, are you okay?" My hands trembled as I waited for his reply.

"Yes, love. We all are. I am going to head back there shortly. No need to worry now, love. I will be there soon."

"Thank God." There were really no words I could think of as the evening started to sink in. I was just relieved that it was over. It was finally over.

"Love you, Cassandra. See you soon," Seth said as he hung up, not waiting on my reply.

Back on the yacht, Jay came back into the salon and sat to join the rest of the guys. He said everything was set. The Coast Guard had taken the pirates and was waiting for the authorities. Seth was free to move the yacht. Jay just wanted to be sure that Jake was okay before he took the small boat and joined the rest of his crew back on the cutter. After he was assured that Jake was fine, Seth walked the medic and Jay down to help them shove off. Before Jay crawled into the small boat, Seth clapped him on the back and said, "You're a damn good friend, Jay. I don't know what I would have done without your help."

"Yeah, well, these guys are the scum of the earth, so no need to thank me. I think we need to thank you, Seth, as you are the one always finding them for us. I know it is risky for you too, and don't think I haven't forgotten that last time you were shot and now Jake . . ."

"Jake's going to be fine, and my little thing was nothing," Seth said, waving off the compliments and the concern.

"No, Seth, it isn't "nothing." You know, Cassandra may have a point when she says that this is really a dangerous lifestyle for you and the others. It was different when you were all single, but now you all have someone in your life who really means something. Maybe you need to rethink this whole scheme of yours?"

"It's been a long couple of weeks," Seth said, being noncommittal. "You probably ought to take some vacation. Go see that pretty wife and baby girl of yours."

"Yeah, I have some leave coming up. But really Seth, you should think about this whole situation," Jay answered as he hopped into the boat and Seth shoved him off. "I'll be seeing you, buddy. Stay in touch."

Compromises

Seth was deep in thought as he watched Jay make his way to the Cutter out in the distance.

Seth turned and went back inside, making his way to the bridge. Jake was resting quietly, sedated for the moment. Robert and Luke were seated on the bench seat behind, waiting for Seth to take the yacht back to the marina on the island.

The last few weeks were catching up with Seth. He was tired and exhausted. He was worried about Jake. Jay's words echoed in his ears, "maybe Cassandra was right . . . you have someone special in your life now. . ."

Seth couldn't wait to see Cassandra. He had missed her so much these past few weeks, and had worried about her. Now he just wanted to hold Cassandra, and never let her out of his sight again. They all remained quiet, each caught up in his own thoughts, as Seth maneuvered the yacht back to the island.

Back at the pier, I was waiting for Seth's return. Ever since he had called my dad, I had been impatient. What in the hell was taking so long? I had run down to the dock waiting for him to pull the yacht back in, as I knew he wouldn't keep it out there in the open water now that things were tied up. Then I saw its lights off in the distance. My parents and the girls were with me. We waited anxiously for them to tie up.

In the bridge, Seth had Robert take over the wheel, saying he and Luke would throw off the lines to the dockhands at the marina.

As I stood anxiously waiting on the pier, I could make out Seth and Luke topside, waiting to throw down the lines. I was practically dancing with pent up nervous energy as I waited for them to get the yacht secure. No sooner had they tied up than I was running up the steps to get to Seth. He was coming out of the bridge as I ran through the salon and into his arms. He held me close to him, kissing the top of my head as I buried it into his chest, holding on for dear life.

"Don't ever, ever do that to me again!" I was angry and relieved at the same time, if that was possible.

"Me? What did I do?" Seth asked, confused as he pulled back just enough to look down at me.

"You walked right into a dangerous situation. I swear, Seth, you will be the death of me yet!" I hugged him close again just to be sure he was real and that he was okay.

Seth couldn't help but laugh. "Me, I will be the death of you? Girl, you drive me nuts when you won't listen for your own good- and you are patronizing me?"

"Well, yes, I guess I am."

He held me back a bit so he could look down at me.

Seth just shook his head, not believing that he was getting chastised. He hugged me close again. "Do you mind if we stay on the yacht tonight? Everyone else can use the hotel rooms we have there. I would like some time alone with you, if you are okay with that?"

"I wouldn't dream of being anywhere else," I said. Then I reached up to pull his head down again for another long kiss. Oh how I had missed him! He moaned as the kiss deepened.

After a few more moments he pulled back. "Love, you keep doing that and no one will see you for a week 'cause I will kidnap you." I giggled in response.

The girls had run past us during this time. Seth pulled me back and called out Jackie's name, but they continued on their way to the bridge. I looked up at Seth questioningly as he looked worried. "Seth?"

I heard a scream from the other room. I instantly let go of Seth and started toward the bridge. "Love," Seth said, as he held me back, "listen, he is okay."

I ignored him, and he let me go. I ran into the other room to find Jackie crying as she held onto Jake, who was trying to calm her down.

Compromises

Mandi looked just as concerned. I walked around Mandi to see that Jake was bandaged and shirtless.

"Oh my . . . what happened?"

"I'm fine," Jake said as he looked Jackie in the eyes. "Stop crying, sweetheart, it's just a scratch, really."

I thought back to the day Seth was shot. Yeah, scratch, I bet. Seth walked in behind me. "He's been checked out by the medic and has something for the pain right now. He's going to need a lot of rest," Seth explained.

"Why didn't you tell us? Why did you say everyone was alright?" I was angry as I turned back to ask Seth.

"Why worry you until you could see that he really is okay?"

"Seth, damn you, will you always try to protect me?"

"As long as I breathe," he answered.

"Well, I, for one, am tired. Can we go to the hotel now?" Jake asked as he stood, wincing as he did so. Jackie quickly dried her eyes and came to his other side to walk out with him, slowly.

I moved so they could pass, but wouldn't look at Seth as I followed our small party off the yacht and to the hotel.

Even though we did go back to the hotel, I wanted to be back on Seth's yacht, in familiar territory and alone with Seth. I was still mad at him, and had a lot I wanted to say, in private. But privacy wasn't something I was going to get right away.

My parents and the girls said they understood when I told them I was going to return to the yacht with Seth. I was grateful that they realized that we wanted some time alone, since we had been separated for so long.

Jake insisted that he was going to be fine, and that the hotel bed would be just as comfortable as his own on the yacht. I had a lot of things I wanted to talk to Seth about, Jake's incident being only one of them, so I was glad I would have him alone tonight.

Back at the hotel, Seth and I packed up our things. He tried to talk to me, but I ignored him as I threw what little he had brought for me into a bag. I told him that I wanted to go to my parents' room to say goodnight. He followed behind, speechless.

"I'm glad you are safe now, Cassie," my mom said, squeezing me tight as I stood in the middle of their room. "I know you want some time alone with your man, but I hope we can spend some time together soon."

"We will probably head back home tomorrow," I said. "I want you and Dad to travel back with us on the yacht. It will take some time to get to Florida, so we will have plenty of time to catch up."

"That's a great idea," my dad said as he kissed the top of my head. "Seth seems like a good guy. I know he was extremely worried about you and that makes him alright in my book," he added.

"Yeah," I sighed, not wanting to say too much, as I was still so angry. "He's a little over- protective, and now I think he will be even worse."

"For good reason," my mom said worriedly.

"Not you guys, too!"

"Honey, he is right. You are too strong willed for your own good sometimes. Maybe you should give the guy a break and listen to what he says."

"Figures," I said as I shook my head. "He's already won you two over. So now I am the stubborn-headed one. Well, we shall see what you think when you get to know him better. The man is impossible when it comes to my safety."

There was a knock on the door, and Seth entered. He had been with the others, ensuring that Jake was settling in. "I was getting worried," he apologized to my parents for interrupting.

Compromises

"See," I said, exasperated, as I lifted my arms in the air in frustration. My parents just laughed, making me realize I had no allies with either of them when it came to Seth and his concern about me. I kissed them goodnight and walked out the room with Seth.

"I just want to say goodnight to the others," I told him as I made my way down the hallway to the girls' room.

"Love, can we talk about this?"

I didn't answer, knowing I needed time to cool down and that soon we would be alone. I knocked on the door to the girls' room. Jackie hollered, "Come on in!"

"Hi, girls!" I said as I made my way in the room. They ran to me and we hugged.

"Good to have you back, Cass!" Mandi said.

I made my way over to Jake, who was dozing in the bed. I hugged him gently. "I'm really okay, Cass. Besides, we won!" he said, slurring his words a bit.

"The drugs the medic gave him are really kicking in," Jackie said. "He seems to be doing really good, though."

She sounded more convinced than I was. "Are you sure?"

"Yeah," Jackie said. "Besides, Luke got the guy back for me," she grinned.

"What?"

Seth answered for Jackie, "Luke took care of the pirate who shot Jake."

"What is it with you pirates and shooting people?"

"Love," Seth said as he moved closer, concern in his eyes, "Jake's fine. The other pirate will live too."

"It doesn't mean that I don't like it!" I answered angrily.

"I know," Seth conceded. He let it drop, knowing that he was probably going to have to hear a tirade from me about this whole ordeal later.

"You'll have to catch me up tomorrow," I told Jackie. "Right now I think I just need to rest." The girls exchanged a look between them. They knew rest was probably not going to be high on my list of things to do tonight.

"Not a problem. We will catch up with you later in the morning," Mandi said.

Robert hugged me. "Glad to have you back, girl," he said.

"It's good to be back with you all," I answered as Seth steered me out of the room, clearly tiring of my goodnight ritual at this point.

We made our way to one last room. Luke opened the door before I reached it. He grabbed me and spun me around the room, before finally setting me on my feet, and kissing me. My kiss with Luke lingered a bit longer than the others. I looked up into his handsome face.

"I love you, Luke," I said.

"Love you too, Cass," he said as he smiled.

"See you in the morning?"

"See you then, Cass. Get some sleep and make sure our man here gets some too. He has really been crabby since you were gone," he added, trying to make light of everything that had happened recently. I loved Luke for the easy caring way he had with me. I was really glad that Seth was over his jealousy of our relationship and understood the deep friendship we had.

"Speak for yourself," Seth said as he clapped Luke on the back. "Thanks again, buddy. If it wasn't for you, we wouldn't have found her so quickly. Not to mention helping out with the guy who shot Jake. I owe you big-time."

"Yeah, don't think I won't be collecting, either," Luke laughed.

"You ready to go home?" I asked Seth, looking up into his beautiful blue eyes, still wanting answers yet getting more tired as the moments ticked by.

"Never been more ready," he said, an unreadable expression on his face.

Seth and I made our way back to the yacht. It was strange having it all to ourselves. Seth went over to the cabinet and poured us a drink. He walked over and motioned for me to sit, but instead I took the glass and drained it in one gulp.

"I'm angry." Might as well get this out in the open, I thought to myself.

"I know, love. I understand."

Damn the man! Couldn't he be unreasonable and fight back? I tried again; "You put everyone, including yourself, in danger. And for what? For capturing a few pirates? Is this the life you want to lead, Seth?

Seth began, "I know you are angry . . ."

I put my glass down and grabbed his hand, leading him down to our stateroom.

Seth questioned, not sure why the mood had changed, "Cassandra?"

Once we got there, I took his glass from his hand and set it on the bedside table. I pushed him back onto the bed and landed on top of him. I stared down at him, and then kissed him. He responded instantly, pulling me closer, and passion overtook any words that we would have exchanged.

I took my time, enjoying the kiss and the feel of him underneath me. He rolled me over and continued the kiss as the heat built between us. He undressed me with ease and impatience, as I did him. When our naked bodies finally met together again, he looked into my eyes and said, "I was so worried about you. I've never seen you so angry . . ."

"Seth," I started to admonish him about his foolish fears, and then thought better of trying to fight with him on this point. I had more pressing issues at hand and reached up to pull his head back down to mine. I could tell he was as anxious to make love as I was, and the passion took over.

Later, we climbed into his Jacuzzi and lingered, taking our time. He positioned me in front of him and washed my hair, massaging my head as he did so. I leaned back into his skillful hands and relaxed. " Mmm," I moaned, "I could get used to that!"

"Yeah, I don't mind it much either," he said, reaching down to kiss the side of my neck as he felt my pulse pick up tempo.

"You were so angry."

"I've missed you more than I am angry. We will talk about this at some point, Seth."

He didn't answer as he rinsed my hair and ran his fingers through it to comb it out. As the heat started to build between us again, Seth jumped out of the tub and grabbed a towel to wrap it around his gorgeous, wet body. He grabbed another towel and held it out for me. I crawled out and let him wrap me up the softness of it. He turned me around and said, "I think I told you once that you were much better wet, do you remember?"

I did remember. It was at the cove that day so long ago when we first met. I had tried to deny my feelings for him for so long, back then. I shook my head in disbelief.

"What?" he laughed at the expression on my face.

"I was just thinking how stupid I was to think I could resist you," I replied.

"Not stupid, just bullheaded. A trait that I see you have installed into your very nature. But," he said as he led me to his bed and laid me down, "I seem to know how to break through your stubbornness now and again." He kissed my face in every spot he could until he finally took my lips with his own. "I've missed you and worried about you so much, love."

"I've missed you, too," I said kissing him back. "Care to show me how much?" I asked, noticing that he was ready once again to make love.

"You are a minx," he chuckled, "but I do love that about you." We didn't speak until much later, after our lovemaking had subsided and we were both sated.

"We need to take a vacation to just be with each other and no complications," Seth said, yawning as he spoke and pulling me close to his side.

"Yes, I think we do," I replied as I snuggled in closer, just relieved to be out of danger and back into his arms.

"We'll plan it in the morning. Right now, I think I have sleep to catch up on."

I agreed and yawned. "Seth," I said groggily.

"Hmmm," he replied, and I wondered if he was far too tired to comprehend what I was saying.

"You scared me tonight," I said, leaning up on one elbow to look at his handsome face as he tried to fight the sleep that was waiting to overtake him.

"Hmmm," he mumbled. "Why is that?"

"This whole pirate act thing. You put yourself at risk when you act the part. And look what happened to Jake this time."

Seth opened his eyes and stifled a yawn. "Baby, I don't want to have a serious conversation right now with you. I feel horrible about what happened to Jake, I do."

"You can't avoid talking to me about this forever, you know," I whispered and then yawned. There would be plenty of time to talk later.

He grinned in the darkness. "Love you, too."

The next morning, I woke to Seth gently kissing my lips. I pulled him down as I wrapped my arms around him to hug him close. "I could never tire of waking up like that."

"I will never tire of waking you like that," he said as he chuckled. "Want some coffee?"

"In a bit," I smiled shyly. "First, I want dessert."

He grinned, catching my innuendo. "They say you spoil your appetite if you eat dessert first," he chuckled.

"Not my appetite," I replied. "I will just want more. I am insatiable, you know," I giggled as he nuzzled my neck.

He smiled down at me and leaned back in for another long kiss before time and everything other than each other didn't matter much. A lot later we made our way to the top deck with our coffee to sit in a lounge chair together. I curled up to his chest, between his legs as we watched the sun rise higher into the sky. It was a truly beautiful day in paradise. For the first time in weeks I was able to really enjoy the scenery around me. Seth had already called and checked on Jake, to find that he was doing fine.

"I don't understand how you ever found me," I said, thinking about what Seth had said to Luke the night before about never being able to do it without his help.

"Luke found out where Alejandro was located. Although we had to look through a few places before we found the exact island you were on."

"How on earth did he do that?" I turned to look at him as I asked.

"He paid a contact to give him information about Alejandro's relatives. Just so happens that he had a very attractive, single cousin that Luke made friends with. Well, maybe more than friends," Seth said as he thought about it.

"He was dating someone to find out information?"

"Yeah, but I think he really cares for the girl now. It has put Luke in an awkward situation."

"He's fallen for this girl? For real? Luke is in love?" I found it hard to believe. This girl had to be something else to catch Luke's undivided attention.

"I think so."

"Wow. Isn't that something," I said, reflecting as Seth pulled me close to his chest and I lay back into him.

"Not to change the subject, but I know you should spend some time with your friends and your parents, yet I want to take you away from all this for awhile, just you and I. What do you say?"

"I say I'd love to." I snuggled deeper into his chest as I took a sip of my coffee. "Are we going to your house in California?" I asked, assuming that he would take me there.

"Actually, I thought I'd take you to England," he said nonchalantly.

"England?" I turned around to face him, not really believing he would take me to his hometown.

"Yes, love. England. I have a house there. One you haven't seen, and I am a bit homesick, as well as that my sister would kill me if I stayed away any longer."

"I'm going to meet your family?" I asked, realizing the implications.

"I met yours," he stated, matter-of-factly.

"I guess you have," I said, as I continued to ponder what he just said and laid back against his chest once again.

"Do you have concerns about meeting my family, love?"

"No, no concerns. I just . . . well . . . it's just that . . . ," I couldn't seem to get the words out.

"It's just that it is a big step for you, to meet my family?" he guessed, correctly.

I turned to face him again. "I'm not afraid to meet them or anything, but what do they think about this most recent turn of events? Do they think that I am more trouble than good for you?"

Seth just laughed. I couldn't see what was so funny. I sat up straighter and pulled my legs in, crossing them in front of me while I waited for him to gain control. "Sorry, love," he said, "it's just that you would stand up to a bunch of pirates, toting a gun in your waistband, and yet you are afraid to meet my family. You have to see the humor in that."

"Humor in what?" Luke said as he walked near us. "Sorry, I don't mean to interrupt, but the hotel was kicking us out unless we paid for another day."

I stood up in a huff, not wanting to answer Seth, and looked at Luke as I said, "I'm getting another cup of coffee and going to check on Jake. See if you can get the buffoon to control himself," which made both Luke and Seth laugh even harder as I turned my back and walked away. "Damn men!" I said under my breath.

I heard Luke ask, "What did you do to her now?"

14

Later, after everyone piled into the yacht and got settled in for the ride back to Florida, I found time to sit alone with my parents and fill them in on my relationship with Seth and how things had progressed until I was kidnapped.

My dad looked around the salon, "I have to say, this is quite impressive."

"Yes, very much so," my mom stated.

They were never impressed by those who had wealth, so the yacht or maybe Seth must have made an impression on them.

"So, what's next?" my mom asked.

"Well," I said as I let my gaze fall to my hands in my lap, "I think we are going on vacation to England."

"Oh, honey," my mom said as she grabbed one of my hands from my lap, "that is so exciting!" I looked up to see that she was genuinely pleased. "That's his home, isn't it?"

"Yes," I answered, knowing that she took this to be a very serious step.

"You're not happy about it?" She knew me so well.

"It's not that I'm not happy..." My dad started to look uncomfortable. He always was when it came to my relationships- although there hadn't been very many that they were involved in or made aware of.

"I think I'll go see what Seth and the guys are up to," my dad said as he made his exit. Just as he left, Mandi walked in.

"Hey, there you are," she said as she sat down. Since she was my best friend and had been through the worst of this relationship, I wasn't shy about sharing my apprehensions with her.

I took up where I left off, "so as I was saying, it's not that I'm not happy about a trip to England, but what if they don't like me? What if I am too 'American' or something for their taste . . . for their son? What if they think I am the one who has put him into danger, time and again?"

"That could never happen," Mandi said in her usual confident manner. "Who wouldn't love you, Cass?"

"Yeah," my mom picked up on the thread of making me feel confident about this next step in my relationship, "who wouldn't love you? Besides, they will probably love the fact that you are bringing their son home. They probably don't get to see him often, and this would be a treat, as he said it was a vacation, so that means he won't be working. And just think what that means about how he feels about you."

I knew that Seth loved me, but now I wondered how we would move past the events of the past few weeks. He was bound to be extra protective of me now. Did he want to whisk me away to England so I wouldn't be in danger? What did this trip mean to him?

We moved into the kitchen to make some sandwiches and snacks for the guys, who were holed up in the bridge. Mandi took some food down to the crew's quarters where Jackie was with Jake, ensuring that he was being nursed back to health. Luckily, Jake had only gotten a graze

Compromises

and wasn't seriously injured. He was getting better with every passing hour. It could have been so much worse.

When we walked into the bridge with a tray of food, they were appreciative of the gesture and grabbed it as if they hadn't eaten for days. My dad drove the yacht, smiling ear to ear, as Seth stood by. I could see those two had hit it off big-time. My mom giggled, and said, "Oh boy, this is something your Dad will never forget." Luke was missing. I asked where he was. Seth said he thought he might have gone topside.

I went searching for him, and found him leaning on the rail looking out over the ocean.

"Luke?"

"Hey, baby," he said as he turned to watch me approach. "What are you doing up here?"

I came up beside him to watch the sun hit the water. "Looking for you," I answered. He put his arm around me. "I love the Caribbean," I said, as we stood there together looking over the expanse of beautiful green-blue water. "Makes you respect it a little more to know how dangerous it can be."

"Yes, it does."

"We won't be in danger on the way home, I hope?"

"No, I checked with my sources. They are keeping a low profile, as the word about Alejandro's arrest has already traveled fast. They will be laying low for awhile."

"So," I said facing him as I turned serious, "tell me about this girl."

"What girl?"

"Luke," I admonished while shaking my head, "you know what girl I am talking about. Seth tells me that was how you found out where I was. And by the way," I said as I hugged him and then kept my arms around him, "thanks. I don't think I thanked you properly for finding me."

Luke smiled crookedly. "Well, if you want to thank me properly, Seth is occupied at the moment."

I playfully slapped at him while giggling, "Don't change the subject."

"She's a good girl. Her name is Jenna. I wasn't really planning on liking her as much as I do. It was a means to an end in the beginning. I found out she's pretty special."

"So, what's next?"

"I don't know," Luke replied, while looking off into the distance. "I don't know what she'll think when I tell her why I met her in the first place. I don't know how she would take that."

"Do you need to tell her? I mean, right away anyway."

"I want to come clean. Lies don't work well in relationships," he said while grinning back at me.

"Seth didn't lie, Luke. He just didn't tell me everything up front, and avoided answering my questions."

"Oh, I know, but it still wasn't right, was it?"

I looked down at my feet while shaking my head. "It worked out in the end."

"Yeah, but not without grief and pain; I saw how you looked when you first got to Florida, before you knew the whole story, the whole truth."

"So you will tell her, and soon?"

"Yup. I will deal with whatever happens after."

"Well, she'd be stupid not to want you, especially when she hears why you did it."

"We'll have to wait and see," he said, as he shrugged, not relaying the true depth of his worry that it might just ruin things between them.

"I do love you, you know that, right?"

"Yeah, Cass. I know. Like I told you, if you ever tire of Seth . . ."

Again, I hit him playfully, as we went back to the stairwell to make our way down to the bridge, where everyone else was enjoying lunch.

During the trip home, I was able to spend a lot of time with the girls and my parents. Seth and I spent our nights making love and reveling in the moments we had together. We would fall asleep at night holding hands. We were growing closer, and without all the secrets and worry between us, we found that we had something that some people only dream about. I felt so totally at ease around him, and knew my heart belonged to him. There was no questioning that now.

Jake was healing nicely, and Jackie found that she actually had a knack for helping him with his wound. My anger about the situation had dissipated, but I knew that sooner or later, Seth would have to have a serious conversation with me about his piracy charade.

As we were heading into port in Florida, everyone was busy getting ready to be back on land. My parents had said that they would be catching a late flight out to the next destination in their retirement plan of visiting the best beaches of the world. They knew that Seth planned on whisking me away to England, and now that they knew I was safe, there wasn't much else for them to do here in the States. Mandi and Robert were going to catch a flight the next day to head back to Virginia. Jackie was taking Jake to the hospital to ensure that everything was healing nicely. Luke was planning on staying in Florida to see Jenna and get things worked out with her. I was worried for him. I hoped that this Jenna would understand and be forgiving. I knew that Luke really cared for her. I hoped she wasn't stupid enough to let the reason he had met her get in the way.

I was still apprehensive about meeting Seth's family. He laughed at me when I told him, saying that they would love me, just like he did. I had told him that I needed to make a pit stop in Virginia to get some clothes, as originally I had only packed enough for one week's vacation. He shook his head and said that I could easily shop for clothes or anything else I needed when we got to England. I told him that I couldn't possibly rely on him for that, but he laughed and kissed me making me forget anything else, but being close to him.

As we docked, Luke called Jenna to tell her he was back.

"Hey, beautiful," Luke said as she answered.

"Hey yourself. Where are you now . . . some beautiful island, having a wonderful tropical drink, thinking of me?"

"Better than that," Luke chuckled, "I'm back in Florida, at the same marina we left from."

Jenna smiled on the other end of the line as her heart picked up its tempo, "Really?"

"Yeah, I was wondering if you would be free for dinner."

"Well," Jenna played with him, "I will have to check my calendar . . . let's see . . . looks like I am free."

Luke laughed. "I'll pick you up in an hour. There's someone I'd like you meet."

"Oh?" Jenna said curiously, "I am guessing you won't tell me now?"

"Nope, but you'll know soon enough. See you in an hour," he said as he hung up.

Because we had been on the yacht for the past few days, we made plans to eat out that evening. Seth called ahead to an upscale restaurant in town. The girls and I took our time getting ready as the guys were busy getting the yacht back into sparkling-clean condition. It always amazed me how Seth would help them, even though he was the owner.

Compromises

He said it was because it kept him humble, and he wouldn't ask anyone else to do something he wouldn't be willing to do himself. It only made me love him more. He wouldn't let my dad participate, though, saying he needed to sit it out. My dad grumbled about not having to primp like the girls, and that he was perfectly capable of washing down a yacht, but Seth was adamant and made him walk around to supervise instead. I could tell my dad had really grown to respect Seth, as had my mom. They were crazy about him, and I couldn't blame them. I felt the same way.

Later, the guys cleaned up as us girls were putting on the final touches to our hair and makeup. Luke left to go pick up Jenna, saying he would meet up with us at the restaurant. He squeezed my hand as he said, "leave us a seat next to you. I may need your help with Jenna tonight, you know, explaining things."

Hoping that Jenna would be forgiving on the reasons why Luke had met her, I tried to see it from her point of view, and wondered how I would react. I had kind of been in her position when Seth had kept secrets from me, but I loved Seth so much that I was able to see past all of that. I only hoped Jenna would feel the same about Luke, as I could see that she meant a lot to him.

As Luke pulled the car up in front of Jenna's house, she came running out as he was getting out of the car, and flew into his arms. They kissed long and hard before Luke set her back down to look at her.

"Wow, I may have to leave more often if this is the greeting I get when I return!"

"Not funny, Luke," Jenna giggled. "I missed you!"

"Yeah, me too," Luke said as he took her back into his arms and kissed her hard and deep. "Hey, what do you say we turn up for dinner fashionably late?" He smiled down at her when they stopped to catch their breath.

Jenna was already dressed for dinner, but she surprised him as she grabbed his hand and led him back into her place, laughing, "I don't see any reason I would disagree with you."

Luke was taken pleasantly by surprise, but added it to the list of things he loved about Jenna. She was spontaneous, and seemed to enjoy being with him as much as he did her. Once inside she started to strip as he followed her to her bedroom. He pulled off his clothes as he followed, laughing all the way.

When they fell into bed, everyone else was forgotten for a time as their lovemaking took over. "Welcome home, Luke," Jenna said as he lay on top of her and she looked up into the beautiful eyes she had missed over the past few days.

"It's always good to come back. Especially when I get a greeting like this," Luke smiled down at her. He closed the distance and wound his tongue around hers. All talk ceased until much later.

After, as Jenna made her way back from the bathroom, she found Luke fumbling around in his pants for something. He smiled as he found a small package and came over to hold Jenna in his arms. "Hey, I saw something, and it made me think of you."

"Oh!" Jenna said, surprised. Luke handed her the box. She looked up into his blue eyes and kissed him.

"Open it!" he commanded.

She opened the lid and then picked up the delicate necklace that lay on the satin inside. The little bear danced around on the chain as she held it up to look at it. Jenna laughed, "You missed the bear so much you had to buy him?"

Luke laughed. "Yeah, guess you could say that. He caught my eye at one of the stores I was walking past, and I couldn't resist him, or maybe it was just that he made me think of you. "

"Oh really?"

"Yeah, and you said our bear had to have a name. Maybe he won't be inclined to bite me anymore."

Jenna laughed. "How about Snowball, because he is a polar bear?"

Luke rubbed his bare foot on the bear rug they were standing on, "Nice bear," he mocked as Jenna laughed again. "Hey, as I much as I would love to stand around with you naked all night, I think we need to get going. Everyone is probably wondering where we are right about now. I am surprised my cell hasn't been ringing off the hook yet." As he said this, it rang, and he looked at the display to see who it was. Flipping it open, he answered, "Hey, Seth . . . yeah . . . we are heading that way now. See you soon."

As he closed the phone, Jenna and Luke laughed. "Fashionably late, huh?"

15

I was at the restaurant with everyone, minus Luke. What could possibly take the man so long? Didn't he realize that we were starving? Seth had called a bit ago, and Luke had said he was on the way. I mean, I realize that he probably was spending "quality time" with Jenna, but my stomach was really getting mad at me and I was about to faint!

"Can we order yet?" Jackie asked, just as my stomach growled again.

Seth laughed and said, "I think Cassandra would agree. Let's go ahead and order and they can order when they get here," referring to Luke and Jenna. As he waved to the waiter to let him know we were ready, Luke and a very pretty girl came into the restaurant. She was dressed in a beach dress with shiny silver shoes. Her long black hair framed a naturally beautiful face. I approved instantly, glad to see that Luke was happy.

As Luke approached the table he apologized, "Sorry we are late. Everyone, meet Jenna," he said for the benefit of the girls, my parents, and me. Then he made introductions, telling Jenna each of our names, saving me for last. He obviously hadn't told her I was home, as the look in her eyes said it all. "This last lovely lady is the best friend, um-besides Seth, that is, that I have ever had. This is Cassandra, Seth's other half."

Jenna stared, clearly at a loss for words. I stood up and shook her hand. "Hi, Jenna. Luke has told me so much about you that I feel I already know you."

Luke motioned for her to sit down and gently pushed her into a chair, as she was clearly still in shock. "Cassandra?" she inquired, "the missing girl who ran away from Seth?"

"Well, yes that Cassandra, but not exactly missing, as you can see. But we can talk about that later, as I am starving!" Luke answered, clearly not wanting to get into a deep discussion at the restaurant.

Oh Luke, I thought to myself, you aren't going to make this any easier. "Jenna, why don't we eat and you and I can chat later?" I offered, trying to assist Luke through this very awkward situation.

Conversation flowed around us. Jenna was really very pleasant, but I could tell she was still very confused at how I just happened to turn up. Seth would touch me throughout the evening. He whispered in my ear and would nibble at it before turning to answer another question from my dad. I giggled as he did this, and then refocused my attention on Luke and Jenna. They seemed comfortable around each other. It was obvious that they were intimate. I caught a glimpse of light at her throat and stared at her necklace. It was a bear.

"Do you like bears?" I asked curiously.

"Well," Jenna smiled as she reached up to touch the bear dangling from the chain around her neck, "I do now." Luke laughed in response as a secret joke passed between them.

"See, Jenna has this rug her granddad gave her and it trips you up when you walk past it. Damn thing has made an impression on me, and I found the necklace while we were in the Caribbean," Luke explained.

Jenna asked, "The Caribbean? Is that where you found Cassie?"

"Yes," Luke answered, glad he didn't have to lie about that.

Before Jenna could ask more, I looked down at my watch. "Dad, Mom, we need to get you to the airport if you want to make your flight on time." They both noted the time and agreed. We all stood up at once.

"It was nice to meet you, Jenna," I said sincerely. "I would like to chat with you at some point."

"Yes, that would be great," she answered politely.

"How about we meet you back at the yacht after you drop your folks off at the airport," Luke said. Clearly he was determined to get the truth out sooner rather than later.

"Sounds great," I said, and hugged him. I whispered in his ear, "Sure you have to do this?" I feared for him. What good would it do now to tell her? I was safe, and back home. She didn't ever need to know. Luke just shook his head in agreement. It seemed as if he was resolved to telling her all.

Later, as Seth and I drove back to the yacht after seeing my folks off, I turned to him and said, "Do you think it will go well for Luke?"

"I don't know, love," he said. "It could be good 'cause he has come clean, but could be bad when she finds out how he set about dating her to get information."

"But he did it to find me?"

"Yes, love, and we are all grateful to him for that. But I don't think Jenna will see it that way. Maybe after she gets to know you she may understand," he said as he grabbed my hand.

"I hope so," I answered, comfortable to leave my hand in his while I looked out the window as we pulled into the marina. "My parents love you," I said as he parked the car.

"They were great. They didn't blame me at all for everything that has happened," Seth added as he shook his head in amazement.

"Why would they? You had nothing to do with my abduction." Seth didn't look completely convinced that he believed that.

We made our way onto the yacht. Luke and Jenna were sitting in the salon. It appeared as if they were just composing themselves, and I had the distinct feeling we had just interrupted them. I smiled, remembering how many times Seth and I were walked in on when there was a boat full of people.

Seth went over to the liquor cabinet and filled glasses of wine, offering to refill Luke and Jenna's glasses. Then he joined me on a couch opposite from Luke and Jenna. I didn't want to tell this girl about the pirate abduction. I didn't think it was going to help Luke at all. Instead, I steered the conversation away from that topic.

"So how did you meet Luke?" I asked, and then regretted the question, afraid that he would start explaining why he had met her.

"Yoga class," Jenna answered matter-of-factly.

"Yoga!" I laughed. "Oh my! Luke, you really are a man of mystery."

"Yeah, yeah," Luke said, clearly having been the butt of this joke for some time.

"What were you doing in the Caribbean, Cassie?" Jenna asked, and I abruptly stopped laughing. Wow, this girl was really direct, and wasn't going to beat around the bush.

Before I could answer, Luke said, "Well, that's kind of why I wanted you to come back here to the yacht tonight. See, I haven't been completely honest with you."

Oh no, Luke, don't do it, I thought to myself. I saw a look of concern come over Jenna's face as he gained all of her attention.

"How's that?" Jenna asked, cautiously.

"Luke," I said interrupting him, "we don't . . ."

"Yes, we do." He continued as he answered me first and then turned to face Jenna. "See, Jenna, Cass didn't leave of her own free will. I am sorry that I made you believe that, but I didn't see any other way. I wanted to keep you safe and not let on that anything was wrong."

"Not of her own free will?" Jenna asked, looking between the three of us.

"No, not of her own free will," Luke continued.

I could see this wasn't going to go well. I interjected, "I was taken, abducted."

"Oh my!" Jenna said as she brought her hand to her mouth after setting her drink down. "How horrible for you!"

"Yes," I said, grabbing Seth's hand for comfort. "Luckily though, Luke and Seth were able to find me, and I was unharmed in the process. Not so lucky for Jake, though."

"Jake? What's the matter with Jake?" She hadn't known about Jake's injury, as he had seemed fine during dinner and had claimed he was tired right after, never giving away that he had been shot.

"Jake was shot while we were helping Cass escape," Luke answered.

"Shot? By whom?"

"Well, pirates, of course."

"Pirates?" Jenna was still not putting it together.

"It's complicated, but we found Cass, thanks to you," Luke added and I shot him a look that told him he didn't have to go there. He ignored me, intent on watching Jenna's reaction.

Compromises

"Me? How would it be thanks to me? I thought she had left Seth, not that she was abducted."

"You told me where Alejandro had his island. Alejandro is the one who abducted Cassie," Luke said explaining.

"Alejandro . . . my cousin? He abducted Cassie?"

I could see she was struggling with this information.

"Yes," Luke answered, "your cousin. We had to lure him out to Seth's yacht, making him think it was full of expensive merchandise. After we saved Cassie, we went back to the yacht to assist in their arrest, and Jake got shot by one of the pirates."

Jenna was quiet. I watched the play of emotions come over her face. I realized when it finally hit her that she was the link that was missing in this discussion.

"All the questions you had about my family. This was the reason why?" she asked as it was becoming more evident at the moment why Luke had found her. "You sought me out. You were looking for information," Jenna said as she stood up.

Luke and the rest of us stood up as well. "Jenna, it isn't like that. I mean it was, in the beginning, but not now."

My heart was breaking for Luke. "He did it for me." I pleaded with her to understand. I could tell she was angry.

"You used me," she said to Luke, clearly ignoring Seth and me. "You lied to me and you used me." Then she walked out, grabbing her purse as she did so. Luke stood there and made no move to go after her.

"Luke, do something! Go after her! Explain!" But Luke shook his head at me.

"I need to let her think about it. She needs to work through this."

"And letting her go is the way to do it? Luke, you need to go to her . . . reason with her . . . make her see."

Luke turned to go down below to the crew's quarters, saying, "She needs time."

I stared at Seth. He took me in his arms and kissed me gently. "Luke's right, love, she needs time to sort through all this information."

"But . . . ," I stammered, before Seth again started to kiss me. "Don't distract me, Seth Hanson! I am worried about Luke."

"They will work it out, love. If they love each other as much as we do, they will work it out."

I couldn't argue with that, but I still felt for Luke. Maybe if I went to see her, to explain and make her understand just how much it was important for them to find me. What could I say, though, that wasn't already said? Seth was probably right. If they loved each other as much as we did, they would find a way through this.

"Listen, you need some rest before we fly out tomorrow," Seth said as he tried to bring me back to the present. I had forgotten about England during the whole thing this evening. My stomach started to get in a knot. I was meeting Seth's family for the first time. It was huge! A big deal for me, as it showed how much Seth really wanted me in his life. This occasion wasn't something to be taken lightly. Seth said I didn't need to worry; but I still did.

"Well, then, I guess that's it," I said as we made our way to our stateroom, but sleep didn't find me until much later that night. Not only was I worrying about meeting Seth's family, but I was worried about Luke. How could I let this situation mess up the girl he finally found that made him happy? I would just need to find a way to get to Jenna and explain in my own words, woman to woman.

The next morning, I went up to the kitchen to find Luke dressed and finishing his coffee. "Going to talk to Jenna?" I only hoped that was his next plan of action.

"Nope, got other things I need to settle up on."

Compromises

"What does that mean?" I asked as I didn't like the evasiveness of his answer.

"Well, I owe someone who gave me information about Jenna."

That meant his contacts. They couldn't be very nice people. "Luke, is this dangerous? Can't you just mail them a check or something?"

Luke laughed as he came and put his arms around me. I leaned into his chest. "You worry too much about me, Cass. You know, I have lived this long without your intervention," he chuckled.

I leaned back to look into his handsome face. "I just worry about you, is all."

"As she does about everyone," Seth said as he made his way into the kitchen, chuckling. I moved out of Luke's arms to go to Seth and kiss him. The kiss deepened and Luke cleared his throat. Seth broke off the kiss, clearly not wanting to. "So what danger are you putting yourself in now, Luke?"

"I was just telling Cass, I need to settle up with the guy who gave me the information about Jenna."

Seth understood that it meant a cash deal. "I'm going with you. I will settle the debt."

"I got it," Luke answered.

"No, Luke, you don't. I know you don't lack for money, but this information wouldn't have been cheap. I am going with you. Besides, Cassandra is right, you shouldn't go alone," Seth stated again.

I instantly had my guard up. "Oh, no! Not you, too! Can't you damn men stay out of trouble for one second? Why am I always the reason you guys are in constant danger?"

Luke and Seth laughed as Luke answered, "You are worth every bit of danger. Besides, this guy is really pretty harmless. He just provides information to the highest bidder and I plan to pay him well to keep his mouth shut about seeking out Jenna. We won't be in any danger at all. Swear!"

Seth obviously wasn't taking no for answer either, and Luke knew how stubborn Seth was. Seth made a cup of coffee and kissed me. "We won't be long." They made their way out, and I sat down to wait. "I'll call when we leave so you won't worry," Seth said to help ease some of the consternation I felt at this turn of events. The only thing that helped me keep sane was that Luke promised me this wasn't dangerous at all.

After I finished my coffee, I showered and changed. I went back topside to look out over the water. Jackie took Robert and Mandi to the airport, leaving Jake to rest down in the crew's quarters. I had said my goodbyes and they had made me promise to call them when I got to England and keep them updated. I was glad for my friends, as they seemed to have good relationships. Relationships . . . it made me think of Jenna.

I went down to the crew's quarters to find Jake watching TV.

"They treat me like I'm an invalid," he complained.

"It's only for a while longer, Jake," I tried to console him. "Hey," I said, changing the subject, "How do I find Jenna?"

"Well, I think Luke has her number written down. I could give it to you, but do you think it's a good idea?"

"Jake, I just can't sit here and do nothing. This was all because of me! I have to try and talk to her."

Jake shook his head and reached over to pick up a black notebook pad. He fumbled through, and after a few moments came up with a number on a slip of paper. I stuck it in my pocket and then hugged him as I turned to leave.

I ran to my stateroom and picked up my cell to call Jenna. I was glad when she answered.

"Jenna, this is Cassie. Please don't hang up," I stated in a rush.

"What do you want?" I could hear the impatience in her voice.

"I just want a moment to talk with you. Can you meet with me?"

"Not at the yacht. I prefer not to run into Luke at the moment," Jenna answered.

Oh, not good. She is still mad at Luke. "Okay, how about this little place next to marina. The little bar is located just out front."

"Okay, when?" Jenna answered.

I was glad she would at least meet with me. "Can you be there in fifteen minutes? Luke and Seth had something to do, and I would rather we do this without them knowing about it."

"Sure, I'll be there," Jenna answered as she hung up.

I checked on Jake first, and found him sleeping soundly. He really was healing fast. Then I left to head for the place I was going to meet Jenna. I was early, as the walk was quick from the yacht to the little bar out front. Walking in, I found a table off to the side, ordered a drink, and waited. My thoughts went back to the night I had walked into this place after the invite from Lisa, Seth's old girlfriend. How long ago was that? I thought to myself. It seemed since forever, and so much had happened since.

I didn't have to wait long, as Jenna made her way in. I waved, and she made her way over to sit across from me.

"Thanks for meeting with me," I said. "Can I get you something to drink?"

"No, thanks, I won't be staying long."

Wow, she was determined. I began with, "Luke is very special. I love him a lot. I need for you to understand that we have a very special bond. What he did, he did for me." I waited and it appeared that at least she was listening. "See, when I was abducted, it had to do with a situation that happened in December when I was traveling with Seth and Luke for the holidays." I told her how I was duped into thinking that Seth and Luke were pirates. I explained the story that Seth had told me about how he had met Luke and how Luke felt responsible for everything that happened to me. She was listening intently as I continued with how I was abducted, and how it was their putting Jason into the custody of the Coast Guard that had set Alejandro off.

"Jason's my cousin," Jenna replied.

I shook my head in agreement, as I already knew that. "I realize that this is a lot to take in right now. Luke should be telling you all this himself. He's a wonderful man. You would be a fool not to see that he only did this out of love for me. Right now he is settling up with one of his so-called contacts, again putting himself in danger because of me," I said.

"Luke's in danger?" At least this registered a response from her. Good, that meant she still felt something for him.

"Yes, unfortunately, again because of me," I shook my head. "They have to pay up for the information that one of his contacts gave him to help to locate you."

"Oh, I see," Jenna replied, and looked down at her hands, which were clasped in front of her. I had to wonder if she did see. Did she see how dangerous dealing with these contacts was for Luke?

"I appreciate what you've told me," Jenna said. "I can see what Luke was trying to do, I do. But I need some time to sort through this thing. It was a setup to meet me and to get me to disclose information about my family. Albeit, that I don't care much for Alejandro, but I wonder how much of what Luke said and did with me was a ploy, and how much was real." She stood to leave.

"I hope you will make the right decision, Jenna. You will be losing the best thing that ever came your way if you don't," I said. I watched her leave as I shook my head. Stupid girl! If it wasn't for Seth, Luke would have been hard pressed to keep me away.

Compromises

I made my way back to the yacht. Seth was pacing on the top deck as I approached. He spotted me walking back, and ran down to greet me. When he reached me, he crushed me to his chest and held me tight.

"What, Seth, what is it?" I was concerned. "Did something bad happen? Is Luke okay?"

"You scared me!" Seth hugged me close and then kissed me deeply.

"Scared you?" I asked the question after catching my breath, "Why?"

"You weren't here when I got home and I couldn't reach you on your cell."

I pulled out my cell and realized that I must have put it on silent while I was talking with Jenna so I wouldn't be interrupted. I could see that it would be some time before Seth would feel that I wasn't in danger when I wasn't with him. "Silly me, I silenced the phone. Sorry honey," I said as I hugged him back.

"Where in the world were you?" he asked, relieved that I was fine.

"I had to try. I met with Jenna," I answered.

"Woman, when will you learn?" he chuckled.

"Probably never," I chuckled back as I reached up for another kiss.

"Don't distract me," Seth said putting some distance between us. "How did it go?"

"I don't know," I answered honestly. "I explained the whole situation. I hope that once she has some time to let it sink in, she will realize the situation Luke was put in." I looked around, "By the way, where is Luke?" Then a thought hit me, "Is he okay? Did everything work out with the contact?"

"Love," Seth said, as he took me back into his arms, "Luke is fine. He's probably in the kitchen making something to eat. I paid off his debt to the contact. Everyone is fine."

"Good," I said, glad that things could maybe get back to normal, although I had never experienced "normal" since meeting Seth.

"You ready to go?" Seth asked as he smiled down at me.

"Go?" I was confused for a moment, as he waited for it to sink in. "Oh, yeah; the flight to England. Well, I don't have much to pack, seeing you won't let me get my clothes back in Virginia."

"I told you, we will take care of that as soon as we land. Besides, wouldn't you like the opportunity to shop in England?"

"I don't want you taking care of me," I answered stubbornly.

"You are something else. Most women would jump at the chance to shop in England and not have to foot the bill."

"Well, I am not most women, if you haven't noticed. I am perfectly capable of taking care of myself," I answered, as he continued to chuckle.

"That's why I love you," Seth said, shaking his head. "You really are something else. Do you think you can be ready to leave in an hour? I have the jet waiting."

I had forgotten he had his own jet, and we wouldn't be traveling through the usual channels. "Yes, let me just pack a few things, and I want to say goodbye to Luke, Jake, and Jackie."

I did find Luke in the kitchen as I was on my way through to go pack. I went in, wrapped my arms around him, and snuggled into his hard chest.

"Wow, what did I do to deserve that!" Luke chuckled as he embraced me back.

"I am flying off with Seth, and I wanted to say goodbye."

He pulled me back to kiss me briefly. "I'll miss you!"

"Yeah, right! You will have some breathing room not trying to protect me for a bit," I giggled back.

Compromises

"I would rather be on guard twenty-four-seven than not have you around, Cass."

"Well, I sure will miss you. Who's going to keep me laughing while I am in England?"

"I'm sure you will be preoccupied," Luke chuckled again.

I laughed back. "Men, you all think the same, don't you?" I gave him another kiss, made my way down to say goodbye to Jake and Jackie, and then packed what little I had.

When we got to Seth's jet, he introduced me to the pilot, Alan. I remembered him from the trip to California, but now that he didn't have to conceal what position Seth was in, he was more talkative. Alan assured me that the flight was going to be pretty uneventful.

I was tired out from all the events of the past few days, and napped along the way. Seth was busy with paperwork, so I tried to avoid distracting him, knowing that once we landed he would be monopolized by his family, as he hadn't been home in awhile. I was still trying to come to terms with the fact that he had all these things, and anxious to see what his home was like in England. He had impeccable taste, so I was sure it had to be spectacular.

As he was finishing up his work and putting it away in his briefcase he turned and smiled at me. "I'm so glad you are coming with me."

I chuckled. "Did I have a choice?"

"You always have a choice, Cassandra."

"Well," I said as I leaned over to kiss him quickly, "I chose you."

"I'm certainly glad of that."

"So, what kind of weather will we be landing in?" I had never been to England, and had only heard a few things. My vision was that it was gloomy, overcast, and rainy. I had no idea what to expect.

"It will be about twenty-two degrees when we land," Seth answered.

"Twenty-two! Gracious Seth, you know how I hate the cold! I absolutely didn't pack anything to prepare for that kind of weather."

"That's Celsius, love," he laughed, clearly enjoying my shock.

"Okay," I said, drawing out my reply, knowing that he enjoyed teasing me like this. "I'll bite. So in American terms, what temperature is that?"

"That would be about seventy-one degrees in American terms, as you call it."

"Well," I smiled, "I think I can handle that." Seth chuckled.

Curiously, I asked, "Does your family know about . . . well . . . you know, your job and secrets and such."

Seth laughed. "Love, my family knows that I deal in technology for a living. They also know that I help Jay, but probably not to the extent that you are aware of. I don't want to worry them unnecessarily. They know I don't let on about my money, and they respect that. I think that my sister and mother will give me a tongue-lashing when we get there, as they are aware that I recently had to rescue you."

I thought it interesting that he tried to protect them from the whole truth, but didn't keep it a secret from them. I settled back into my chair and looked out the window as we approached his homeland.

We landed in London, as that was where Seth's family lived, and he also said he wanted to show me the sights and shop. He said it was comparable to shopping in New York City. I wished he had let me stop in Portsmouth to grab some items, but he had been so intent on whisking me away. I don't know if he was afraid that if I stayed in the States something bad would happen or if he was just anxious to get here. Somehow, I thought it was probably a mixture of both.

There was a car waiting in the garage. Seth pulled out his keys and loaded my bags into it. He explained that his sister had driven it over earlier in the day so we would have transportation when we arrived.

Compromises

It was weird sitting on the wrong side of the car and watching him maneuver down the streets, driving on the wrong side of the road.

First, he took me to a pub, one of many that I could see as we drove through the streets, and we had a great sandwich and a warm beer. One of the many things I noted that they did differently in England was the warm beer; that was going to take some time getting used to. Then he took me shopping, to buy a few items I would need for the next few days. I didn't like the fact that he was paying for everything, but he insisted, and I found it hard to resist when he would drown out my protests with his kisses. Besides, I did need to have some clothes while we were here.

We hopped into the car after I absolutely would not let him take me to another store, and then drove out of town. As we drove he showed me some of the more interesting tourist spots. He said we would take the next few days to visit sights as I ticked off the different things I wanted to see, including the Changing of the Guard, Stonehenge, and some beautiful old castles.

We pulled up to a grand home in the outskirts of the city. The outlying area was beautiful and I was amazed how lovely the home looked. It was older, but sprawled out on a green rolling hill with lots of flowers and shrubbery.

"This is where I grew up," Seth said as he pulled into the circular drive. I tried to imagine what he would look like as a child, running across the beautiful green lawn with the wind blowing his black curls, laughing with friends. The thought made me smile.

A woman and man came out the front door. They were handsome people and in great shape. I could see he resembled his mother, as she ran around to the driver's side and barely waited for him to get out as she enveloped him in an embrace. Seth hugged her back. "Hi Mom, Dad," he said, as his father walked up behind them to clasp his hand.

They moved over to where I was coming out of the car, and his mother embraced me and then stepped back, "I'm sorry if I startled you, it's just that I have heard so much about you that I feel I know you already."

I laughed, "Not a problem at all. I wasn't expecting that kind of greeting, as I have heard the English are so formal- it took me by surprise, is all."

They all laughed. Seth put his arm around my waist, "Love, you watch too many movies or talk to the wrong people. We are a very welcoming bunch. Besides, my mother is American, as you will soon tell from her lack of accent."

"Oh, I see," I said as we made our way into the house. I took in the modernized kitchen with a table and chairs off to one side. Seth motioned for me to sit while he held a chair out for me at the table.

"Would you like some tea?" his mother asked and then added, "I made coffee as well, knowing Americans prefer that over tea."

"Coffee would be grand," I commented.

"I'll grab it, Mother. Why don't you sit and chat while I take over." Seth seemed at home in their kitchen as he was in his own. His mother smiled as she shook her head and took a seat next to me.

"So you are safe now! After Seth finally got you back, I heard what those scoundrels did. Just horrible, horrible!"

Before I could answer, Seth interrupted, "Mother, let's not dwell on things we had no control over. Tell me, where is that meddling sister of mine?" he asked instead.

"Right behind you, big brother," answered a beautiful, slender girl with long black, curly hair and bright blue eyes. I could see the resemblance instantly. Seth grabbed her and hugged her tight.

"Sis," he said as he put her back on her feet, "meet Cassandra." I went to rise, but his sister ran over to me and hugged me while I sat in my seat. It wasn't hard to get caught up in her enthusiasm over seeing us.

"I have been dying to meet the woman who has captured the heart of my brother. I can see why," she grinned as she took the other seat next to me, while Seth remained standing in the center of kitchen, taking it all in with a smile.

"You haven't let her get a word in edgewise," his mother said as a little girl came running in from outside and attached herself to Seth's leg. A handsome man, carrying a small baby girl, followed her.

"Uncle Seth! Uncle Seth!" the little girl chanted as she danced around him.

Seth bent down and tried to retain his balance as she clung to his neck and kissed him. She was beautiful, and if it wasn't for the difference in her eye color and slightly lighter hair, I would've thought she was Seth's daughter. He chuckled, "Alex, you are about to knock me over, and that would definitely make Cassandra laugh."

She looked over at me with a mischievous grin on her face, and I could see that she wanted to do just that - make her uncle embarrassed. Seth stood up quickly, obviously aware that she would take him up on his offer if he wasn't on solid footing. She ran to me and hugged me briefly before throwing a thousand questions about where I was from and what was it like to be taken captive by pirates. I laughed in spite of myself as her mother told her it wasn't polite to ask such things from someone who just came out of a horrifying experience, and shooed her out into the other room.

"It's okay, really," I replied with a chuckle. "I was imaginative as a child myself, and can understand how the mystery would be intriguing at such a young age."

"Nonsense," Seth's sister said. "I will have none of it, and she had better learn better manners before she re-enters the room," she said, loud enough to be heard in the other room- which prompted silence from Alex.

Seth set my coffee in front of me and gave a cup to his mother. "Tea?" he asked his sister, who waved him off as she refocused her attention on me.

"So, how long are you here? Do you like to shop? I know some of the best places in town to buy the best bargains and still look like you bought the latest fashion. What about seeing the sights?"

Seth chuckled, "Liza, I would love the opportunity to show her my homeland without an entourage, if you don't mind."

"But, I do mind! You can't do her justice in the shopping area, and I am so much better at being a tour guide."

Seth threw his hands in the air while looking at me. "I think that I will have to whisk you away to my home sooner rather than later if I am to spend any time at all with you while we are here." I chuckled, as did everyone else.

The rest of the evening was spent with me as the center of attention, something I was not used to. Seth's family wouldn't let it be any other way, as they directed the conversation around me at every turn. Liza- short for Elizabeth, I learned later- was really quite fun to be around. She told me childhood stories of her and Seth, and I learned more about the man I had fallen in love with. I marveled at how welcoming his family was to me and how comfortable it was to be in their company. I thought back to the time I was in Seth's home in California and how he had said that missing the holidays with his family would be a welcome break. I could almost see why, as they didn't give you a moment to breathe, but then again, I thought that he just didn't know how lucky he was to have a sibling who loved him so much. They had an easy camaraderie, and it made me wish I had grown up with a sibling rather than being an only child. The children were adorable. I noticed that Alex gravitated

Compromises

toward Seth at every turn. She hung on his every word, and he seemed to encourage her interest in his stories by embellishing the facts.

At one point, he was telling them how he had met me at Benny's. He told Alex- short for Alexandra- that I was wearing a ball gown and a crown. That he had stared at me the whole time. I laughed as I corrected him; "I beg to differ, Seth, I was in Capris and a T-shirt, with flip-flops, to boot." He ignored my interruption and continued his story of how when swimming at the "cove" he had to sweep me into his arms to save me from a shark. I raised an eyebrow at him when he glanced my way: he just chuckled.

He tousled Alex's hair and said, "Well, it almost was like that."

"It wasn't like that at all," I giggled.

The little girl frowned at me, "I like Uncle Seth's story better."

Seth pulled her close to kiss her cheek, "she's learning, Alex. She'll come around. How about I tell you a "Fat Butt" story?" His sister clued me in that Seth made up stories about two dogs, one called Fat Butt because she was a fluffy poodle and the other, a dachshund, called Cupcake. Alex wouldn't let him rest when he was around until he told her a story about these two dogs and their adventures.

Later, when we were alone, as Seth showed me the bedroom we would share for the evening, he took me into his arms and kissed me lightly on the lips. "I love you, Cassandra."

"I love you too, Seth," I said, with caution in my voice, wondering where this conversation was headed.

"You were so gracious today with my family. I know they can be overbearing at times, but they mean well."

"No, they were perfect. Not what I expected at all. You know, I expected them to be very reserved or something."

"Again, love, you really do have to get out more and learn about other countries. You can't believe everything you read. You should see how some people here stereotype Americans. You definitely don't fall into any of those categories."

I didn't think I wanted to know how they stereotyped Americans. I changed the subject to our sharing a bed. "Are your parents okay with this?" I motioned to the large double.

"Honey, I am well past being under their 'rule', and they know that we have been together for quite some time. I think it's pretty obvious to everyone that we are intimate."

"It just feels weird," I said as I moved to sit down on the edge of the bed.

"Don't worry," Seth chuckled as he leaned against a dresser, "I'll try to contain myself while we are here."

I shook my head as I smiled at him, and forgot anything else I might have said as he moved over to take my face his hands, pulling me up tight to the length of his body while he kissed me. "Contain yourself?" I asked when I caught my breath moments later.

"Well, maybe not," he chuckled as he moved away and grabbed my hand to show me the rest of the upstairs. Later that evening he showed me just how much he was not going to behave himself.

The next few days passed quickly. I had a shopping excursion with his sister and mother and declined any spending cash that Seth tried to give me. They took me to Harrods at Knight-bridge, a shopping mall that covered over four acres and held every type of store you could ever want. We were able to pamper ourselves in luxury. It was definitely a tiring day. They were helpful in translating the dollar exchange rate, which baffled me at every turn.

Over several days, Seth showed me more tourist attractions and although I had previously never had any desire to visit England, I was glad now that I had the opportunity to come to such a lovely place. We hopped on a double deckered bus and made our way to

Compromises

Kensington Palace to view the Crown Jewels. We visited Windsor Castle in Kensington and Seth explained that it was one of the three official residences of the queen as well as the largest inhabited castle in the world. As I looked at the overwhelming size and beauty of it, I teased him, saying, "I thought this was your home."

Seth laughed and grabbed me around my waist to pull me to the length of his body, igniting a fire within me. He kissed me and released me to pull me behind him as we ran to catch back up with the tour group.

Seth knew a lot about England and about other sights. When we visited St. George's Chapel at Windsor, he explained that it held the tombs of the "ten sovereigns". The gothic architecture was quite impressive; I gazed up at the roof, amazed at the beauty of it.

As we walked around Stonehenge in Southern England, I got caught up in the mystery of how these huge stones were set so precisely. Seth's sister and her family had joined us that particular day. Little Alex told me that some believed that aliens set the stones there. His sister added that it was believed that it was thought to have healing powers and many traveled here to cure their ailments. Either way, it was mystical.

At the Changing of the Guards at Buckingham Palace in London, the guards truly didn't move or stare at you. Seth laughed as I did a little dance around one of them and then was sullen that he didn't even smile. He told me some of the things he had done as a small child to try to get a guard to react, to no avail. His homeland was beautiful and I was growing very fond of the place.

At night, we would gather in one of the "reception rooms"- which was really another way of saying "living room"- and I would listen to them talk about current events or to stories about Seth as he grew up. Little Alex always had a place in Seth's lap as she sat content to hear him talk about whatever he was doing. When she wasn't by his side, she was grabbing my hand and smiling up at me. I marveled at how good he was with both his nieces, and couldn't help but think of how he would be if we had children. It was inevitable to think about it as we were around them. I tried to keep my thoughts to myself for fear of what Seth would think if he could decipher my thoughts. One night as we lay in bed he pulled me close to his side and kissed the top of my head.

"Wondering what our children would be like, love?"

Now how did the man do that? He had an uncanny ability to read my mind. "Why do you ask?" I said, afraid to meet his gaze.

He wasn't about to let me go that easily and he put his finger underneath my chin to raise my head and meet his eyes. "I have seen you watching me with my nieces. To answer your question, I love children; would love to have them with you." My heart beat triple time, trying not to dive too deep into that statement and what it meant about our future. When I didn't answer he prompted, "Wouldn't you like to have my children, Cassandra?"

Oh wouldn't I, I thought to myself; but I answered calmly, "Yes, Seth, I would."

"Good," he said, as if that settled everything. He kissed me, slowly intensifying the passion that never ceased. "I say we start practicing right now," he chuckled, as a look of horror overcame me. "Kidding, love; when you are ready, of course, to have children," he corrected himself, "not sex." I wound my arms around his neck and pulled him in close.

"I love you, Seth Hanson."

"Show me," he said as his hands moved lower to bring me in close to length of his body.

Later, I lay there for a long time, taking in what he had just admitted to. He wanted to have children with me. Sleep didn't find me until much later that evening.

16

The next day we headed out to go to his own home, in the Channel Islands on a little island called Jersey. As I hugged his family goodbye, Liza made me promise that I would call her soon. Little Alex clung to me and begged her mother to let her go with us. Liza was adamant and said maybe another time, but that Seth and I needed some adult time alone.

As we headed to Jersey, Seth explained to me that you had to be either native born or a very rich man to own land there. From the looks of the huge house that we pulled up to later that day, I had to believe he fit the latter category. What lay at the end of the driveway was a beautiful stone house. It looked like stacked stone. The windows were large and everywhere, reflecting the sunlight that shone down on it. There was the feel of a castle about it. I wondered what little Alex thought of it. I could close my eyes and imagine a castle with my man riding a white horse coming out to meet me as I picked flowers in the large gardens around the house. Yes, my imagination was running away with me.

As we pulled around the drive, a familiar man came out of the house, rushing to meet us. As soon as the car stopped I jumped out and ran toward him. I hugged Luke before kissing him. "What in the world are you doing here?"

"Well, I was lonely since I got dumped, and figured you would be just the person I need to perk me up."

Seth walked up behind us and shook Luke's hand. "Well, at least you can keep her busy while I catch up on some work."

I frowned. "Seth, I thought you said you were on vacation!"

"I know, love, but I can't totally ignore my business for any length of time. Part of the pitfalls of owning your own business is having to keep your thumb on the pulse at all times."

"But you have me," Luke grinned, as I again turned to hug him.

"Still won't talk to you?" I asked, knowing that he knew I was speaking about Jenna.

"Women are so stubborn. I really am at a loss when it comes to trying to get someone to forgive you; never had to worry about it before, as I never came back. I just moved on to the next one all the time. That was until I met you," he put his arm around me and steered me into the house. I shook my head, wondering how Jenna could be so blind. Luke changed the subject to explain what Mandi, Jackie, Robert, and Jake were up to since I had left.

When I entered the foyer I stopped listening to Luke's chatter and took in the cathedral ceilings and big open rooms. I knew that Seth must have had the house built, as it wasn't the usual style of home I had seen in England. Everything was tastefully decorated. Luke, obviously no stranger to the house, offered to take me on a tour. Seth said he wanted to get some calls out of the way before dinner, and told me to run on ahead with Luke; he would meet up with us later for dinner.

Each room was tastefully done. The windows let the sun in

and showed beautifully tended gardens around the outside. It was breathtaking. Luke laughed when he got to Seth's room, a large canopied king-size bed in the center. "Guess you will be staying here, unless Seth is so busy with work and you decide to warm my bed, that is." I playfully slapped him as I walked into a huge closet. I touched the sweaters and slacks hanging there. I thought to myself that this closet was probably half the size of my boat! The bathroom itself was huge. Seth's taste for luxury was not squandered there, either. It reminded me of how beautiful his California home was. I found the piano in a room downstairs, on an elevated platform surrounded by windows. I ran my hand over the keys, thinking how I missed hearing Seth play. I hadn't had the pleasure since he had rescued me. I would have to rectify that soon. I might just straddle him on the bench this time, but unlike the last time, I would have no reason to stop.

When we got to the kitchen, Seth was busy making dinner. He actually allowed Luke and me to assist with making up some vegetables and a salad. We laughed and had a good time. Every chance he got, Seth would encircle my waist with an embrace and kiss me. Luke laughed and said, "Boy, do you have him wound around your little finger or what?"

Much later, as we were sitting down to dinner, Seth's phone rang. He looked at the number and excused himself as he took the call, walking away from the table.

"I can't believe he is working," I said as I took another bite of my steak.

"Yeah, he should throw the damn thing in the moat and have the Royal Guards keep away his business partners," Luke said in all seriousness, as I broke out in laughter.

"Luke, I swear, you would get along really well with Seth's niece, Alex. Moats and Royal Guards," I said as I shook my head. I wasn't about to admit that I had thought about those very same things when first seeing his home.

Seth returned, but I could tell the call had put a damper on his mood. Although he waved off my concern, I could tell that whatever was said preoccupied him throughout the rest of dinner.

Luke tried to keep things lively, talking about the Loch Ness Monster. Nessie, he called her, like they were old friends or something. He had me in stitches most of the evening talking about taking me out hunting to see if we could catch ole Nessie on film. He said we should wear rain boots and raincoats as it was surely about to downpour since we were in England, after all. I laughed as the weather was actually perfect since I had been here.

Luke's chatter finally brought about laughter from Seth. I looked at him, questioningly.

"Love," Seth laughed, "the Loch Ness is in Scotland and not England."

"Oh," I replied, a little embarrassed that once again, I had fallen prey to Luke's stories.

"Sorry," Luke chuckled, not looking sorry at all. "You are just so gullible, Cass, and I love to tease you."

"One of these days . . ." I let the threat dangle in the air, as I joined in their laughter.

Later, as I snuggled close to Seth in bed, I tried to see if he would open up about the call he took at dinner.

"I am going to have to leave for a bit," Seth said.

"Leave?" I questioned, "When? Here? Why?"

"Tomorrow," he said as he turned to me. "I'm sorry, love, I really wanted this to be our vacation. I'd like for you to stay, either here or with my family in London, until I return."

Compromises

"Do you want me to go with you when you leave? Would you prefer I go home to wait for you? I don't mind cutting my vacation short."

"No," he answered adamantly. "I want you to remain here."

"Seth, if this is your silly over-protectiveness again . . ."

"It's not that simple. I wanted to do something with you before we left England, but it will be delayed." He wasn't giving away anything, which was starting to concern me. "Please stay until I return." He kissed me deeply, but I pushed back, concerned about the turn of events.

"Seth," I hesitated, not sure where he was going and why, "how long will you be gone?"

"I'm not sure right now, but I promise I will make it back as soon as possible."

"Well, I could stay here at your house, if Luke will be here," I answered.

"That would be fine, love."

Then a thought hit me, "Seth, this isn't to do with pirating is it?" I waited with trepidation, hoping that wasn't the case.

"Love, it truly is just business and it isn't anything you should worry your pretty little head about. Now, I am going to be gone for a bit, so won't you give me something to remember you by?" Seth said, as he moved his hand to my hip to pull me in closer. He promptly stopped any reply by taking my lips with his. As I snuggled in closer to his body, the heat that always engulfed me when around him made all conscious thought disappear. All my concerns about why he would be leaving were put aside as our lovemaking took over.

By the time I awoke in the morning, Seth wasn't in the bed. I thought it was strange that I hadn't heard him leave. Then I noticed a note on the bedside table. I picked it up and read,

Love,

You will notice I have left by the time you get this note. You looked so peaceful I didn't want to wake you. Besides, it would have been harder to leave you if I had. I do hope you will go to stay with my family in London if Luke should leave before I return. I so want to accomplish one thing with you before we head back to the States. Be a good girl and do what I ask, just this once. Luke will keep you company. I will be back shortly.

All my love, Seth.

Well, now what? I thought to myself as I sat down to stare at the note. Well, if Seth wanted me to stay and it seemed important to him that I spend time with his family, then that was what I would do.

I called Liza, as Seth had left her number as well as several others for me.

Liza's surprise was evident when she answered. "Seth's gone? Oh for heaven's sake, Cassandra, you should fly back here to be with us."

"I will probably be doing that shortly and I appreciate the offer, but Luke is here and I really wanted to sightsee here before Seth returns."

"Was he being secretive again?" Liza answered tiredly. "I swear, that brother of mine and his secrets!"

I laughed in spite of myself, as I felt the same way. "Look, Liza, I didn't mean to tie you up on the line, but I did want to give you the heads-up that I would be there in a few days."

"I can't wait to spend more time with you, and this time, you will have to stay at my house." We agreed to meet up in a few more days.

Compromises

I called Seth next. He answered on the first ring. "Hi babe, everything okay?" He sounded concerned.

"Are you in flight?"

"Yeah, I had to make my way back to the States. Are you going to spend some time getting to know my home before I return? Luke will make an entertaining tour guide. Just remember, you love me though, right?"

I laughed, "Like you would have to remind me? Seth, when are you coming back? Why are we always getting separated?"

"I told you, love. It's business. I don't like this any better than you do. I plan to be back straightaway, so you stay put and enjoy my homeland."

"Business that meant you had to sneak out in the early morning to go away without waking me and not saying goodbye?"

"You looked so peaceful and I needed to catch a really early flight out. I do want to spend some uninterrupted time with you when I return, so don't plan on leaving. Promise me."

"I just worry about you," I answered solemnly.

"As I do you, love. Now be a good girl, enjoy Luke, and then go stay with my family. They would love to entertain you while I am gone. Besides, I know my sister will have a pub or two that she will want you to go to while she leaves the kids with her husband."

I laughed, knowing that he was right. His sister had said as much before we left to come to Seth's home."Okay, but hurry back to me."

"I will be there as soon as I can," Seth replied. "Love you."

When I got downstairs, Luke was making coffee, enjoying some kind of Danish. "Morning, sunshine," he smiled as I pecked him on the cheek on my way to grab a cup to make coffee.

"Spill," I said, while stirring my sugar.

"Huh?" Luke asked, confused.

"What do you know?"

"I have no idea what you are talking about, Cass," Luke said as he sat down at the kitchen table, taking another bite of his Danish.

"Luke," I admonished, "you know damn well what I mean. What's going on?"

"Look," he said as he set his cup down, "if he was doing anything dangerous and involved in pirating, I would be going with him, right?"

I thought about it, and he was probably right. "Then why all the secrecy?"

"It's work. You know these Brits; they don't like to divulge all."

"I hope you're right, Luke. I hope you're right." He was making me feel absolutely foolish about being anxious. He was right. If it was involving pirates, Luke would have gone with him. I decided to put it out of my mind and enjoy my vacation with my very best male friend.

"Can we do some sightseeing?"

"Well, sure we will," Luke laughed.

We had a great time in the Channel Islands over the next few days. I was surprised that Luke knew the area so well. He said that he had been there before, as Seth was always generous with his things and allowed them to vacation there when they wanted. He talked about Jenna, and we tried to formulate a plan of action. I told him that she seemed concerned when I said he was in danger, so that meant she had feelings for him. After a couple of days of sightseeing, Luke said he wanted to get back to the States and see if he could touch base with Jenna. Besides, he wanted to let me have more time with Seth's family.

We said goodbye at the airport in London. "I hope you work things out with Jenna," I said as I kissed him briefly.

"You and me both," he replied.

Liza was waiting for me. The girls were nowhere in sight, so that meant she had left them with her husband. We stopped at a pub on the way home. I looked down into my warm beer, trying to relax over lunch. Liza reached over and placed her hand over mine.

"You're worried about Seth. I really think he didn't mean to take off like that. I know he really wanted this to be time for the two of you to get to know each other."

"I thought so, too," I said shaking my head. "Why your brother has to keep me in the dark, I don't know!"

"He's overprotective that way. When he first told me that he had met someone, and I wanted to fly out to meet you, he wouldn't let me. He said he didn't know where it was going and he promised that once things were ironed out he would bring you here to meet the family."

I was curious. "So when exactly was that?"

"Last fall? It was right around Halloween, I believe."

Wow. We hadn't even really gotten to know each other by then. We were attracted to each other, yes, but I hadn't thought he had fallen for me like that yet.

"Well," Liza said as she raised her glass to toast and I did the same letting our glasses clink together, "here's to my secretive brother. May he find his way back to his beautiful girl soon!"

"Amen to that," I replied.

17

Luke met up with Seth in Florida on the yacht. Seth had also invited Jay, so they could talk and get a plan of action.

"How did things go after I left?" Seth said to Luke.

"I think I threw her off. She's pretty smart. Came right down that morning to get me to spill my guts on what I knew. I told her that if it had involved pirating I would have left with you. Are you sure you shouldn't be a little more open with her now that she knows about you?" Luke asked tentatively, not wanting to get Seth angry.

"I can't, Luke. She'd worry too much. I want out of this thing, and it may be messy. She's better off thinking I had my usual business, and when I get back to her I can explain all."

Jay interrupted, "I don't know Seth. This could be pretty dangerous. After all, isn't a relationship about truth and about knowing that someone will have to worry over you from time to time?"

"You haven't seen my Cassandra when she wants to protect me. Remember on the island? She just up and walked away from me on that last night I snuck in to see her, knowing that she was staying in danger

Compromises

to keep me safe and catch Alejandro. No, if she knew what we were about, she would be right here and demanding to go with us." Seth was adamant, and it seemed as though both of his friends were not going to be able to sway him into divulging anything to Cassandra.

"Jackie and Jake are due back any moment," Jay said.

Luke questioned Seth on what he had said to keep them out of the loop. Seth said he had told them he stopped by to pick up a few items before heading out to his business meeting.

The three of them knew they had little time to accomplish what they needed to do next. Hopefully it would keep Seth and Luke safe for a long time.

"One more for old time's sake?" Luke asked.

"Let's hope it is for a really long time," Seth said.

Seth hadn't told Cassandra for good reason. When he and Luke had settled up with their contact prior to going to London, they had also obtained information on where the pirates were meeting. The contact, Mike, had liked the money that Seth flashed in front of him, and since he thought they were pirates, he had no qualms about giving up information. Seth didn't want to lie to Cassandra, but he was about to make a huge change in his life, and he needed to make sure that he and all his friends would be safe for a long time to come. It was risky, yes, but he had to try. It was the last act he hoped to do for a long time. He wanted to get back to Cassandra quickly, before she got too suspicious, so it meant they had to act fast.

He had been busy while Luke stayed to entertain Cassandra and to help keep her from being suspicious about his abrupt departure. That was why he hadn't waked her to say goodbye. He knew that if she had begged him to stay, he would have faltered. He couldn't chance that.

Seth packed a small overnight bag, dressed down in ragged jeans, and a T-shirt, with his baseball cap on backwards. He pulled his wavy black hair into a ponytail. He holstered his gun on his hip and walked upstairs to meet with Luke and Jay. Luke was dressed similarly. They looked dark, handsome, and extremely dangerous. Exactly the look they were going for. They made their way out quickly, so Jake and Jackie wouldn't catch them.

They flew out on Seth's jet and landed on the southeastern-most tip of Puerto Rico. There they went to a marina that had a fast boat waiting for them. It was white, with red flames on the side; the outboard motors had enough horsepower to push you back into your seat when it was in full speed ahead. They said goodbye to Jay, saying they would keep in touch.

"Be safe, my friends," Jay said as they clasped hands in a strong handshake.

Seth handed Jay his cell phone. "If Cassandra calls, please tell her that a business partner found my phone at my last meeting, and since you were listed as the emergency contact, you had retrieved it."

"She's too smart for that, Seth," Jay said, shaking his head. "She will have expected you to call her."

"I am going to do just that," Seth said as he produced another phone. "Thus, the plausible reason why I have a new number. Besides, when we finish here, I don't want the pirates having anything to contact me with. That will now be in your possession."

"Sometimes you are so sneaky it scares me," Luke laughed. "Just glad I am on your side."

They jumped in the small fast boat, as Jay untied them from the pier and threw in the ropes.

"Keep in touch!" Jay hollered out over the roar of the engines.

"You'll hear from us in a couple of days!" Seth hollered back as he kicked the boat into gear and sped off, headed for the Caribbean islands and a meeting place that was known only to pirates.

Compromises

It was approaching dusk as they got to the small island. Several armed men were waiting as they pulled in. No one, except pirates, was expected on this side of the island. Locals knew to stay away, and visitors were warned against going there if they didn't want to lose their life or possibly be held for ransom.

Seth threw a line to a man who tied them to the pier. He didn't question them. They looked like the rest of the men who came this way, except maybe they were just a bit more handsome than the others. Not that this man would ever admit that to anyone who might ask. Pirates were a touchy bunch.

Luke and Seth made their way to a bar that was overcrowded with men and some very buxom women who did nothing to hide what they had. They walked up to man sitting in the corner who, at the moment, was preoccupied with a woman with a T-shirt pulled up through the center of her shirt and tied off to show off both her midriff and her large breasts. Her shorts were so short she might as well have been wearing just underwear. She was sitting on the man's lap, laughing as he whispered in her ear.

"Johnny," Seth said as he took a seat across from the man. "Long time no see."

"Ahh," Johnny replied, "the Englishman. Good to see you." He nodded his head at Seth and then at Luke as they sat down.

The girl, noticing that the two new men were far more attractive than any others in the whole place, quickly made her way over to Seth. He smiled but shook his head as she attempted to sit in his lap. "Sorry, honey, but not tonight."

She looked over at Luke, hopeful.

Luke looked at her. She would be a welcome distraction. She was quite fetching, and he knew that it wouldn't be a permanent romance she was looking for. He looked at her face. But Jenna clouded his mind. Damn the woman; did she ruin him for anyone else?

"Sorry, but we have business tonight. Maybe another time," Luke added, hoping that indeed there would be another time, if Jenna truly blocked him out of her life.

Seth grinned as Luke looked over at him. "You too, I see."

"Rub it in, why don't you?" Luke answered angrily.

Seth laughed, throwing his head back, enjoying his friend's discomfort at not being able to want another woman.

Johnny interrupted them. "So, you boys in on the next job? We recently had two incidents in the Caribbean that wound up putting some of our guys in jail. We are running low on numbers."

"So we heard," Seth answered, not giving anything away. "That's why we are here."

"Well, see if you can try not to get caught or anything. Damn Coast Guard is all over the place lately."

"Yeah," Seth said, and added to himself, silently, "that's what we are counting on."

"So what's the plan?" Luke said, as the girl settled back into Johnny's lap.

Johnny grinned. "Well, there is a lot of travel going on in the upper Caribbean, it seems. I want to have you boys grab one of our new recruits and head over toward the Bahamas. I will be headed farther south with my own little crew. We should be able to be occupied for a bit."

"Great," Seth said. "We will head out in the morning. Right now, I think a drink or two is order, gentlemen."

Several hours and drinks later, Seth and Luke stumbled into their hotel room, leaning on each other for support, singing an old tune.

Compromises

They plopped down on their respective beds, not bothering to change but kicking off their shoes.

"I wouldn't quit your day job," Seth chuckled, referring to Luke's singing.

"You either! Hey is it like that for you all the time, Seth?" Luke asked while staring up at the ceiling, his words slurring slightly.

"Huh?" Seth asked, already half asleep and not sure what Luke was referring to.

"The girls . . . They don't do anything for me anymore. I mean they are nice to look at, but I can't get Jenna out of my mind. She's the only one I want in my bed. Am I sick or something?"

Seth laughed. "Lovesick, my friend, just lovesick. And yes, it is like that all the time. I want only one woman to warm my bed, and right now she is far away in England, safe and sound."

"Damn," Luke cussed. "Thought so. I better get this chick to take me back, then. I don't relish being celibate the rest of my life!"

Seth laughed as he closed his eyes and dreamed of Cassandra, wanting to get this ordeal over with so they could start fresh together.

The next day was a flurry of activity. Seth snuck a quick phone call to Cassandra, glad to hear that she hadn't tried to reach him on his cell; she was surprised when he told her the story about having to get a new phone because he had lost the old one.

She was spending time with his sister, and doing more sightseeing. They were planning on taking the girls to a picnic on the grounds of Leeds Castle, and then run through the maze at Hampton Court Palace later on with little Alex. He so wished he could be there, and told her so. Seth added that he had to run, and not to worry if he didn't call regularly, as his meetings were running late. Cassandra never suspected a thing.

As they headed out, Luke and Seth went into the bar to grab one of the new recruits Johnny had told them about. They wanted someone "green" and pretty impressionable. After they selected one and talked up how they were going to make enough on this one run to live on for the next year, they all climbed into the fast boat. They needed a witness; someone who would make it back to tell the pirates what they wanted relayed. Seth nodded at Luke, who nodded back. Off they went.

The Caribbean was beautiful but hot that day. They would have enjoyed the day more if they hadn't known that what was about to happen was dangerous and perhaps deadly. They spotted a vessel off in the distance. Seth reached down to his radio and punched in a couple of numbers while Luke and the other pirate- they called him Sandy because of his light-colored hair- were looking out at the vessel they were fast approaching.

"This will be an easy take!" Sandy said. Excitement was just oozing from him. He was like a kid at Christmas, waiting for the moment to open his gifts.

"Nothing's easy, my man, nothing," Luke said. The kid was young. Luke was feeling sorry for him. Seth glanced his way in caution: you never knew how deep some of these kids got in with the pirate thing. The kid had a taste for it, and wasn't ready to be saved from it. Luke looked away, but he got the message. Can't save 'em all.

As they approached the yacht, Seth fired a couple of shots across its deck. Instantly, the boat slowed. The owners knew they were a sitting duck in the water, as pirates could shoot holes in the yacht and sink her if need be. An elderly man came walking out on the deck, and Seth's stomach sank. He hated this part of his charade. If only he could tell the old man that it was going to be okay and no one would get hurt, if he was careful and didn't do anything stupid.

"Gentlemen," the old man said, clearly afraid, but not willing to show it, "What can I do for you fine men today?"

Compromises

"You can give up your yacht or your life!" Sandy said with a cocky grin as he aimed at the old man.

Luke stepped in front of the gun Sandy was holding, clearly blocking his path, while keeping his own gun pointed at the yacht, but not at the old man. "Just let us aboard and we will let you take your dinghy there on the back. No one has to get hurt today, mister."

Seth knew this was where it got tricky. He hoped the old man wouldn't try to be a hero and save his boat and do something stupid. But before he could say or do anything, the old man's wife came out through another door, brandishing her own gun, and shot Luke in the leg. Before Sandy could respond, Seth grabbed his gun and pointed it down. He looked at Luke who just nodded his head, indicating he was okay. Seth knew it must hurt like hell. He had been shot in the leg before.

"Now ma'am," Seth said, training his weapon on her as the old man took in a breath, "I would advise you not to be shooting at my friends here. It won't end well if you do."

Luckily, she lowered her gun as her husband rushed to meet her. Seth let out a sigh of relief, but kept his gun trained on the couple. "Throw your weapon down, ma'am." She did as he asked. They would never know that the last thing that Seth would do was shoot anyone innocent. But he had a charade to keep up. Seth told Sandy to tend to Luke, giving him orders to hand him some clean white towels from one of the storage cubbies. Then he had Sandy jump on board the yacht and make his way up to the couple.

"Luke, you okay?" Seth asked, still warily watching as Sandy approached the elderly couple, keeping his gun trained on them. He saw Sandy retrieve the woman's gun and stick it in his back waistband and then motion for them to move toward the back of the yacht, where their dinghy was tied.

"Yeah," Luke said, as he wound more towels around the wound. "She got me good."

"It works in our favor. I am leaving you here. You know Jay will be here shortly, so hang on. I have a plan to make Sandy think you are gone for good."

"How come I don't think it will be pleasant for me?" Luke said.

"That's 'cause it isn't, Luke, but it will secure your future without piracy." Seth leaped out onto the deck and tied the fast boat to the yacht.

Sandy had the old couple release their dinghy into the water and climb into it. The old woman pleaded, "But we are so far from shore and we won't last a day without food and water!"

"Hey," Sandy said rather cockily, "at least you live, right?"

"But wait," the old woman began before her husband hushed her.

"Now darling," the old man said, looking at his wife with caution, "things will turn out okay if we just do as they say."

"But . . . ," the old woman was insistent.

"Let's be smart about this," the man said, "we don't need to draw attention where it shouldn't be drawn."

Sandy looked at the couple, not sure what was going on. Seth seemed to have been preoccupied and to have missed their exchange.

The couple pushed off and made their way away from the boat. Seth wasn't worried, as he knew they would meet up with the Coast Guard momentarily. He walked with Sandy back up to the flybridge of the yacht. "Okay, man, let's get her under way."

"What about Luke?" Sandy asked apprehensively.

"He will slow us down, unfortunately. Besides, that shot looked really bad and I think he will probably bleed to death unless you are a doctor?" Seth tried to keep all emotion from his voice.

"Right," Sandy acknowledged, not wanting to be thought of as anything other than a seasoned pirate. "So you want me to untie the boat, or what?" he asked, as they moved into the bridge.

"You grab this wheel here and just push this level here straight forward when I give you the signal, you hear?"

"What are you going to do?" Sandy asked as he took his position behind the wheel.

"Going to make sure our friend doesn't suffer," Seth said.

Sandy had no idea what he intended, but didn't have time to ask, as Seth walked swiftly out of the flybridge to make his way to the fast boat tied to the side. Sandy couldn't see inside the fast boat from where he was, and didn't dare move from his spot, as he didn't know when Seth would give the "go ahead." From below he heard a large splash and tried to look down, still not seeing anything. He heard Seth start the engine to the fast boat and heard it being pulled around back. Then he heard the crane on the stern, probably wrenching the boat aboard. A few moments later he heard Seth holler, "Okay Sandy, nice and slow, pull that lever up and head straight.

When he came back up, there was blood on Seth's pants. "What the hell happened?" Sandy asked.

Seth replied, as he took over the wheel, "Gave our man a good burial at sea, is all. The sharks will take him if he doesn't drown first."

Sandy tried to contain the horror on his face as Seth nonchalantly continued to make his way forward. "Damn shame," Seth said. "He was one of my best men, too! Why don't you take stock of what's on the boat so we know what kind of fortune we are looking at?" Seth wanted Sandy out of the way while he radioed Jay and give his location.

Sandy went down onto the lower deck, and saw that Seth had winched the little fast boat up on the stern where the dinghy had been before. He shivered as he saw it, thinking how callously Seth had thrown Luke overboard to die.

Sandy made his way through the yacht and became excited when he found several expensive-looking pieces of jewelry. He stuck them in his pocket, not about to share them with Seth. He was a pirate, after all. He was tallying up all the things they could strip down off the yacht to make money when he got to the last stateroom below. Hearing a whimper, he moved quickly toward the closet it came from, drawing his gun.

Sandy opened up the closet door and aimed, excitement and worry running through him as he contemplated that he might just have to shoot someone.

A beautiful blonde was cringing in the corner, tears streaming down her face as she held a hand to her mouth.

Sandy smiled as he held out his hand to the beautiful lady. She had to be in her mid-twenties and she looked like an angel, a scared one at that. "Come on out here, Miss. I ain't gonna shoot ya."

The girl ignored his hand and tried to straighten her spine, wiping the tears from her face as she came out of the closet. Resignation was clear. She was ready to face whatever these pirates had in store for her.

"What have you done with my parents?" She seemed determined to put on a brave face.

"They will be fine. Someone will find them in a few days. What were you doing down here?"

"Where is the rest of your group, the one in charge?" The girl seemed determined to get answers, but not answering any in return.

Sandy took his finger and gently trailed it down her strap to her top. She took in a deep breath, but didn't move. Sandy just smiled. Man, if he didn't think Seth would come looking for him, he would just love to have this little thing underneath him. He started to think he might just chance it, when the boat slowed. "Now what?" the young pirate thought to himself.

Compromises

He grabbed the blonde's arm, forcing her to follow him as he made his way up to the flybridge to see what was happening.

"What's going on?" he asked, as he made his way into the flybridge with a firm grip on the girl.

Seth pointed to a speck on the Radar not bothering to turn around. "See that? It's big and moving in on us; could be Coast Guard."

"Seth?" The girl said, surprised.

Seth turned around and stared at Lisa. "Damn!" he thought to himself. He wasn't expecting this turn of events.

"You know him?" Sandy asked, flabbergasted that this pretty lady knew Seth.

"You're a pirate?" Lisa was having a hard time coming to grips with this information. First, her parents had been overtaken by pirates. They had told her to hide, and now . . . now . . . she had found out that Seth was one of them!

"Where did you think I get my money from?" Seth shrugged, letting her believe it was so.

Lisa's face turned completely red. "Damn you! Damn you to hell!"

Seth laughed. He really was enjoying her discomfort. This was going to work out well for him, far better than he had hoped for. He would be able to get Lisa out of his life forever now. He knew her well. He taunted her, "What, not good enough for you now? You were only interested in my money after all."

Lisa's face contorted with anger as she replied, "I may be a bitch who preys on eligible men for their money, but at least I am honest about it. I didn't lie and pretend to be something I wasn't."

Seth laughed again. Oh, if only Cassandra could have heard this! He was certain that she would have enjoyed it as much as he did.

In the meantime, Sandy had been watching the radar. "Damn, what do we do?" Sandy asked as he pointed to the object moving in.

"Here," Seth said as he handed the radio to Sandy, "call Johnny. Give him a heads-up on what's happened so far and what it looks like. Tell him to keep his guys away from us, or the Coast Guard could get more of us. Find out where they are at so we can make sure we stay far away from them."

Sandy did as he was asked. Seth had to keep from smiling as the kid relayed that Luke had been dumped overboard due to a life-threatening injury while taking over the yacht and at the shock that registered on Lisa's face when she heard this.

"You are unbelievable! You threw your own best friend to the sharks?" Lisa asked, wondering what she ever thought she saw in him.

"You should see what I would do to you, now that you know!"

Sandy continued on the radio and relayed that Seth saw a large ship on the radar, suspecting the Coast Guard. He asked for their coordinates so they could make sure they didn't steer the "law" in their direction.

Johnny gave out his location, saying that he also had taken on a large yacht. He wished Sandy the best, and told him tell Seth that he was sorry to hear about Luke. "Luke was a damn good pirate," he said.

As Sandy put down the radio, he ran out to the stern and saw that the ship was moving in on them. It did look like the Coast Guard. He ran back into the flybridge. "What do we do now, Seth? I don't want to go to jail!"

"Well, son, that's the nature of our business. It's a risk we take every time we go out on the water. What did you think? That being a pirate was easy?"

"This was my first time out," Sandy said as he sunk in the chair next to Seth. "I didn't expect we would just throw one of our own out in the ocean, and I sure as hell didn't expect to go to jail."

"You joined the wrong profession, my friend. Now we have to face the music. We can't outrun them and we sure as hell won't win a gunfight. All that's left to do is to surrender. At least we didn't steer them toward Johnny and the others."

"Damn!" the kid said as he slumped in his chair. "This totally sucks."

"It does," Seth agreed. "It does."

Lisa, knowing that rescue was imminent and determined to make it out of this alive, kept quiet and sat down, waiting.

"What?" Seth asked, goading her, "no one last roll in the hay for old times' sake?"

"You disgust me, Seth! I hope I never see you again."

Seth just laughed as he grabbed her arm and made his way down to the lower decks to await the Coast Guard.

As the patrol boat approached and boarded them, they took both Seth and Sandy in custody. Sandy saw the old couple they had thrown off the yacht not too long ago, looking over the side and pointing, saying, "That's them. Those are the pirates who took our boat, and our daughter, Lisa."

"Mom, Dad!" Lisa ran over and embraced them. She would never tell her parents that the man who had overtaken their yacht was one she had dated for a couple of years. She couldn't bear to have them know that little piece of information. They had never met each others' families, mostly because Seth wouldn't allow it. Now she realized why.

As the Coast Guard boarded the yacht, one of the Guardsmen asked Sandy, "We heard there were three of you. Where's the other guy?"

Sandy replied, "He didn't make it, too injured."

When Seth and Sandy were led onto the boat to take them to the

Coast Guard ship, Seth suddenly said to the kid, "I ain't going to jail, friend," and jumped out into the water. Immediately the guy next to him started shooting in the water. Blood rose to the surface as they pushed Sandy forward. Lisa put a hand to her mouth as a single tear dropped.

The Guardsman commented, "Well, he's fish food for sure," and they all laughed, all except poor Sandy and Lisa.

18

Jenna was miserable. There was just no other way to put it. Weeks had dragged by. When she finally got the courage up to try to see Luke, she heard that he had flown out to London to see Cassandra and Seth. It was amazing what people on the docks knew when you asked. She didn't even have to find Jake or Jackie to get that information. That could be a good thing, as people watched out for each other that way. They had seen Jenna with Luke and thought they were a couple; thus, they relayed the information pretty easily.

There was so much that she needed to talk to him about. She had talked with Cassie and gotten most of what she wouldn't listen to before when Luke tried to explain, but now she wanted to hear it from the horse's mouth. Had he fallen for her, or was everything a ploy to get information in order to rescue Cassandra? She absentmindedly reached up to play with the little white gold bear that hung around her neck. She didn't have the strength to remove it before and now . . . well, now . . . it was as much a part of her as the hand that held it. Damn the man!

He confused her. He said he wanted her, yet he also said he wanted to give her space to figure all these emotions out.

Well . . . she'd figured them out, and gone through them again. It boiled down to one thing. She felt used. He had used her. But had he fallen in love with her? That was the burning question in her mind. Oh, she was by no means ready to forgive him for the deceit and lies, but she needed to know how he felt about her.

Kirsten jolted her out of her daydreaming. "Jenna? Did you hear me?"

Jenna shook her head to clear the cobwebs, "Sorry . . . what?"

"I asked," Kirsten said again, clearly irritated that she had to repeat herself, "have you heard anything from Luke lately?"

"No," Jenna replied sullenly. "I can't reach him on his phone. I don't know if he won't answer because it is me or if he's afraid to answer."

Kirsten laughed, "If he knew what was good for him, he would answer."

"You're not helping," Jenna said, exasperated.

Kirsten stopped and immediately apologized. "Look, I know this is really hard for you, but he did say that things changed when he got to know you right?"

"Yeah, but I don't know what kind of change that means."

Before Kirsten could answer, Jenna's cell rang. She jumped as it startled her. She recognized Luke's number. Jenna let it ring a couple of times, staring at her phone like it was a foreign object. Now that he was calling she was afraid . . . afraid of what to do and what to say to him.

Kirsten, looking questioningly at her friend asked, "Well, are you going to answer that?"

Jenna picked it up and said tentatively, "Hello?"

"Jenna, thank goodness you answered," a female voice said on the other line.

Compromises

Jenna looked down at the number again as she pulled the phone from her ear to make sure it was Luke's. She brought it back to her ear and asked the question that was burning in her mind. "Who is this?"

"This is Jackie. I have Luke's phone and it was the only way I knew how to contact you."

"Jackie?"

"Yes, remember, from Seth's yacht? I'm Jake's girlfriend?"

"Yes, I remember. Why are you calling me? And why do you have Luke's phone?"

"Listen, I need you to come to the yacht. I can't tell you this over the phone. Something bad has happened and I think you need to come."

"Bad? What is it? Is it Luke?" Jenna grabbed her chest, short of breath. Kirsten was mouthing at her, "What? What's happened?" but Jenna waved her questions aside.

"Like I said," Jackie was insistent, "I need you to come over straightaway. I can't do this over the phone," and she hung up.

"What?" Kirsten was practically dancing around her, "What is it, Jenna?"

"It's Luke. Something bad has happened and Jackie won't tell me over the phone. That must mean it is really bad news. I need to get over there right away." Jenna grabbed her purse and headed for the door, leaving Kirsten standing behind, yelling with instructions to call her when Jenna found out what happened.

On the drive over, Jenna couldn't think. She kept playing the phone conversation over in her mind. Something bad had happened. Jackie had Luke's phone. Something was so bad she had to tell her in person. Jenna wouldn't even think it. No, she wouldn't let herself believe it. Luke couldn't be . . .

She parked the car and ran to the yacht, racing up the stairs and into the salon. Jake and Jackie were sitting there solemnly on the couch.

There was another man there she'd never met before. He walked up to her and said, "You must be Jenna." Jenna shook her head in agreement, still not sure what to ask . . . afraid of what she might hear. The man continued to talk to her, and she told herself to concentrate on what he was saying.

She felt faint. The room was spinning. Dimly, from far away, she heard this man introduce himself as Jay. He was from the Coast Guard. He wanted to tell her that Luke had been shot and he needed for her to sit down. Jenna fainted as the last words dropped on her ears . . . Luke was shot . . . Luke was shot.

Jenna was dreaming. She had to be. Luke was whispering her name, telling her that everything was alright. She looked up into his face, the face of an angel. Heaven . . . she had died too, and was in heaven with Luke. Then he kissed her and she responded. As he deepened the kiss, her senses came alive and . . . she was being shaken awake, and there was a cold cloth on her head. She stared up at Jackie, who was looking quite distraught. "Jenna, Jenna, are you okay? I think you fainted."

Jenna turned her head and saw that she lay on one of the sofas in the salon. Jake and the other man, Jay, she thought she remembered him saying, were watching, concern in their faces. Jenna didn't see Luke anywhere. She started to cry. She couldn't help it. It was too much. She didn't want to hear anymore. She didn't want to know that Luke was dead, gone from her forever. No she couldn't handle it . . . refused to. She hadn't even gotten the chance to tell him . . . tell him . . . that . . . oh, now it was too late! The tears continued to flow.

"Jenna, shhhhh, its okay," Jackie said, wiping a tear that fell from her own eye.

"He's dead, isn't he? That's what you couldn't tell me on the phone," Jenna said, as more tears streamed down her face. Damn her foolish, foolish heart. She had wasted time being angry. She should have listened to him, to Cassie, to all of them. Damn! Why was she so stupid? He might still be there with her now, if she had only listened. She might as well have been the one to pull the trigger. She was at fault. If he was with her, he would never had gone off and gotten shot . . . her fault.

"Jenna, listen to me," Jackie said. "Luke is alive. He's pretty laid up, but he will be okay."

Jenna sat up instantly, and then was sorry she had as a wave of nausea came over her. She put a hand to her head to steady the spinning room. "What? He's alive? Where is he? I need to see him!"

Jackie gave her a glass of water, but Jenna waved it away. Jackie said, "Are you sure you are okay now? I can't have you fainting when you see him. It will make him crazy, and we have had a tough time of it trying to keep him down as it is. That's why I called you. He threatened to come over to your place as soon as the doctor left. He's been obsessed with trying to see you. So I called, but didn't want to tell you over the phone. I am glad I didn't, seeing how you reacted."

Jenna stood as Jake grabbed her arm to steady her and make sure she wouldn't pass out again. "I'm fine," Jenna said, to convince not only herself, but everyone else around her. "Where is he? I want to see him right away."

"Okay, just be careful. He's trying to be all brave, but his wound is pretty bad and he really shouldn't be moving around a lot."

"Now!" Jenna said, forcefully.

Jay shrugged, and Jackie said, "Follow me, then." Jackie led her down the front stairwell, but not to the master suite where Seth stayed. Rather, they went to a stateroom down the hall. Jenna prepared herself for the worst. She didn't know what to expect, but she damn well wasn't going to faint again. Jackie knocked on the door and said, "Luke, are you decent?"

"Yeah," a voice answered. It was Luke, but he sounded so . . . tired.

Jackie opened the door and whispered, "Remember, he was just shot, so even though he won't let on, he's in pain." Jenna nodded her head in agreement and made her way through the doorway.

Luke lay on the bed, propped up with pillows. He was wearing cutoff jeans, and they were cut away above a bandaged leg. Other than his cutoffs, he was naked. Even injured he looked irresistible. Jenna swallowed the lump in her throat and willed herself not to cry again.

"Hey, gorgeous," Luke said as she made her way to the bed, "is that all I have to do to get you to see me? Get shot?" He was joking, of course, but Jenna didn't find it funny.

"Damn you, Luke! What have you done to yourself?"

"Done to myself? Honey, I didn't do this to myself. This was the result of an old lady protecting her own yacht. She had every right, too. Good thing she wasn't a perfect shot, or maybe she wasn't aiming to kill me, not sure. Glad the shot wasn't a little higher to the left or honey, we wouldn't be able to make love."

"Luke!" Jenna admonished as she moved closer. "For heaven's sake, will you be serious for once?"

"Okay," Luke said, giving up. "I can see you're in no mood for laughter. Look, it's really nothing. They are literally babying me. I really don't have to be bedridden, but they won't let me up; doctor's orders to stay in bed for a few days. Hey, care to join me?" Luke smiled seductively, and if she wasn't so damn mad at him right now, she might have laughed and crawled in with him.

"Don't distract me. What happened? Why did an old lady shoot you?"

"Well, I figured . . . no wait, Seth and I figured . . . we are done with the whole pirating thing. I think Cass explained how we play at being a

Compromises

pirate to help catch them and keep ourselves safe. Well, now that Seth fell in love and I am done with the whole risky business myself," he purposely avoided saying how he felt about Jenna, "we decided it was a good time as any to end the charade."

"So you do that by getting shot?"

"Well, they think I'm dead, actually. They think that Seth threw me overboard once I got shot. Burial at sea . . . gone forever . . . no more Luke, the pirate. A good ploy, although we hadn't planned on me actually getting shot. That part was a mistake, but one to our benefit."

"So the pirates think you're dead?"

"Yes, and we want to keep it that way."

"Won't they recognize you?"

"Well, see, everyone has a twin, and besides, this hair needs a new style anyway."

Jenna, finally relieved that he really was okay, sat down beside him. He took her hand and brought it to his lips. She let him, but didn't move. Then he reached up to gently grab her chin and drew her closer. He gently kissed her lips. Again, but with more pressure, and then she had no more will to fight him. The emotions of the past few weeks came pouring out and she kissed back. He scooted her around until he pulled her into bed with him. He went to roll and instantly hollered out in pain.

"Luke?" Jenna asked worriedly.

"I'm okay. Damn thing, I just forget, sometimes, my limitations. They just don't make drugs strong enough these days."

Jenna finally laughed, and Luke chuckled. "Well, I'm glad you found your sense of humor," Luke said. Then on a more serious note he said, "I'm so sorry. I'm sorry I didn't just come right out on day one and tell you why I found you. I wasn't planning on feeling the way I do about you. I never have felt this way about anyone before, and frankly,

I botched the whole thing. Can you forgive me? And please tell me you can, as it seems that I can't have anyone but you."

"You tried?" Jenna asked, teasingly.

"Believe me, darling, I was nearly attacked by a big-busted woman just a few short days ago, but it seems you have ruined me. All I want is to be with you."

Jenna smiled in spite of herself. "Really?"

"Yeah," Luke chuckled as he tucked her into his side, "Really."

"Well," Jenna answered as she laid her hand on his bare chest, "I guess I will have to forgive you then. But you still have a lot of explaining to do."

"I have lots of time to tell you anything you want to know. It appears I will be laid up for a few days."

Jenna thought of something that hadn't occurred to her before. She sat up and looked at Luke straight on. "You said they had to think both you and Seth were dead. What happened to Seth?" Jenna asked tentatively, not sure she was going to like his answer.

"Well that," Luke said as he got serious, "is a whole other story."

19

I had been with Liza, Seth's sister, for about a week. I was getting anxious. Seth hadn't called in a couple of days, and when I called his cell, it was answered by Jay. Jay said that Seth had lost his phone while on a business trip, and since he was the first number on it his business partner had called him and Jay had gone to get it. Jay assured me that Seth was fine, but probably very busy. "So busy he can't call me?" I thought to myself as I walked in the garden that mid-afternoon.

Alex came running from nowhere, laughing as she encircled my waist in a hug. "Hurry, hide me," she giggled. I saw a little blonde about two years older than Alex running towards us.

I laughed as I pointed to a bush just a few feet away, "There! Hide there!" I told her as she took off.

The little boy was a neighbor next door. They played together all the time, although Alex told me he was so much like a brother that she thought he was annoying. I laughed, as she didn't seem annoyed at the moment. In fact, I had seen them play all week, and they got along more than they fought. I think they just didn't want to admit how close they were as friends.

The little boy looked up at me and with his cute English accent asked, "Where'd she go, Cass?"

"Oh, no, you don't, Gabe, I can't tell. Girls' secret bond, you know."

"Girls' stinking bond," he mimicked me and ran off to try to find her as I laughed.

I continued on my way, worrying about Seth, when I felt, rather than heard, someone approach me from behind. I was pulled back into a familiar muscular chest as hands closed over my eyes.

"Guess who?" his English accent was a dead giveaway.

"Hmmm, let me think. Luke?" I asked, playfully.

"You wishing, love, or teasing?" Seth inquired.

"Teasing, of course," I laughed, as he released his hands and I turned to embrace him.

"Ouch!" Seth cursed and stiffened a bit when I squeezed him around his back.

"Seth, are you hurt?" I asked, instantly concerned.

"Just a little sore, love, nothing you can't cure," he said as he took my lips with his own. He deepened the kiss until we heard children laughing. He released my lips, but not the hold he had around my waist.

"Something funny, Alex?" Seth asked and then chuckled.

The kids ran off, probably to tell Liza that they had seen us kissing. It was such a big deal for kids that age. It was like kissing was taboo. Well, it should be for them, but not for us. I looked up into his beautiful blue eyes and said, "So why are you sore and why didn't you call me? I was getting worried about you."

"Love," he replied as he stole another quick kiss before continuing,

Compromises

"You should never worry about me. Ahhh, I missed you so." I didn't think about it until much, much later. He had avoided all my questions, but I was so caught up in seeing him again, I didn't pay attention at the time.

We walked into Liza's house as we continued to talk about how much we had missed each other, and what I had been doing while he was gone. We decided to stay for the night and leave early in the morning to head back to Seth's home.

After dinner we gathered around as Seth pulled Alex on his lap to tell her another "Fat Butt" story. She giggled as he told her how the little dog drove a car. "Uncle Seth, he can't reach the pedals of a car."

Seth laughed, "That is why, my dear child, he had a cat take over the wheel while he pushed the levers." We laughed as he rose and said it was time for bed, and he would tuck Alex in. I followed, watching as he helped her climb into bed.

"Uncle Seth?"

"Yes, angel?" he replied.

"Will you promise to come around more now that you have Cassandra?"

"Why, do you like her?" He asked with a smile as I stayed in the doorway.

"Yeah! I want to keep her."

"Well, then, I can't argue with that!" Seth laughed as he kissed her lightly and turned off her light. He saw me in the doorway and led me out into the hallway and into the guest bedroom we were staying in.

"You're a hit with my family, as I knew you would be."

"Trying to butter me up, Seth?"

"Now who needs to butter you up?" He laughed as he moved me closer to the bed and started to undress.

I searched his body when we landed in bed, but found no evidence of why he was in pain, other than tiny little black and blue marks. He shrugged off my questions, saying he wasn't really in pain and would explain all later, but right then had more important things to take care of, as he rolled me onto my back and undressed me.

We arrived at his home late in the afternoon the next day. When we got there, he pulled me into his arms and swung me around. I laughed as he finally set me on my feet. "What was that all about?"

"Do you realize, love, that we are truly alone? We have never been fully alone without the threat of someone interrupting us. Don't get me wrong I love all our friends and family, but we haven't been alone since California."

He was right. I had never thought much of it, but on the yacht there was always Luke, Jake, or Robert. At my home there was the addition of Jackie and Mandi. Then there was his family while we were in London, and then Luke's unexpected visit the last time we were here in his home. I wrapped my arms around him and he swept me up, walking me into the room with the piano before setting me down.

"I have a gift for you," he said, as he moved to sit at the piano.

"I can't wait," I said as I sat down in a chair behind him. He played the piece that I had bought him for Christmas. It was beautiful, and I went to stand behind him as he finished playing so I could lay my hands on his back to feel his muscles move underneath. Tears were in my eyes.

He turned to me, and a frown furrowed his forehead as he noticed the tears. "What, love?"

"It's so beautiful- it just moved me, is all." I leaned into him and cradled his head to my breast, running my fingers through his dark curls. "Make love to me, Seth." I didn't have to ask twice, as he stood up and carried me up the stairs to lay me down on his bed.

Compromises

"I love you," he said as he kissed the remainder of the tears from my cheeks.

"I love you, too, Seth," I said, as all other thoughts flew out of my mind and I concentrated on how perfect he felt.

Later that night, we made our way down to the kitchen. He lifted me to sit me on the counter and then moved over to his center-island countertop. I was wearing one of his button- up shirts, and was busy rolling the sleeves up so as not to get them messy. He handed me chocolate and two graham crackers and then turned to roast a marshmallow over the grill. I laughed, never having cooked s'mores inside before. He brought the melted marshmallow back to me and I grabbed it between the crackers and chocolate. I delicately licked around the edges, moaning in pleasure as I took the first bite.

Seth laughed. "Love, you keep that up and I might have to ravish you right here in the kitchen." I giggled in response, enjoying my treat as he made one for himself.

"You know I love you, right?" Seth asked, as he intently watched the marshmallow turn brown.

"Yes," I answered cautiously, wondering what he had up his sleeve.

"So much that you would forgive me, love?" He asked as he grabbed a piece of chocolate and two graham crackers to slide the marshmallow into.

"Seth . . ." I wasn't sure where the discussion was heading, but I had a feeling it wasn't going to be good.

"Well, I have to tell you about my business trip, and you aren't going to like it."

I was getting a little nervous, and sucked a piece of melted marshmallow off my thumb as I finished my treat. "Okay," I said tentatively, waiting, and braced myself on the counter, anticipating what he was going to tell me. He still hadn't explained why he was sore and why there were some small rounded bruises on his back.

Seth came and stood between my legs, holding me securely in place, as if I would run.

"I want to give up the pirating thing, for good. I've thought a lot about it these past few weeks when you were abducted and then when Jake got shot . . . well, it is just too risky."

I smiled as I wrapped my arms around him, "Good, I am glad about that. But what does that have to do with your business trip?"

"Well, I wasn't quite truthful with you."

I frowned, letting my hands drop from around him, jumped off the counter to pace in front of him, and then stopped to stare up at him. "Okay, what weren't you truthful about?"

"It was business, pirate business." I took in a breath quickly as I waited for him to explain. "I wanted out, and so does Luke. It was going to be tricky, though, and we had to make everyone believe that we were gone, really gone, for good."

"Gone?" I wasn't following. Something was missing.

"Yes, they need to think that Luke and I are dead."

"Dead!" I practically screamed at him and he came to hold me still, but I struggled out of his hold. "What did you do to make them think you are dead?"

"Well, we took one of their fresh recruits with us on a pirate expedition. We were counting on the fact that he could relay all that happened to the others when they got caught by the Coast Guard."

"Damn you, Seth, you try my patience! How do they think you are dead if you are standing right here in front of me?" I stood, exasperated and angry, waiting for his reply.

"Well, Luke got shot . . ."

"Luke got shot!" I hollered out, unbelieving.

Compromises

"Love, let me finish. Yes, he did, by the wife of the owner of the yacht we were overtaking. Unexpectedly, of course, but it worked in our favor." When he noticed how I had slumped into a chair, white as a ghost, he added, "Luke's fine. It was a minor wound. He's really playing it up, though, let me tell you!" Seth avoided saying anything about Lisa: he must have figured I had enough to deal with right then.

"I need to see him," I said as I stood up.

"Love, there will be time for that. Let me finish the story, please." Seth pushed me back down in the chair and I sat down, not sure that my legs would hold me up as he continued.

"I had him hide out in the fast boat we used to overtake the yacht. I made the kid we had with us think that I pushed Luke overboard before the Coast Guard arrived. Told him it was customary for one of our own if he wouldn't make it. Kid took it hook, line, and sinker. Then I had him relay that information to one of the major players in the pirate ring. So now they think Luke is dead. Not to mention I had the kid get the coordinates on the location they were at so the Coast Guard could arrest others at the time we were overtaken. Since the ringleader told the new recruit where they were, they will never suspect that it was Luke or I that turned them in."

"So how do they think you are dead?" I asked, not sure I really wanted to know the answer.

"Well, that was trickier. Jay and I worked out a plan . . ."

"Jay was involved with all this?" I asked incredulously, interrupting Seth once again.

"Love, you need to listen, please . . ."

"Okay, so you worked out a plan."

"Yes, we worked out a plan. I told him that they need to think we are dead. The only way to do that is to see blood. Well, Luke's turn of events was unexpected, but to our benefit."

"I don't see how Luke getting shot is to anyone's benefit." I replied, quite distraught. It made me think about Jake and how he had suffered through his recovery, not to mention Seth being shot this past holiday.

"We didn't expect it, but it worked in our favor. Believe me, Luke is fine. So anyway," he continued with his story, "I pretended like I wasn't going to go to jail for anyone or anything, so I just jumped in the water, and Jay shot rounds of bullets where I jumped in."

"Seth, oh, my . . ."

"Love, it was a plan. He waited just a moment before shooting, as he and I planned it. I swam quickly toward the back of the yacht while the bullets went in a different direction. The bullets weren't real bullets, but these pellets that disintegrate and release red food coloring in the area where I jumped, and it looked like blood. A few of them got me, thus the bruises you saw earlier, and my soreness."

"I . . . don't . . . want . . . to hear . . . anymore," I stammered, as I thought I was going to be sick. Luke shot, and then Seth putting his life in danger once again! And . . . he had lied to me . . . again. I needed air. I got up and walked out of the kitchen onto the patio, taking in deep gulps of air.

"Love," Seth came up behind me to grab my shoulders, but I shook him off.

"I need to be alone, Seth. Please . . ."

"I understand," Seth said, his head hung low, "Just remember, I did this so I could get out of pirating . . . for good, for us . . ." He walked back inside silently to leave me to my own thoughts.

I played it back in my mind. It made sense. They would never let Luke or Seth go if they didn't believe that they were dead. Seth was right about that part. But, why didn't he tell me? Why did he continually keep me in the dark? And Luke . . . oh, my . . . Luke . . ."

Compromises

I picked up my cell and made the call. Luke answered on the first ring, "Hey girl, guess he told you."

"Luke, I don't know whether to kill you myself or run home to tend to you," I answered honestly.

"I am fine. Actually, I am going to use it to my advantage. Not only did it get me out of pirating forever, but I am getting some major sympathy from Jenna. I had Jackie call her, and she came right over. We are talking through things, and she's finally listening. She's upstairs right now getting me something to eat. Look, I know you are hopping mad at Seth right about now, but honey . . . he did it for you, for me, and in the long run, for himself. Try to give the guy a break. He loves you more than anything or anyone. Really, trust me . . . I know. Look, I gotta run, but be a good girl and cut the man some slack, will ya?"

I didn't know what to say other than, "I will see you soon. I'm still mad at both of you though, and don't think you are getting off so easily."

"Didn't think I would, darling . . . gotta run . . . I have to play the poor injured Luke and gain some sympathy. Talk to you tomorrow. Go easy on Seth, would you?"

Before I could reply, he hung up. Damn men! Thick as thieves they were. Now that I knew Luke was really okay, I could concentrate. So Seth wanted out of piracy. He had done it for all of us. Luke was extremely happy about it. Shouldn't I be?

Yet he had lied, again. I made my way inside to go find Seth. I didn't have to look hard, as I heard music coming from the piano room. I walked in tentatively as Seth concentrated on the piece he was playing. It was like he was pouring his heart out on the keys. I listened and allowed myself to relax. When he finished, he wiped the sweat from his brow and then turned, realizing he wasn't alone. He didn't make a move toward me, waiting to see what I would do.

"You lied to me again!" It was all I could think of to say at the moment.

"I knew you would never let me go if I told you the truth. You would have either talked me out of it or insisted you put yourself in danger by going with me."

He was so right. He knew me so well. "It was still wrong," I said, not yet ready to give up the anger I felt.

Seth got up and walked over to me. He placed his hands on either side of me as he gazed into my eyes. "I swear," he said, "I won't ever have to lie to you again. It's over . . . done . . . forever."

I looked up into his eyes. I wasn't quite ready to forgive him. I turned and walked away and headed upstairs to bed. Seth didn't follow me, probably knowing I needed some time and space to figure it out. He stood at the end of the stairwell, watching as I made my way up to our bedroom, his bedroom. He hung his head and turned to walk back into the living room to plop down on the couch. He turned on the TV, with the volume low, while he gazed at the images as they flickered across the screen. He was probably trying to concentrate on the show that was playing, to no avail. He loved me and hoped I would see it his way.

I slept fitfully and finally, around midnight, woke when I screamed out loud. In my dream there were pirates . . . and the Coast Guard . . . and guns . . . and lots of blood . . . Seth's blood. It had startled me awake. I had a sinking feeling in my stomach. It took me a moment to remember that I was here in London, in Seth's bed. But he wasn't here with me. I knew I could never live without Seth. I had tried it once before, and it didn't work then. I knew it wouldn't work now. He just really exasperated me when he lied to me and did things in secrecy. He was right, though; I would never have let him go, and I would have insisted on going with him or made him give up such a dangerous plan.

Compromises

I went downstairs to get some water from the kitchen. After getting my glass, I made my way into the living room. I found Seth sleeping on the couch, the TV still on. He looked so gorgeous, with his beautiful head of curls framing his face as he slept with his head on a sofa pillow. I turned off the TV, found a blanket, and laid it over him. He stirred just momentarily and whispered my name. Damn the man! Why couldn't I stay mad at him? I curled into his side and he pulled me close, smiling in his sleep. "Yes, Seth Hanson," I said to myself, "you've won me over, but I'm not happy about it."

The next morning I awoke, alone, on the sofa. I smelled something wonderful cooking in the kitchen, wrapped the blanket around me, and made my way into the kitchen. He had undressed me at some point in the night, and we had made love. Well, they say make-up sex is the best. I just didn't like that we had had to fight.

Seth was busy cooking and whistling the tune from the song he had played for me the day before. He was dressed only in shorts, looking totally hot and sexy. I could never get enough of the man.

"Good morning," I said as I took a stool at the counter and sat to watch him work his magic in the kitchen.

"Morning, love," he said as he leaned over to kiss me. Then he handed me a glass of champagne and cranberry juice. I smiled as I took the first sip.

"Are we celebrating?"

"Yes, love. I am, at least. You have forgiven me."

"Well, don't push your luck. I may not be so forgiving the next time. You're just lucky that neither of you got hurt . . . bad that is, and in the long run, it seems to have helped Luke with Jenna."

"Ahhh," he said as he came around the counter to embrace me. "I see, only for those reasons?"

"Aren't you afraid you'll burn something?" I giggled as he kissed my neck.

"I can always start over," he said as he took my mouth with his.

When he finally released my mouth and turned to go back to his cooking, I said, "Please don't ever put me through that again."

Seth turned to look at me seriously. He came over and grabbed my hands, "I promise, love, no more secrets . . . well, of that kind at least. Listen," he said as he moved back to the stove, "something else happened to our advantage while I was on this little stint."

I couldn't imagine what else he could have taken place during that adventure. I crossed my arms and waited.

"Well, it appears we took over Lisa's parents' yacht. She was on board when I took it over."

"Lisa? Like your old girlfriend, Lisa?"

"Yes. She was downright disgusted with me. It was hilarious, love. You would have so enjoyed seeing her, screaming at me that she might be a bitch who dates for money- her words- but at least she was honest about it."

I laughed as I tried to imagine Lisa saying these things to Seth. "You never let on to her that you weren't a pirate?"

"Nope, better that she think that way."

"But what if we cross paths with her?"

"Love, believe me, I try not to do that anyway. But if we do, you will have ammunition and you can tell her that you knew about me all along."

I laughed, picturing it. I could see us now, at some fancy gathering and her look of disgust as she saw us together. Her, trying to pull one over on me again, saying that she knows something I don't. And I, I would answer, 'What, being a pirate? Oh, he told me eons ago!"

Seth laughed with me. "I thought you would find that funny."

Compromises

Much later, we spent time going through town. We walked through the quaint stores as I picked up little gifts for the girls and my parents. I even found a little something for Luke. Later that night we found a little restaurant to eat in.

"I really love your homeland, Seth," I said, as I took another bite of my steak.

"I'm glad you do." He seemed pleased.

"How do you do it?" I asked, perplexed. "I mean the yacht, the home in California, and this?" I gestured as I opened my arms. Anything was better than talking about the recent events.

"It's a struggle. I love being in all three places, but rarely have time to truly enjoy it all. I am seriously considering slowing down a bit so I can enjoy them more."

"And the pirating?" I broached the topic with trepidation, not wanting to start another fight, but making sure he didn't have any other plans in that area, as he promised.

"I have made some compromises," Seth said.

"Compromises? What compromises?"

"I gave up the pirating part, entirely. I want to lead a normal life with you, Cassandra. To do that, it meant that I need to stop putting us all in danger. That's why I did what I did. It was the only way out of it. I never thought about it before, but when I met you and fell in love with you," he stopped to take in my expression and saw from my expression that I had registered this last piece of information, "well, I had to stop."

I let his words sink in. I knew the pirates wouldn't let Luke or Seth go. It would have had to be something drastic to get them out of this forever. I could see that now. He loved me, and he had risked his life to do it. "That makes me happy," I finally said, as I looked down at my hands in my lap.

Seth grabbed my chin, forcing me to meet his eyes, "Which? Me . . . giving up the pirating thing . . . or spending my life with you?"

"Both," I said as I looked into the blue eyes I had grown to love. It was a huge step for us both. It was enough to know that he wanted to spend his life with me.

When we got back to his home, he went to the kitchen and filled two glasses with wine. Then he led me out to his back patio. It was a beautiful clear night. There were lights strewn through the trellis that covered the small area out back. He walked over to one of the rosebushes that grew up the side of the trellis and pulled off a rose, handing it to me. I smelled its fragrance and looked out at the scenery as he came up behind me to kiss the top of my head. We stood there, looking out at the beauty that surrounded us, comfortable in each other's company, as he wrapped his arms around me.

After awhile, he turned me around and took my glass, setting it beside his on a nearby table. Then he got down on one knee. I held a hand to my chest as I realized what was about to happen.

"The business I had to leave so unexpectedly for was to not only to end my life as a pirate, but to get you this," he said as he pulled a black box out from his pocket.

"Seth," I said, but he stopped me as he said . . .

"I spoke of compromises earlier. My love, my Cassandra, will you do me the pleasure of marrying me if I promise to stay away from pirating and never lie to you ever again?"

Tears welled up in my eyes as I took in the single large diamond on a white gold band. I leaned down to take his face in my hands and to kiss him as he rose.

"Love?" He questioned me finally, as I hadn't answered. He clearly was confused why I hadn't given him any answer yet. He wiped a tear away that rolled down my cheek. "Cassandra?" He asked, as a frown furrowed his brow.

"Yes, Seth, oh yes!" I finally got around the lump in my throat to answer him.

He kissed me deeply. When he finally pulled back he said, "That's why I was so secretive. I wanted to ensure everyone's safety as we started our lives together and . . . I wanted to get you this ring. I called your parents when I was out. I didn't dare tell anyone other than them, as I was afraid that someone would spill the beans, so to speak."

"Well," I smiled, "I forgive you for all the secrecy and taking off like that, then. But don't you ever . . . ," I stressed the word *ever*, "ever, lie to me again. Do you hear me?"

"We will have a lot of family to call tomorrow, but Mrs. Hanson, I would like to spend the evening relishing this moment with you."

I smiled as I kissed him. "I could get used to that . . . Mrs. Hanson . . . I like the sound of that."

"I'm glad you have decided to forgive me, Cassandra," Seth said.

"I can't stay mad at a man who only tries at every turn to protect me. But I swear, if you ever lie to me again . . ."

Seth laid his fingers over my lips, "Don't say it. It will never happen again. Promise," he said, as he leaned down to take my lips with his own.

Later, as we lay in bed, cuddling each other, I thought back over the past few months. Never in my wildest dreams did I think that less than a year later, I would be engaged to the most handsome, perfect man in the world. We fell asleep wrapped in each other's arms.

20

The next day we called his family. They were ecstatic, and insisted on a huge get-together with all their friends to announce the news. While Seth's mother and sister called all their family and friends to gather that week at the house, I called my parents. Since they were already aware, they extended their congratulations and made plans to head back to Portsmouth to meet us after our vacation in England was over. I called Mandi and Jackie, and they were so excited that they wouldn't let me off the phone until Seth said we needed to pack and get ready to head back to London. We were ignoring his family, and there would be hell to pay if we didn't get back to them soon.

When we got to his parents' home, they rushed to meet us with hugs, kisses, and best wishes on our engagement. As we made our way into the house, Liza explained that there was a lot to do to get ready for the huge gathering, which was going to involve all their friends, acquaintances, and family. We spent the day shopping and cooking, and then finally it was time to dress for the event. I was amazed at how

Compromises

quickly everyone they knew would make it to their home, considering how little notice we had given them.

I wore a jersey silk dress that clung to my curves, and Liza did my hair up in pins, letting some of my natural curls escape to frame my face. Later, as I was alone while Liza was getting ready and dressing her children, I finished my makeup. Seth walked in, looking absolutely gorgeous in a white collared shirt and black slacks. He walked up behind me as I was applying my lipstick, and our eyes met in the mirror. He laughed. I laughed also, remembering many months ago when he had told me that applying lipstick was a waste of time as he would just kiss it all off of me. He turned me around and did just that.

"Seth," I admonished him.

"What, love?" He tried to look innocent. I couldn't help but laugh, and then kissed him back.

Liza cleared her throat from the doorway. "Don't mean to interrupt, but we have guests arriving and they want to meet the future Mrs. Hanson."

Little Alex came running in from behind her mother, looking absolutely beautiful in a pretty dress and her hair done in curls. "Can I call you Aunt Cassandra now?"

I leaned down to hug her as I replied, "I have no problem with that, but you will have to ask your uncle and mother."

"Wouldn't have it any other way," Liza laughed.

"She needs to get used to that very prestigious position in the family." Seth laughed. "She might as well get used to it, right, Alex?" Then he turned to me and held out a hand as he said, "Are you ready, Mrs. Hanson?"

I was still finding it hard to believe, but I loved to be called by his last name. We walked arm and arm as Seth said, "Well, let's not keep them waiting."

Later, as things were in full swing and I had met so many people that my head was spinning, not remembering any of their names, I snuck away to call Luke. I dialed him as I stood in the kitchen and Liza and Seth's mother came in to grab another tray, smiling at me as they did so and rushing back out to feed the guests.

Luke told me was doing just fine. Jenna had stepped out of the room and he couldn't talk long. I hated to tell him about Seth and me, given his circumstances, but didn't want him to find out any other way.

"So, he has gone and stolen you away from me," he laughed.

"Yes, I guess he has truly captured my heart, and my last name, it seems," I laughed.

"When's the big day?"

"We haven't really discussed the when and where piece yet. We are just trying to get through telling everyone at this point. There are so many people to tell. He has a huge family, it seems, and you can't offend anyone, so we are trying to make sure everyone is aware."

"That's Seth for you. Guy never does anything small," Luke joked.

"Tell me about it. You should see the rock he bought me. I'm scared to wear the thing for fear pirates will find me and steal my treasure."

Luke laughed at my joke. "Well, I wouldn't know anything about pirates, only read about them in the paper. Doesn't seem like a very good thing, being around pirates."

I laughed, "Indeed, Luke, indeed." I said goodbye, telling him that as soon as I was back I had a bone to pick with him about lying to me and duping me into believing that Seth really had left on legitimate business.

Seth put his arms around me as I hung up. "There you are. I missed you," he said as he kissed me and then steered me back to where his family was gathering. He whispered in my ear, "I can't wait to get you all to myself again. This family thing is taking its toll on me."

Compromises

I giggled in response as Liza pulled me away to introduce me to more cousins. Once again, when I was separated from Seth, I would search the room and our eyes would lock. No matter when I looked for him, he was always staring right at me. It made me feel like I was the only thing worth looking at in the room, and I smiled back at him, glad that he had chosen me to spend his life with.

The next day we made preparations to return back to the States. Seth knew that I was anxious to see Luke, although Luke sure sounded fine on the phone and it seemed that things with Jenna may have taken a turn for the better. We said our goodbyes to Seth's family. Liza made me promise that she would be involved with the wedding plans as soon as I had an idea of when and where. I told her that I was going to lean on her pretty heavily, as I would with my two friends back home. I wasn't good at planning a huge event, and this was clearly going to be one, so I would need all the help I could get. Alex kissed me on the cheek and promptly announced that I needed to get married soon, or she would be too old to be a flower girl. I laughed as I replied that if that was the case, she would just have to be one of the bridesmaids.

As we boarded Seth's jet and headed home, I stared again at the ring that now was a permanent part of my hand. I pinched myself.

"You okay, love?" Seth asked with concern.

"Yes. More than okay, actually I am a little overwhelmed. I just wanted to make sure I wasn't dreaming."

"You aren't dreaming," he said and then kissed me deeply to prove the point. Don't stress over the details, love. I can hire someone to do it all, but I think between your friends and my sister, we won't need any help."

"I agree," I laughed. "They can't wait to plan it all."

Seth kissed me once more before leaning his head back to catch some shut-eye. I hadn't thought much past the recent events, and wondered what was next for us. I fell asleep only to be woken a few hours later as we landed.

"Where are we?" I gazed out the window and saw palm trees in the distance.

"Florida. The yacht is here love, remember? Besides, I know you won't rest until you see Luke is fine for yourself."

I had forgotten we would need to get back to his yacht. One of the things I would have to get used to as his wife would be traveling with him. I was anxious to see Luke. "I forget the life you lead sometimes," I said as we made our way to depart from the jet.

"As long as you don't forget me," Seth laughed as he grabbed my elbow to assist me off the plane. "And don't forget the fact that you made me fall in love with you, Mrs. Hanson."

I laughed as he was relishing the feel of my new last name on his tongue. "I beg to differ, sir. I believe I had no choice in the matter. A pirate came into my life and stole my heart!"

"And you made an honest man of him to boot!"

We laughed as we made our way out to the welcoming party that was anxiously waiting for us.

"Will you look at you two," Luke said as he grabbed me and I clung to him, glad to see he was truly okay. He was using a crutch to steady himself. Jenna was standing behind him. "You went and made an honest man of him, Cass!"

"Shoot, I think I am the one tying her down," Seth laughed, as Luke and he clasped hands in a firm handshake.

"Jenna," I said as she came up to hug me, "are you keeping him from straining too much?"

"Luke is not a very good patient, which is just as well, as I am not a very good nurse." She shrugged her shoulders and then shook Seth's hand. She laughed as she looked at Seth and me. When I looked at her in question she replied, "It is good to know that the Seth I met a few short weeks ago wasn't actually pining away for some love that wouldn't ever return."

I laughed as I hugged Seth close.

We made our way back to the car. I walked hand in hand with Seth, with Luke by my side, thinking I was luckiest girl in the world.

Later as we sat in the salon of the yacht, we talked about plans for taking it back up the coast to Portsmouth.

I had a moment, when Luke and Seth were caught up in the when and how to leave, so I could sneak over to chat with Jenna.

"So, how are things with you, Jenna?" I asked politely, not wanting to pry, but curious as to how things had or hadn't progressed with her and Luke.

"Let me tell you," Jenna replied as she shook her head, "the man scared me to death. I rushed right over when Jackie called me. I never gave him the chance to explain until much later. I actually fainted for the first time in my life when I thought they were going to tell me he had died. It scared me to think I had let him leave my life without his knowing how I felt about him."

I smiled, remembering how I had felt after leaving Seth over the first pirate incident. I remembered how hollow I had felt inside, and the feeling of loss. "Our men are quite unforgettable," I acknowledged.

21

The next day I awoke to find the sun streaming in the window. It lay across Seth's face, and I watched as his chest rose and fell while he breathed heavily, sleeping soundly. I couldn't resist him, and reached over to kiss his lips. He smiled in response and rolled over to pull me close.

"Morning, Mrs. Hanson," he said into my hair.

"Ummm . . . I like the sound of that. Can't we just elope and make it official?"

"What and cheat your friends and my sister out of the biggest event they will plan this year?"

I pulled back, staring into those beautiful deep blue eyes. "This year?"

"Well, love, do you expect me to wait much longer?"

"That's not enough time to plan it, Seth. What about everything we need to do?"

"Love, I am sure that you will find a way. I am leaving it in your capable hands. I just don't want to wait too long."

Compromises

I snuggled down into his chest, "It's happening so fast. I will have to get busy right away."

"I'm sure you will have it all organized in no time."

"Is there some reason you are in such a rush?" I asked.

"I'm impatient to make you mine, legally. Besides, why wait?"

"Why, indeed," I giggled as I crawled out of bed, but not before he grabbed my hand to pull me down to him again. "Seth," I laughed, "morning breath."

"Right," he said as he kissed me quickly and released me.

Later, I went up to the kitchen to find Luke drinking coffee with Jake. Jake was completely healed, and back to his old self.

"Where's Jackie?" I asked, as my friend had stayed in Florida to nurse Jake back to health.

"She's making arrangements with Mandi about going over some details about your upcoming wedding."

"Not them, too!" I sat down in a chair next to Luke.

"Girls and a wedding . . . what did you expect?" Jake laughed, as Luke joined in.

Seth walked in the kitchen, kissing me briefly before going to make a cup of coffee for both of us, as he noticed I hadn't made mine yet. He set my cup in front of me and added sugar and stirred it for me.

Luke laughed. "You spoil her, Seth. You are going to make it difficult for the rest of us men who liked to be waited on."

"I love taking care of my bride," Seth replied.

Jake and Luke looked up in surprise. I answered, "We didn't run off to Vegas or anything, but in Seth's mind, we are already married. It can't happen soon enough for him."

"I just am anxious to have you as my wife," Seth explained.

"As I am, Seth, but really . . . you are going to have to be patient."

"Seth's never been a patient man," Luke laughed, "at least when it was something he really wants."

"He waited for me," I replied, thinking of the many months he spent courting me and then separated from me because he thought it was good for me.

Seth kissed the top of my head and then sat down next to me. "I'll be patient, but I'm not going to wait to call you my bride or my wife."

"Goodness," I said looking to Luke for help. He just shook his head and got up to rinse his cup.

"Jake, did you make sure everything is set to go? And when does Robert arrive?" Seth asked, as I took a sip of my coffee and then almost choked.

"We're leaving so soon?"

Seth looked surprised. "I thought you would want to be home. Your parents were making arrangements to fly home to Portsmouth soon."

"Well," I stuttered, "I do, but what about Jenna and Luke?"

Luke turned from the sink with a smile. "Don't you worry your pretty little head about me and Jenna. I have the girl right where I want her."

"What exactly does that mean, Luke?"

"I'm going to be seeing a lot of her. I am going to fly back down after we dock in Portsmouth. Granted, she will have to get used to my travels and all, but so it is with a life of a sailor."

"You're going to leave her?" I asked, incredulously, wondering how I would have felt to be in her shoes.

"Yeah, people do it all the time, Cass," Luke said as he leaned against the counter with arms crossed. "I only know the water. Could you imagine me trying to do anything else for a living?"

He was right. This was all he, Jake, and Robert knew. I hadn't given it much thought. I, obviously, hadn't given much of anything thought.

Compromises

Things like, would I work? Would we live on the yacht? England? California? My head was spinning.

I stood up, as Seth watched me, confused by my sudden movement. I smiled in spite of the turmoil I was feeling inside. "I need to get showered and changed."

"Want company?" Seth asked, but I wanted time to think.

"I am sure you will be busy getting ready. I will catch up with you in a bit." I kissed him briefly, and practically flew down the stairs.

When I got to the stateroom, I leaned against the door as I closed it. I let out a big sigh. I loved Seth, and didn't ever want to be away from him, but this was too much to take in. My head was spinning with thousands of questions.

The knob moved behind me, and I jumped away from the door as Seth peeked around it when he felt resistance. "Can I come in, love?"

I moved away and let him come in. He took one look at me and frowned. "What is it, love?" He came and held me as I leaned my head into his chest.

"I'm . . . overwhelmed . . . with all of . . . this," I said, not looking up.

He took his finger and lifted my chin. He looked into my eyes, saying nothing, then gently kissed me. Soon the heat built between us and I pulled him back into the room until I felt the bed at my knees and we fell into it. We took our time, relishing the moment, the feel of flesh upon flesh. Our lovemaking had tenderness to it; like he was afraid I would break if he touched me too hard. After, we lay in each other's arms.

"Better?"

"Seth," I said as I leaned up on an elbow to gaze into his beautiful eyes, "we can't solve all my worries with sex."

"Why not?" he chuckled.

I smacked him playfully in the shoulder and grinned as I answered, "Because reality has to set in at some time."

"The only reality I need is with you by my side. Here or anywhere. Did your conversation with Luke make you think that I would be leaving you in Portsmouth while I traveled? Is that what this is all about?"

"Well," I said as I looked down at his perfectly toned chest and lay my hand over his heart to feel it beating, "I don't know, exactly. I panicked. You knew that though, didn't you? Because you followed me down to the room."

"Love, I know you. I can feel your emotions better than ever before, and you have never been that good at hiding them from me. I don't ever want you to feel you can't talk to me. A marriage is about working things out together, being there for each other, knowing the other person so intimately that you are almost one. Why do you think the marriage vows say that two become one? I want to be one with you, Cassandra, through everything."

He always had a way of saying exactly the right thing at the right time. I smiled, "You are a beautiful man, my love, both inside and out." I leaned down to kiss him and he deepened the kiss. "I love you," I said as he finally pulled back.

"Hmmmm," he moaned. "I could stay here forever, but we have to head out soon. There's some weather I want to miss on the way home."

I noticed he was referring to Portsmouth. "Home?" I questioned him, intent on his answer.

"Home, is wherever you are," he said as he climbed out of bed and moved toward the shower. "Sure you don't want to accompany me in the shower?" he threw over his shoulder.

I ran and beat him into the bathroom, turning on the shower,

Compromises

laughing as I responded, "I couldn't say no to such a proposition as that, Seth Hanson." I turned serious as he crawled in with me and held me close. "I do worry about everything, just like you said. I don't know what the future holds. What you want me to do, where I should live . . . "

Seth caught me by surprise as he laughed. "What?" I asked, a little frustrated.

"Love, now don't be getting mad at me, it's just that you are so silly, sometimes."

I stood with my hands on my hips, "Exactly what am I being silly about?"

He tried to contain his laughter. "You are delightful." When he saw that that wasn't helping, he grabbed me and held me close. "I love you, and whatever you wish is my command. Better?"

"I'm not sure," I said as I pulled back to look at him.

"You can do anything you wish. I would like for you to travel with me, whether it be to my homes in California or England, or on my yacht. But I want you happy, and I am not going to tell you what you can or can't do. My home is where you are. You tell me what you want and I- well, I- will try to do everything in my power to ensure you get it."

"Seth," I pushed at his chest, "you can't just give me everything I want and not consider what you want."

"Oh, I am not, my love, 'cause I have a feeling that we both want the same things. You are just a bit overwhelmed by all of this right now. You will see, once you have time to think it through." He said this last piece as he jumped out of the shower, wrapping a towel around his hips and then handing me a towel. "You'll figure it out, love," he grinned as he helped me step out of the shower.

"I do so love you, Seth Hanson," I said as I wrapped my arms around his neck. "Sometimes, I think you know me better than I do."

"That's because we are soul mates, love."

"Soul mates?" I hadn't thought of it like that before. Soul mates; destined and created for each other. One without the other wasn't whole. Soul mates . . . Yes, I was beginning to think maybe we were.

I followed him out to the stateroom to change. It got me thinking. Yes, I was thinking a lot clearer now. Maybe he was right; I was just overwhelmed by all the recent changes.

The days followed, traveling by sea to make our way to Portsmouth. I couldn't wait to see everyone there. I spent time with Seth in the bridge as he started to teach me how to read all the gadgets and even let me take the wheel for a bit while he stayed by my side. He said there was no reason I couldn't learn how to drive one of these things. I loved the way he stayed behind me as he instructed me on what to read and what to do. Like the time he had taught me how to shoot a gun, I was distracted as his chest made contact with my back. He laughed, as he knew exactly what it did to me.

Luke did indeed have a very heart-wrenching goodbye with Jenna, and I could see he was torn about leaving her behind. He promised to see her after we docked in Portsmouth- he was going to fly down to stay a few weeks with her. He was doing well with the injury to his leg; he barely limped any more. I tried to keep him occupied on the trip home by laughing about some of the old stories he told me the first time I had come with them down to Florida. After the first day, he seemed to do better.

Robert had flown in by himself, saying Mandi had to work and was waiting for our return, back in Portsmouth.

Jackie tried to get me to think about the wedding, but I waved her off, saying that I had a few ideas, but wanted to think them through before doing anything specific. She looked curious, but I told her that I only planned on doing this once and it would be done to perfection, my perfection.

As we pulled up to A-dock in Portsmouth, everyone gathered on the pier. My A-dock family was waiting to give us a hearty welcome home. The dock was lined with tables, laden with food. Coolers held drinks, including wine and beer. The guys quickly tied the lines and soon I was engulfed in hugs. I was pulled quickly in every direction, as everyone wanted to hear about everything that had happened. They hadn't seen me since I left for Florida, not knowing that I was going to run into Seth there.

Seth and the guys were busy washing down the yacht, and said they would eat after they were done. Mandi arrived shortly after we docked, and she hugged me close. "I've missed you!"

"And I you," I giggled.

"Let me see the 'rock'." She, of course, meant my engagement ring. Everyone crowded around to get a glance.

"Wow," was all Mandi could say.

"Yeah, I know," I laughed.

Later, I made a plate for Seth and set it aside as I went to find him on the yacht. He was just putting away some of the cleaning supplies as I approached him.

"Hi, love, miss me?" He smiled as he pulled me in close.

"Always, when you aren't around," I grinned back as we made our way back to the dock and the party.

The next few hours passed quickly with stories about what had happened while I was gone and with getting caught up on the news at home. My parents were due to arrive the next day.

Later, I walked on board the Mainship, feeling it had been years since I had been home. Seth followed me on.

"Missing it here?"

"Not as much as I would miss you if I didn't have you," I answered. "Remember when you said that you would do whatever I want?"

Seth looked cautious as he answered, "Yes."

"I know what I want to do."

"Are you going to keep me in suspense? Or are you going to tell me?"

"I want you, Seth. Always did. I don't want to be apart when we don't have to be. I like to be busy, but having a job would be impossible with your schedule, so I would like to find a national charity that I can work with as we travel, if that would be okay with you."

He grabbed me and kissed me before answering. "That would be more than okay with me. What about your friends, your family?"

"Well, my parents are traveling a lot, and my friends, they can fly to wherever we would be when they can."

"Sounds like a wonderful plan to me," he smiled down at me.

"I have an idea about our wedding, too."

"Wow, you have been thinking. Okay, what will it be? Huge church here, castle in England? What?"

"Well . . ." I trailed off as I told him my plan. He shook his head, knowing that I would choose to do it my way.

22

The weeks flew by as the wedding preparations were completed. Seth's family came in to Portsmouth a few days early. They opted to stay at a hotel close by, and were spending time getting to know my folks.

Liza, Mandi, Jackie, little Alex, and I were busy getting the last-minute items done. We sat in the salon of the yacht with ribbons, lace, and little wrapped candies strewn about as we made items to put on the tables for guests. Seth walked in and saw the mess, laughed, and stopped only long enough to kiss me as he continued on his way to the kitchen. Since the wedding was fast approaching, Luke was flying back with Jenna and was due to arrive shortly.

The day before our wedding arrived before I knew it. I found a moment to walk downtown on High Street with the girls in tow. We stopped at the kiosk on the corner to have a bagel knot, delicious bread with a cream-cheese center, and some of the best coffee in town. We wandered into a nautical store along the riverfront on our way back to the marina as I searched for a gift to give my soon-to-be husband. We chatted with the owners, wonderfully friendly people, as they helped me select a scrimshaw pocket knife with a pirate emblem. After all, piracy was something that had brought us together and kept us apart. It would always be a part of the history of our lives together.

It was a beautiful day, and everyone hustled about to make sure everything was ready. I had opted to stay on the Mainship that night with the girls. We partied with all of A-dock and our families until a late hour. When it was time to go in, Seth grabbed me close.

"Who made up this stupid rule of not seeing each other the night before?" he asked, clearly not ready to let me go. "Maybe I should just steal you away and lock you in my room until morning."

"Well, my darling," I said in a fake English accent, "that just wouldn't be proper."

He laughed and hugged me close again before taking my lips with his own. "I hate this ritual. Why do I need a night of reveling in kinship with my friends when I could be making love to you?"

"Because," I answered laughingly, "everyone else would be disappointed if we didn't follow through with the bachelor/bachelorette party thing. Besides, we broke the tradition by not going out dancing or to a strip club."

"We did, at that," Seth laughed.

"Goodnight, Mr. Hanson," I said as I turned to leave.

He pulled me back for one last kiss. "Goodnight, soon-to-be Mrs. Hanson."

Later, when we were finally settling in around the horseshoe table with my girlfriends and decaf coffee to wind us down, Liza said, "How is Seth going to survive the night without you?"

"I am sure that Jake, Luke, and Robert will keep him busy."

"They probably are watching some sports show and drinking beer," Jackie laughed. Actually she wasn't far from the truth. They were watching a game on TV and knee deep in beer cans. Seth was missing

Compromises

me already, but knew that tomorrow was special and it would be good for me to have my time alone with the girls. A smile played across his lips as he formulated a plan and then told the guys his idea.

Jenna smiled as she said, "I can't believe that you chose Portsmouth for your wedding location. You could have been anywhere in the world. The Caribbean, England, the choices were endless . . ."

"I'm a simple girl," I grinned back. "Besides, this is my home and these are my friends. I wanted to share this very special day with all of them. It isn't about the huge church, the huge gathering, the pomp and circumstance. It's about a bond that I take very seriously, and I wanted the day to be absolutely perfect with my friends and family at my home."

"Well," Mandi said as she sipped her decaf, "don't be surprised if Seth surprises you."

"Do you know something?" I was curious.

She shrugged her shoulders and rose. "I know nothing. I only know that Robert has been very secretive and changes the topic whenever I walk into the room if he is talking with Seth."

"Hmmm," I said. "I wonder what that man of mine is up to now . . ."

We all moved onto the pullout couch and popped in an old favorite romance in the DVD player, armed with tissues and popcorn. It was late when we all went to our own beds.

I had just brushed my teeth, thrown on a long T-shirt, and crawled into bed, wondering if I would be able to sleep.

I was startled as I heard a knock on the window above me. For a moment, I thought it was Seth, and was brought back to a memory of when he had knocked on the window to get me to talk with him. Startled back to the moment, after another knock, I opened it and was surprised to see Luke.

"Luke?"

"Can you spare a moment for an old friend?" He waited for my reply.

"Be right there," I replied. I jumped off the bed, threw on a pair of jeans, and silently made my way to the back of the boat as I snuck around the girls strewn about it, sleeping.

When I got outside, Luke was standing on the dock, looking out toward Norfolk and the lights reflecting off the water. It was calm, and the moon was bright. It was a perfect night.

"Luke?" I again, inquired, curious to what made him seek me out.

"Come with me," he said as he grabbed my hand and led me down toward the yacht.

"Luke, I'm not supposed to go there tonight." He didn't answer me as he continued to hold my hand tight and lead me down the dock, walking past the yacht. As we got to a slip down at the end, the small boat that was usually hoisted on Seth's yacht was waiting.

Luke motioned for me to climb in. I did, and then wondered why he didn't follow. Then I saw Robert walking toward me with a bottle of wine and two glasses. He put them into the small boat without a word, even as I questioned, "Robert?"

Jake came next, carrying a blanket. He dropped it on a seat beside me and did a bow.

Last, I saw Seth. He was practically running down the dock toward me. I laughed, as it seemed the guys were all in on this little escapade. As he approached me I asked, "Seth Hanson, what are you up to?"

"Well, I believe that the groom is supposed to enjoy his last night of the freedom of being single, correct?"

"Yes," I laughed, wondering where he was going with this discussion. He started the engine and maneuvered the small boat onto the Elizabeth River, heading toward Norfolk.

Compromises

"Well, I am celebrating. I just chose to celebrate it with the one person I felt should celebrate it with me."

"I don't think it's supposed to work that way," I laughed.

"I like to make my own rules, and who knows, maybe this will be one that catches on. What do you think?"

I wrapped my arms around him as I answered, "I think I don't deserve you."

"We," he said as he drove the small boat into a small inlet of water called the Hague, "deserve each other, love." I couldn't have agreed with him more.

As we pulled into the quiet area, we looked at the homes, all darkened except by the lights that lined the streets. He cut off the engine, and since the water was calm, we just floated. Seth popped open the wine and poured us each a glass. He had turned on the radio, and music played softly. We just sat there, watching as we saw a lone dog walking along the shoreline.

"If the girls wake up and find me gone . . ." I started.

"They will know that I have kidnapped you, as the guys are fully prepared to keep everyone from worrying."

"Do you always have everything under control?"

"Everything, but you, love . . . everything, but you."

We relished this quiet moment in time, and my last night as a single woman. I knew I wasn't missing out on anything. My life was just beginning, or so it seemed as I lay my head against Seth's chest.

The next morning was a flurry of activity. The guys had moved to the hotel where Seth's parents were and gave us girls the use of the yacht to get ready. A-dock was a flurry of activity, wrapping ribbons with flowers all down the poles that led to the yacht. Some friends were on the yacht, preparing the upstairs for the party after, placing tables, chairs, and flowers everywhere.

Down in the master stateroom, Mandi was putting the finishing touches to my hair and little Alex was dancing around with pleasure, watching as her dress flew out around her. Her mother looked on, laughing and taking photos of everything. As Mandi tucked another flower into my hair she asked, "Are you nervous?"

"Extremely," I laughed.

"You'll be fine," Liza said as she took another picture of me looking into the mirror. "My brother loves you so much, he will always take good care of you."

"I know," I answered as Jackie rushed in, with Jenna behind her.

"You should see the dock, Cass, it is just absolutely beautiful."

I stood and went to the side window, looking through it. It truly looked gorgeous. There were flowers and satin streamers everywhere. The sun was shining, and everyone was gathering, dressed in their finest, with flip-flops on. I giggled as I looked down at my "Bride" flip-flops on my feet. They were my mom's idea. She knew how the dock wasn't conducive to wearing heels-and they were "just adorable" she had said. I had to agree. She had found them while shopping abroad. She had picked up a pair for Seth that said "Groom."

My mom entered the room, and the others quickly departed, letting me have a moment with her alone.

"You look gorgeous," she said as she took in my kerchief-styled dress. From my waist down it was made of a thin sheen of white-gauze looking material. It came up to hug my waist and breast, which was adorned with pearls and white sequins that overlaid the white material there. My hair was done up in pins to allow just some of the natural waves escape, with little white flowers strewn throughout. The pins had pearls, which accented the flowers in my hair.

"Thanks, Mom, for everything." A tear started to escape from my eye and she shook her head at me.

Compromises

"You'll make your mascara run, dear. No time to get all sentimental on me now." She reached down to pick up an item she had laid on the bed. She opened a jewelry box, and in it lay a perfect strand of tiny pearls. Moving behind me, she clasped it around my neck. "This is from Seth. He said to tell you that he knows you will be as perfect as these are."

"I love that man," I said as I touched the pearls to feel their smoothness.

"These," she said as she handed me earrings that were made of pearls that cascaded from a post end, "are from your Dad and me."

"Mom," I said as I hugged her, "you shouldn't have."

"Well, it is our only daughter's wedding day," she said as she tried not to cry. "We know that you will be well taken care of and that you will be so happy with Seth."

"I love you Mom," I said as I hugged her.

Liza popped her head in, "Ready, Sis?"

I laughed. Seth's family had included me as one of them ever since he had announced we were engaged. I was truly a very lucky woman. "I am."

"Oh, wait," Mandi said as she came toward me. "Seth said the necklace was something old, passed down in the family, your Mom's gift is new, so you only need something blue." Jackie came in at that moment and swung a blue garter around her finger.

"There's your something blue," my mom laughed.

In my "Bride" flip-flops, I made my way up to the kitchen. Seth, dressed in a white tux, waited at the end of the stairs outside on the dock. Luke, dressed in a beautiful blue-green tux the color of the Caribbean water, stood beside him, with Robert and Jake just a step behind. I was surprised to see Jay, the Coast Guard friend of Seth's, but it made absolute sense that he would be there. A beautiful woman and a little girl stood next to him. Little Gabe, Alex's friend from England, stood waiting patiently for his cue to produce the ring.

Mandi, my maid of honor, dressed in a cute sundress that matched the guys' tuxes, waited on the other side with Jackie, Jenna, and Liza. Little Alex was waiting in the kitchen with me, holding a basket of flower petals. My mom handed me my bouquet as she kissed my cheek. My dad took my arm, and Luke walked up to help my mom down the stairs. I gazed out at the sea of faces and could see Seth's parents and all of my A-dock friends, lined down the dock. Little Alex went first, dropping petals as she went.

"Love you, baby," my dad said. I hugged him close.

"Love you, too, Daddy," I said, feeling very sentimental.

"Ready?" he asked. I nodded, for fear I would cry if I spoke.

Someone started music. Piano filled the air. My dad led me down to the dock. The pastor stood there and started the ceremony with, "Who gives this woman to wed . . ."

As Seth and I held hands and listened to the pastor, I thought back over the past few months. I remembered meeting Seth that day at Benny's: so handsome, so dangerous. Yes, dangerous to my heart. I had lost it to him, but what better person to lose it to?

I thought back to the time I was abducted and he had snuck in to see me. I remembered how we lay under the stars, knowing that we would be apart for a bit longer. The trip to England, his dangerous ploy to get out of piracy forever; so many things had come our way, and yet, here we were, together and about to become one in marriage.

Seth smiled down at me, and I smiled back. He mouthed the words, "I love you."

I mouthed back, "And I love you."

We turned our attention to the pastor as he said that Seth had written something that he would like to read.

Compromises

Seth took both my hands in his, gently rubbing his thumb over my hand. "I wanted to tell you, that this very special day will always be held as the highest memory in my life." I tried not to cry as he continued. "I fell in love with a beauty that caught my eye from the moment I saw you. Not only are you perfect in every way, but you have a beautiful soul. I couldn't imagine anyone else I would want to share eternity with. And so, I ask you again, before I place the symbol of my love on your hand, will you spend forever as my wife, Cassandra?"

The tears would no longer hold. As they trickled down my face, I kissed him.

The pastor tapped me on the shoulder as I tried to regain composure. "I haven't gotten to that part yet."

I grinned at him and answered Seth, "Yes, my dearest Seth, forever and always, I will be your wife. I was just thinking over the past few months and everything we have been through. We have suffered through turmoil, pain, and loss. Yet our love carried us through and so, without any doubt, I know that our love will survive whatever life throws at us. Come what may, I will always be yours."

The pastor continued at that point with the exchange of rings, and finally pronounced us man and wife, forever as one, to go forth into a world filled with danger and hardships. But we had what it took to conquer them all. We had each other.

We partied on the top deck of Seth's yacht with our friends and family. Seth danced with me, reminding me again that he would always take the lead. I laughed, remembering so long ago when we were on this very deck in the Caribbean and Mandi had told him that I was afraid to dance with anyone because I had been told so many times that I tried to lead. Seth had told me that I just hadn't had the right partner to dance with. He couldn't have been more right. I smiled as he spun me around the deck.

I already had so many wonderful memories with my new husband, and we were just beginning our journey through life.

As I twirled about in the arms of Luke, he kept me laughing, saying that he was always available as a backup.

"What about Jenna?"

"Well, I figure you will never leave Seth, so I had to find someone," he jokingly answered me.

"You are incorrigible," I laughed.

"So I've been told."

Everyone took their turn dancing with me, even little Gabe. Alex insisted that the girls all dance together, and we all clasped hands and danced around in a circle.

I had such a wonderful time with everyone, and it was truly an event that would be remembered for some time to come.

Later, as we said goodbye to everyone, I shooed the last of my A-dock family out of the kitchen as they were cleaning up. After the last of our guests left, I went looking for Seth, who had disappeared just a short while ago. I found him standing at the rail on the top deck. The stars were out and the moon shone brightly, reflecting off the water. I walked up behind him, and he held my arms in front as they encircled his waist and I leaned into his hard, lean back.

"You okay?" I asked, as he seemed to be lost in thought.

He turned in my arms and looped his arms around my back. "Better than okay."

"Anything I can get you?"

"Just you, I want you," he answered before taking my mouth with his. We watched as the guests departed down the dock, going to their respective boats or to the hotel. As I watched them, I caught a glimpse of someone standing on the walkway, at the end of the dock. I swore it

Compromises

looked like . . . no, it couldn't be . . . but it looked like . . . Alejandro. I rubbed my eyes and opened them again. But the man was gone.

"Love, you okay?" Seth asked as he looked at me.

"Yeah, I just thought . . . it was nothing." I smiled, determined not to allow a dark cloud cover my day.

Seth led me down to the stateroom. Someone had put flowers all around the room, and the scent filled the air. The bedcovers were pulled back, waiting and inviting us in. Seth lifted me into his arms, effortlessly. He had to turn sideways to get us through the door. He didn't put me down, and kissed me as he walked to the bed to gently place me there.

He lay down beside me, and started to pull the pins and flowers from my hair as he kissed me gently in between pulling out pins. He ran his hands through my hair to shake it loose. "I love you, Mrs. Hanson," he said, as he started to undress me.

"I love you, Mr. Hanson," I replied as I undressed him.

I looked up into those eyes that I had come to love so much.

He said, "Love, there is one thing that I would ask of you on our wedding night. One request that you would honor for the rest of our lives together."

Perplexed, I answered, "Anything, Honey."

"My grandparents had a thing that they kept sacred through all their lives together, and my parents after them."

Totally curious now, I rolled onto my side and supported my head on a bent arm. "What was that, Seth?"

"They made a pact that no matter what the day brought their way, they would never go to bed angry with each other. If they had some sort of fight, they had to work through it and go to bed without any anger. It didn't mean that they might not have agreed on the day's events or that they were happy about the situation, but they would kiss each other and know that whatever it was, they would work through it."

"That's so beautiful. I mean, I don't know how anyone could do that, but it is beautiful."

"It's hard to do, especially when you want to be stark raving mad. But they said, you never knew when the good Lord would call you home. So, no regrets . . . no anger."

"I'll promise to try really, really hard," I smiled at him.

"Me too," he grinned back before talking my lips with his own. "Love, we have to get back to reality now, unfortunately."

"I figured that would happen at some point," I smiled in response.

"I have to fly out to California for a meeting for a few days."

"Oh," I said, not relishing the separation.

Once he realized that I thought I would be staying here, he rolled on his side, supporting his head on a bent arm while the sheet fell away from his muscular chest. He said, "I want you to fly out with me, stay at house there with me, if you want to . . ."

I could see he was trying to let me make my own decisions. I thought I would play a little with him. "Well, I was hoping to stay here . . ." I let my sentence trail off as he looked so lost and forlorn. "Seth," I laughed, "I'm joking. Of course I am coming with you."

He tried not to smile, "Not funny, Cassandra." He circled my waist with his arms as he pulled me in close. "Don't make me resort to my old pirate tactics and take you now."

I laughed, "You wouldn't dare."

He did just that, and then rolled me over, lying on top of me.

"Oh," I said as I rolled him over and jumped out of bed.

"Love, where are you going?" He asked as I rummaged through a dresser drawer until I found what I was looking for.

Compromises

I jumped back in bed, holding a gift box. He sat up next to me as I handed it to him. "It's a little something I bought for you as a gift."

"Love, the only gift I need is you."

"No, this one has meaning and will always remind you of me when I am not with you, brief as those moments will be," I laughed.

Seth opened the box and took out the pirate carved knife I had bought him earlier. He flipped open the knife and then slid it back into its holding space. He smiled.

"You're my pirate. Forever, my heart is in captivity."

I looked into those blue eyes and then kissed him. "I will always love you, Seth Hanson, and of that you can be sure."

He answered before silencing me with a kiss, "And I will always love you, Cassandra."

Much later, before falling asleep, I thought back to the day on an afternoon that was unusually warm for September when I had heard the intermittent hum of a bow thruster. Had I known then what I did now, I would have been running down the stairs to greet a dark and handsome captain of a mega-yacht that pulled in to block my view of the Elizabeth River. Then I thought of the man I thought I saw earlier in the day. Did my eyes deceive me? Was it Alejandro? Or was I thinking up things because I finally found peace with Seth? I drifted off, uneasy about what I thought I had seen, wondering if I should tell my new husband. If I did, would he be pulled back into a dangerous double life again? I finally decided not to say anything, convincing myself that I couldn't possibly have seen Alejandro. Eventually, sleep found me, and I dreamed of my new life with a man who had stolen my heart.